Bunking D
by Ch

It had been so
had taken care of her.

So long since she didn't have to think or
make decisions. She needed peace, just for
a moment. And Sam Beaumont seemed to
understand.

Morning birds chirped, their song soothed.
Caroline closed her eyes, breathing deeply,
fully aware of the man next to her.

He'd been part of the reason she hadn't slept
last night. Since her husband had left, Caroline
hadn't been held intimately. She hadn't been
kissed.

Sam Beaumont had reminded her of all the
things she was missing. His kiss, the look in
his eyes, right before their mouths touched,
was enough to remind her that she wasn't just
a single mother raising a daughter alone, but a
woman, through and through.

Holiday Confessions
by Anne Marie Winston

ᗞ᙮ᏢᏇ

"Lynne, why are you downplaying what's happening between us?"

"I'm not," she protested. "But I don't have any claim – "

"Maybe I want you to," he said in a low, ferocious tone that caught her by surprise. And before she knew what was happening, he jerked her towards him and set his mouth on hers.

He kissed her with a stunning, single-minded intensity that rendered her too shocked to move. His lips dominated and devastated her pitiful defences. Finally she put her hands up to his shoulders – to push him away? – but he only reached up with one hand and dragged her arm behind his head.

There was nothing tentative about his touch as he eased her onto the couch. He didn't say anything, just fanned the wildfire of desire deep inside her.

She couldn't speak, couldn't move, couldn't think, she could only lie there and feel as he removed her clothing.

It was then she wondered if a person could die of pleasure…

Available in December 2007 from Mills & Boon® Desire™

The Unexpected Millionaire
by Susan Mallery
&
To Claim His Own
by Mary Lynn Baxter

ᗧ᙮ᗁ

Bunking Down with the Boss
by Charlene Sands
&
Holiday Confessions
by Anne Marie Winston

ᗧ᙮ᗁ

Bending to the Bachelor's Will
by Emilie Rose
&
Secrets in the Marriage Bed
by Nalini Singh

Bunking Down with the Boss
CHARLENE SANDS

Holiday Confessions
ANNE MARIE WINSTON

MILLS & BOON®
Pure reading pleasure

*First published in Great Britain 2007
by Harlequin Mills & Boon Limited,
Eton House, 18-24 Paradise Road, Richmond, Surrey TW9 1SR*

The publisher acknowledges the copyright holders of the
individual works as follows:

Bunking Down with the Boss © Charlene Swink 2006
Holiday Confessions © Anne Marie Rodgers 2006

ISBN: 978 0 263 85609 5

51-1207

*Printed and bound in Spain
by Litografía Rosés S.A., Barcelona*

BUNKING DOWN WITH THE BOSS

by

Charlene Sands

Dear Reader,

When I created the fictional town of Hope Wells, Texas, in my book, *Like Lightning*, the town and the cast of characters I created just wouldn't go away. I fell in love with these people and knew I had to write another story to bring back some of my favourite characters.

Caroline Portman surely has her work cut out for her when mysterious drifter Sam Beaumont enters her life and begins giving her orders at the ranch, as if he's the boss. Belle Star Stables, the ranch Caroline is so desperate to save in this story, was created out of my love for horses. They have always fascinated me and I have always longed for my own horse. And now I have a whole stable… I wonder what Caroline would say about that?

Maddie, Trey and Jack Walker, along with my heroine, Caroline, have all returned to tell a heart-tugging story of sacrifice and love and second chances. I hope you enjoy reading Sam and Caroline's story as much as I enjoyed writing it!

All the best,

Charlene Sands

CHARLENE SANDS

resides in Southern California with her husband, school sweetheart and best friend, Don. Proudly, they boast that their children, Jason and Nikki, have earned their college degrees. The "empty nesters" now have two cats that have taken over the house. Charlene's love of the American West, both present and past, stems from storytelling days with her imaginative father sparking a passion for a good story and her desire to write romance. When not writing, she enjoys sunny California days, Pacific beaches and sitting down with a good book.

Charlene invites you to visit her website at www.charlenesands.com to enter her contests, stop by for a chat, read her blog and see what's new! E-mail her at charlenesands@hotmail.com.

This book is dedicated to the memory of my childhood friend, Los Angeles County Deputy Sheriff, Jack Miller, the true inspiration for the sheriff in this story. You paid the ultimate price, Jack. Your service and sacrifice will always be remembered.

Special heartfelt thanks to my wonderful editor, Jessica Alvarez.
Thank you for all that you do.

One

Tie-One-On Bar and Grill was known for two things: earsplitting country music and beautiful female patrons. Sam Beaumont indulged in both. He sat at a corner table in the honky-tonk listening to Toby Keith's latest, while eyeing a tall blonde up at the bar. She'd caught his attention the minute she walked in. The thing of it was, the Texas bombshell had stared back at him with interest, then spent a minute deep in conversation with the bartender before grabbing two Coors and walking over to him.

"I need a man," she said, with a shake of her head. Her long locks gyrated right back into place. She set the two bottles down on the table and gave him a good long assessing look.

"Yeah?"

"Chuck over at the bar says you might be interested."

He surveyed the leggy blonde, sweeping a leisurely look over her body. She was beauty-queen pretty, but Sam had seen more than a fair share of pretty women in his day. No, it was something in her eyes that spoke to him, a guarded look he knew too well. It was that vulnerability, even as she stood there brazen as all hell, claiming she needed a man, that intrigued him.

Sam sipped his beer slowly, keeping her waiting, and a surge of something he hadn't felt in nearly a year traveled through his veins. An unhurried rush, a tingle of awareness that he had believed long buried, surfaced.

That, in itself, was enough for him to send the woman packing. He didn't *want* to feel anything. Not ever again.

"So are you?" she asked. "Interested?"

He swept her a look. "What'd you have in mind?"

Even through a layer of smoky haze and dim light, he couldn't miss her face color to tomato red, but the woman seemed determined. She slid into the booth at the same time she slid a beer his way. "I need a month's work, for a month's wages, room and board included. Chuck vouched for you. He said you're looking for work."

He sipped his beer and thought about the events that had brought him here. The CEO of a major construction company on the run, not from the law, but from his own guilt-ridden past—Sam was running from things he could no longer face. He didn't need the cash, but hell, staying real busy kept those agonizing thoughts at bay. And Sam needed that, almost as much as he needed his next breath.

"Maybe." He surprised himself with his answer.

Truth be told, he wouldn't mind staying in one place longer than a week. So far, nobody had caught up with him. And he wanted to keep it that way. When he'd left his CEO position with its staggering responsibilities and his old life behind, he'd called his younger brother Wade occasionally, at his insistence, but Sam had never disclosed his location. Trust only went so far. He needed running room and manual labor to keep his tortured mind from remembering.

"I'm Caroline Portman." She held out her hand and Sam took it. Well, hell, he wasn't in the habit of shaking hands with women. But her handshake was firm, even though her skin was soft as butter.

"I'm kinda desperate for help right now, so you can take advantage of me, but only just a little."

She smiled briefly, and he noted two dimples peeking out from both corners of her mouth. Like he said, beauty-queen pretty. He felt another unwelcome surge travel through his body.

"I've got one month to get my place up and running. It's hard work and long hours, but I can pay well."

"What kind of work?"

Sam cursed himself for asking. He'd pretty much determined that those sparks he felt a moment ago weren't anything he wanted to feel again. He'd spent the better part of this year numb to the outside world. Keeping the status quo was essential. If those tiny sparks nudged away the numbness to any degree, then he'd never survive. He'd have to say no to pretty Miss Caroline Portman.

"I'm rebuilding my stables. The place sort of went

downhill, and, well, I'm planning on bringing it back up to the way it was before, uh, before…"

She stopped, blinked several times, biting down on her lip, unable to get the words out. It wasn't an act—he'd had enough experience to know when someone was downright lying. The lady had choked up, and Sam saw the heartache there, the pain she tried so bravely to hold back.

He didn't want to know. He'd had enough grief of his own to last a lifetime. Hell, he'd been drifting for months, heading from one Texas town to another, trying to forget, and that was what kept him going. The forgetting.

He liked this town. Hope Wells reminded him of the place he'd been raised since the age of five, a small friendly place where life was simple and fair. But looking into Caroline Portman's eyes, maybe he needed to amend the fairness part. Sam knew that life held more unfair uncertainties than sometimes a man could take.

Or a woman.

Damn if he didn't love horses. Rebuilding a stable and working with horses again appealed to him. He had spent his young life around ranches. He knew a thing or two about livestock and would enjoy the work, but he still didn't think this a good idea.

"Not interested."

Caroline blinked her big baby-blue eyes.

Sam rose from the table, finishing off his beer. "Thanks for the offer."

Stunned, the blonde sat there wearing a disappointed look.

He set a few bills on the table and strode out of Tie-One-On. If nothing else, meeting Caroline Portman had added a little spice to an ordinary day.

He walked along the sidewalk, heading toward the motel adjacent to the honky-tonk. He'd almost made it to his room, but a shuffling sound from behind alerted him. He spun around.

"Wait up, Mr. Beaumont!"

Caroline Portman walked briskly toward him. Out of breath and flustered, she looked even sexier, like a woman who'd just had a wild night. Sam envisioned putting that look on her face and his momentary slick-hot fantasy made him shudder.

She came up to face him. "I need to know—why?"

"Why?" Sam kept walking, but at a slower pace.

She stayed with him. "Why did you refuse my offer?"

"I don't recall telling you my name," he said, as old instincts kicked in.

"It's a small town. I know a little about you. You're here looking for work, aren't you?"

"Yep."

"I'm offering you a job."

"Yep." He kept walking until he reached his motel room. He leaned against the door to face her. Moonlight streamed onto her form like a spotlight and Sam noticed the snug fit of light-blue jeans and a chambray shirt with some sort of rhinestone work on the chest. Not gaudy, but with style, the color bringing out the true blue in her eyes. She was a woman who didn't flaunt what she had, but yet she couldn't conceal the perfection of her body. "Don't men say no to you very often?"

Caroline blinked and shot him a stern look. "Men say no to me all the time, Mr. Beaumont, but that's not any of your business. I know you're looking for work. The man I had lined up broke his leg, and now I've run out of time. Seems to me we could make some sort of arrangement."

He glanced at his motel door, raising his brows.

"Not that kind of arrangement," she hurried out.

Sam chuckled.

She folded her arms and waited.

Sam pursed his lips. He admired this kind of determination. Damn, if he wasn't the biggest kind of fool. "I need to know something first."

Caroline nodded.

He pulled her into his arms, and leaning back against the door he brought her with him. She was too stunned to protest, so he did what he'd wanted to do the minute he'd laid eyes on her. He kissed her.

It wasn't long, and it wasn't sweet, but rather a deep exploration of lips meeting and mating. Sam steeled himself against her honey-soft mouth. He braced himself against the onslaught of holding a beautiful woman in his arms. He breathed in her female scent, some fruity fresh concoction that reminded him of a lazy summer day, and willed his body not to react. It didn't. Not in the least. Relieved, he released her immediately. He'd learned everything he needed to know.

He stared into furious blue eyes. "I accept the job."

Caroline smiled with sugary sweetness and stepped out of his arms. "Good, because now I can fire you, Mr. Beaumont."

Morning dawned way too fast for a woman who hadn't slept a wink. Caroline Portman rose from bed, dressed quickly and went out to the kitchen to make breakfast. Her head ached and her eyes burned, but she couldn't afford to waste any more time. She had work to do. And keeping busy kept her from thinking about Annabelle, her sweet five-year-old, who she had unselfishly sent off to Florida for a vacation with her grandparents.

How she missed her daughter. She and Annabelle had never been apart. But Caroline's mother and father had insisted on taking Annabelle home with them, especially as they lived just minutes away from every child's fantasy come true, Disney World.

Her parents' offer had come once they'd heard Caroline's plans to refurbish the stables. They had given her their blessing, backing her up one hundred percent. Her parents knew what the stables had meant to her, and how much it had hurt her that her ranch had been run down nearly to ruin. She'd given up her heart and her trust to the man she'd married and he'd abused both. He'd run her livelihood into the ground, putting her so much in debt that she'd only just now surfaced in the black again.

Gil Portman hadn't the mind for business. He'd entered into one bad deal after another, running up bills that he couldn't pay, then trying to recoup the loss by entering into one dubious deal after another. The last one had been investing in a shady stud-service scheme that had nearly bankrupted them. Caroline had been busy raising Annabelle, placing her trust in her husband, but she'd learned a hard lesson with Gil, and she'd never place her life or her livelihood in the hands of another man again. Caroline had vowed when Gil had run off, abandoning his family, that she'd never allow a man to run roughshod over her good intentions again. She knew better now. She could only rely on herself and her two very loving, supportive parents.

Edie and Mike Swenson knew that their daughter would need time alone to achieve her goals without a five-year-old distracting her. They wanted the ranch to succeed again, because they knew that the ranch meant stability for Caroline, but it also meant something more. It meant independence. Caroline needed both now, for herself and for her daughter. Her parents hadn't flinched, but had stepped in, offering to help with her little bundle of energy. And, as they'd put it so tenderly, they'd missed seeing Annabelle. Spending time with their granddaughter would be good for all of them.

Caroline had finally relented, agreeing to let them have Annabelle for one month. In that time, she planned to work harder than she'd ever worked to get her stables back up to par. She'd come up with a new name to signify all the changes she'd planned to make. Annabelle Star Portman would be excited to know that Portman Stables would now be known as Belle Star Stables.

Caroline stuck a piece of sourdough bread in the

toaster oven, set the coffeepot to brewing, then sat down at the table to check the classified ad she'd placed in yesterday's *Hope Wells Reporter*.

The telephone wasn't ringing and no one was breaking down her door looking for work. Her last hope had been dashed yesterday, with Sam Beaumont. But she wouldn't think about him, not when she had a problem to solve. Finding a suitable worker on a temporary basis wasn't easy. But Caroline knew without a doubt she'd have to find someone or her plans for Belle Star would crumble.

Fatigued, Caroline slumped in her seat, struggling to keep her eyes open. She glanced at the *Reporter,* blinking her eyes, but the newspaper print blurred, her eyelids drooped and her mind all but shut down. Maybe if she just slept for a few minutes, she'd feel better.

Maybe if she laid her head down on the table, just for five minutes…

The explosion rocked Caroline to a sitting position. She snapped her head up from the kitchen table where just minutes ago, she'd laid her head down to rest. Dazed from her little nap, it took a moment for her to come to grips with what just happened. Her toaster oven had overheated. The appliance, literally "toast" now, had ignited the can of cooking spray she'd left nearby. Caroline was covered with the greasy effects of that combustion.

And within seconds, flames erupted, catching on to the overhead oak cabinets.

Caroline screamed, "Oh God!"

She ran for the fire extinguisher on the wall next to the refrigerator and yanked it free. Fumbling with the handle, she couldn't get it to work. She'd never used an extinguisher before. Heat burned her cheeks and smoke billowed from the cabinets. The fire spread.

Panicked, she fidgeted again with the extinguisher and cursed the husband who'd left her in this mess, the husband who'd abandoned his wife and child when the going got rough, the husband who had recently died, leaving her a widow. "Damn you, Gil!"

She didn't take time to worry about speaking ill of the dead. Since Gil had abandoned his family, nothing much had gone right in her life. She couldn't help but lay the blame where it seemed to fit. Marrying Gil had been the biggest mistake she'd ever made, yet without him, she wouldn't have had Annabelle. That was the only good thing he'd ever given her.

Caroline gave up on the extinguisher, opting to call the fire department instead. Of course, she knew her entire kitchen might burn to the ground before they arrived, but she had little choice.

And then the choice was taken from her.

A pair of masculine hands reached out to grab the extinguisher. Stunned, Caroline turned sharply to find *him,* the man who had caused her sleepless night, standing beside her, taking control.

"Get back," Sam Beaumont said, commanding her with a quick nod.

Caroline stepped back and watched as he pulled the pin and operated the fire extinguisher, putting out the flames with long sweeping motions. He did a thorough job, making sure all the flames were put out, before turning to look at her. "You okay?"

Numb, she nodded, biting her lip.

He swept a quick gaze over her body as if he had to make sure himself. She must have passed inspection because he set the extinguisher down and assessed the damage to her cabinets.

Caroline glanced at her once-tidy kitchen, where just minutes ago everything had been neat and organized. Now, the place looked like a disaster, but her kitchen was still standing, and so was she. "What are you doing here?"

He turned to face her, his lips quirking up in a charming smile. "Apparently, putting out your fire."

Tears stung her eyes, from the smoke and the flames and from the relief she felt at this moment. She gazed into Sam Beaumont's dark-brown eyes, seeing not the hard man who had refused her yesterday, but a man who appeared genuinely concerned. He'd shown up in the nick of time.

And Caroline owed him. But he still hadn't explained what he was doing here.

"Want to tell me what happened?"

Caroline shrugged, numbed from the thought of what might have happened. The little appliance mishap might have escalated into a full-blown house fire if Sam Beaumont hadn't shown up. "I guess the toaster oven overheated. It's old and I should have known the other day when…it…sparked…that I…" A lump formed in Caroline's throat. She couldn't finish her thought.

Sam took her arm gently and guided her out of the kitchen. "Let's get away from this smoke."

He opened the back door and they both stepped outside. The fresh air was like a balm to her out-of-whack nerves. She breathed in deeply.

"Wanna sit?" he asked and led her over to the back-porch swing. She sat down, and to her surprise he took a seat right next to her.

Still reeling in shock, Caroline remained quiet. It had been so long since anyone had taken care of her. So long since she didn't have to think or make decisions. She needed peace, just for a moment.

And Sam Beaumont seemed to understand. He sat beside her in silence.

Morning birds chirped, their song a harmonious cluster of sounds that soothed. Caroline closed her eyes, breathing deeply, listening, fully aware of the man next to her.

He'd been a major part of the reason she hadn't slept last night. Since her husband had left nearly two years ago, Caroline hadn't had any physical contact with a man. She hadn't been held intimately. She hadn't been kissed.

Sam Beaumont had reminded her of all the things she was missing. He'd taken her into his arms, pulled her close and brought his mouth to hers. He'd made her feel feminine and alive with just one kiss. He'd sparked something in her that Caroline had buried a long time ago. She knew she was no longer that young, naive, innocent girl who believed in happily ever after. No, a bad marriage had erased all of those thoughts, but she hadn't realized that she'd been dry, like an arid desert, wasting her womanhood away.

Sam Beaumont's kiss, the look in his eyes, right before their mouths touched, was enough to remind her that she wasn't just a single mother raising a daughter alone, but a woman, through and through.

Enough of a woman to realize that the man sitting next to her was sexy as sin. The tight fit of his jeans and the broad expanse of his shoulders hadn't escaped her.

"It's nice out here," he said.

Caroline nodded in full agreement, but then she turned to look at him as curiosity set in. She asked once again, "What are you doing here?"

He didn't hesitate this time. "I could lie and say I was passing by on my way out of town. That's what I'd planned on saying. But the truth is, I found your ad in the newspaper and came out here deliberately."

"Why?" Caroline asked, realizing she should be concentrating on how to fix her newly burned kitchen cabinets instead of shooting the breeze with Sam Beaumont, but somehow she couldn't quite tear herself away. She had questions for him and she hoped he would give her the satisfaction of truthful answers.

"I came here to apologize."

"Oh." It was the last thing she expected him to say. Caroline wasn't accustomed to having men apologize to her. Gil hadn't had the civility or manners to do so.

His arrogance wouldn't allow it. Caroline only saw her husband's good side when he wanted something from her. And sadly, she hadn't realized his tactics until after he'd abandoned his family. She'd been blinded by love, or what she'd thought was love, and now, as she gazed into Sam Beaumont's dark eyes, she wondered if she could believe him.

"I stood behind your door, ready to knock, when I heard the explosion. Then I heard you scream. Your door was open, and, by the way, you should keep your doors locked, especially when you're all alone out here. The rest is history."

Caroline stared out into the morning light, squinting her eyes and holding her breath. "You say you came to apologize?"

"I was way out of line yesterday. It kept me from sleep last night and I knew I had to make it right."

So, she hadn't been the only one who hadn't had a good night's sleep. She felt herself softening to him. It seemed he had scruples and a conscience, but she wasn't letting him off so easily. She'd learned her lessons the hard way. "I see. So was it your refusal, the kiss or your arrogance that you're apologizing for?"

Sam chuckled and lifted up from the swing to lean against the porch post. He faced her squarely. "I deserved that."

"I know," she said, but a smile she couldn't contain emerged. There was something extremely charming about the man, yet, Caroline wouldn't let her guard down completely. She stood up to face him. "What I can't figure is why you kissed me."

Sam's gaze traveled to her chest as sunlight beamed down. She felt piercing rays of heat, not from the sun but from his direct perusal.

He ran a hand down his face and finally, he lifted his eyes to hers. "You've got, uh, something wet splattered on your blouse."

Caroline glanced down. She'd been through too much this morning to be embarrassed, but the fact remained that she'd been splattered with cooking spray, and grease stains made her blouse almost transparent. And of course, the moisture had hit the most protruding target. Her breasts. She folded her arms over the wet area, hiding what he'd already seen. "Hazards of wet cotton."

Sam agreed, "Yeah, what a bummer."

She caught his smile, but he had the good grace to maintain eye contact with her.

"Will you answer my question?"

He set both hands in the back pockets of his jeans and sighed quietly. "Why does a man kiss a beautiful woman?"

Caroline soaked up the compliment. Oh God, did it feel good to hear those words. Yet she steeled her resolve, not letting him off the hook so easily. She had to know. "You tell me."

Sam averted his gaze, looking off in the distance. She doubted he was studying the scenery. After all, broken-down barns and stables, along with a neglected yard chock-full of weeds, weren't all that interesting.

"Okay," he said, "you deserve the truth. It was a test."

"And I passed? Or failed?" Caroline tried to make sense from his words.

He shook his head. "Don't take this the wrong way, but the test had nothing to do with you. It was *my* test. I had to know something."

"What? What did you have to know? I offered you a job and you kissed me? What kind of test was that?" Caroline asked, exasperated. She didn't understand any of this. The man seemed to be speaking in riddles.

Sam just stood there, looking guilty.

It was that look that got her to thinking. Then, as if a light clicked on in her head, she figured it out. "You kissed me to see if you were attracted to me," she stated with certainty. "And...and once you did...you accepted the job."

Sam's mouth twisted.

"Meaning, you decided you could work with me...because...because..." Caroline blinked her eyes, keeping both fury and tears in check as the niggling truth began to surge forth in her mind.

"Look, it was a mistake, a damn fool thing to do. But you've got one heck of an ad campaign, lady, walking up to me in that bar claiming you're looking for a *man*. I'm just looking for work. Period."

"I could have phrased that better," she said defensively, "but you had no right to put me to your test."

Caroline closed her eyes, willing away the pain as realization dawned quite clearly. Sam Beaumont had made her come alive last night, with a hungry mouth and steady embrace. He'd made her feel things she hadn't felt in years, while she, on the other hand, had been so uninspiring that he'd decided he could work with her. She wouldn't be a temptation at all. Caroline Portman wouldn't shake his resolve in any way.

Caroline didn't think her day could have gotten any worse. Sam Beaumont had touched her last night with an embrace and sexy kiss that had revived what she believed dead inside in one quick unexpected moment.

"Look, I'm here to apologize. I know I made a mistake. And I'm real sorry."

Caroline heard the sincerity in his tone. She stared deeply into his eyes and saw it there, too. His expression never faltered, the apology written all over his handsome face. For some strange reason, she believed him. Which was saying something. After what Gil had put her through, Caroline didn't put much faith in any man. "Okay, I accept your apology."

"Listen, let me put my words into action. Since I'm here anyway, and I know a thing or two about carpentry, I can fix your cabinets for you. Unless you've hired someone already?"

She shook her head.

"It'll take me the rest of the day, but I'm not heading anywhere special, so I don't mind doing the work."

Caroline inhaled deeply. The offer had merit. "I don't know if I can afford you."

"No charge," he said immediately.

"That's not what I meant, Sam."

He stared into her eyes for a long moment. Too bad he had a sinful body, a handsome face and dark eyes that could burn into your soul, because sexy Sam Beaumont found Caroline completely lacking as a female. Boy, she didn't know if she'd ever get over that one.

"I'll be on my best behavior."

She could bank on that but the thought didn't comfort her. Sam wasn't good for her ego, but Caroline had put that part of her life on hold anyway, so what did it matter if she wasn't the kind of woman Sam Beaumont thought attractive? Right now, all she needed to know was if he could help her out with her cabinets. "You sure you know how to fix cabinets?"

"I've had some experience." He peered at the damage with a gleam in his eyes as if calculating exactly what he needed to do and how he'd accomplish it.

It was good enough for Caroline. She surely didn't know anything about repairing them and it didn't look as if anyone else was coming to her rescue today. "You're on."

He nodded, then approached her with a purposeful stride. Their gazes locked as he stood before her. "Tell me something."

His probing look told her she wasn't going to like his question. "What do you want to know?"

"When I was behind your door, I heard you scream out. So, who's Gil?"

Two

Caroline appeared shaken by his question. She'd flinched when he'd mentioned Gil's name, and then a somber expression stole over her face. For a moment, Sam thought she'd keep that information to herself, but then she spoke up, albeit quietly. "Gil was my husband. He died about four months ago."

"Sorry. That's rough." How well he knew about losing someone you loved. How well he knew the heartache involved, the day-to-day agony of living without the ones you love. Sam hadn't been able to face his demons any longer. He'd taken off trying to escape the truth, to dull the pain, to find some way of surviving.

Caroline sighed, a brief smile emerging before she spoke. "As long as we're being honest with each other, I can tell you that Gil only did two really good things in his life. He gave me a daughter for one. She's five years old and the light of my life. And two, he kept up his life insurance. We have enough money to live and, if I'm real careful, there'll be enough to refurbish our ranch."

Caroline had a five-year-old daughter? Sam's gut clenched. A searing jolt shot straight through him and he winced as if he'd been sucker-punched. He hadn't suspected, though he should have known she might have been married, she might have had a family.

"Where is your daughter?"

"Annabelle?" A winsome expression stole over her face and she smiled. Sam saw the joy there and the love she wouldn't even try to hide. God, if only Sam had shown that same kind of love to his own daughter. If only he'd been…more. "She's with her grandparents in Florida. They've got her for the whole month. I miss her terribly."

Sam missed his daughter, too. Only she wasn't ever coming home. His heart ached and old pain surfaced. Pain he'd tried to run from. He'd endured months and months of agonizing grief and then it had turned to numbness. He liked the deadened feeling best. He'd managed to drift for months this way. Forgetting.

Good God, Caroline's daughter was the same age his daughter would have been—had she lived.

And little Tess *would* have lived if Sam had been there for her.

"My parents took her so that I could have this month to bring Belle Star Stables up to snuff again."

Sam brought himself back to the present. "So, you need to find help really fast."

She nodded. "Time's a wasting."

"Any prospects?"

"None at all."

Sam pondered this for a moment. His first instincts were to get out of Dodge the minute Caroline confessed to having a young daughter. Sam didn't think he could take the day-to-day reminder, but her daughter wasn't here. And she wouldn't be for a month.

And Sam had had enough of drifting from town to town every few days. He wouldn't mind staying on in Hope Wells for the month. But he'd already made a big mistake with Caroline and he'd hurt her feelings, as well.

He figured he'd be doing her a favor if he stayed on. He knew his way around a ranch and truth be told he'd spent the better part of his adult life running one of the largest construction companies in the southwest, the Triple B, his father's namesake, Blake Beaumont Building. He'd been CEO and top of his game, professionally. He'd helped his father bring in more business than they could handle, building up a small enterprise into a multi-million dollar corporation. To say he had some experience in carpentry was an understatement. Sam had made a fortune, but he'd paid a heavy price for his success. The cost of his dedication to work had been the untimely death of his child.

Yet as he stood there, looking at Caroline, he knew he could help her. If she'd agree, he could have her place up and running in one month's time, then he'd move on. Actually, he missed the hands-on work of creating and building something from scratch. Refurbishing her stables would be a challenge he'd love to take head-on.

And he'd already determined he could work side by side with Caroline, pretty as she was, he simply wasn't interested in getting involved with a woman. Good thing too, because the whole widow-and-child package would do him in otherwise.

"Listen, I have a proposition for you. If by the end of the day, you like the work I've done, and if no one comes knocking on your door for the job, I'm reapplying."

Caroline lifted her brows. "You are?"

"Yep, if you're agreeing."

She folded her arms, contemplating. "I don't see as I have much choice."

"Fair enough. Is it a deal then?"

Caroline hesitated, but he knew he had her over a barrel. She was desperate for help. One determined lady. She had a plan in mind, and Sam had no doubt she would succeed, with his assistance. "Let's see what you can do with those burned-up cabinets."

"Yes, ma'am."

Caroline reassessed the damage, not to her kitchen, but to her heart, and decided that it was a good thing Sam Beaumont was only interested in an honest day's work. He'd been up front about it. He'd been truthful. That's a heck of a lot more than she'd ever gotten from Gil.

Caroline had more than her ego on the line. And if

Sam Beaumont was the man for the job, then she was one step closer to seeing her dream come true. She hadn't gone into that honky-tonk last night looking for love. She'd gone looking for an employee.

Caroline grabbed the bag of food she'd bought from Patsy's Pantry, burgers fully loaded, fries and two caramel and fudge sundaes, still frozen she hoped, and exited her truck. She'd left the house three hours ago to run errands and then, because her kitchen was in turmoil, she'd picked up dinner.

It was after seven o'clock when she walked through her front door. Sam had been working all day, and if the cabinets looked half as good as the man fully immersed in the job, wearing a tight white tank and those faded blue jeans, then Caroline had found herself an employee.

"Dinner," she announced, setting the bags on the kitchen table.

When she glanced up, she found Sam standing back from the cabinets, admiring his work. "Almost through," he said.

Caroline swallowed, looking at the work he'd done. He'd managed to reface the existing cabinets so that they appeared an identical match. No one would have guessed that there had been burnt and charred wood there just hours ago. "They're beautiful."

"I couldn't find a match to the old doors, so I put on all new ones."

"I see that." Caroline loved the new look, but she hesitated. "I hadn't planned on renovating my entire kitchen. Those new doors must have been expensive."

"Nah," Sam said, finally glancing over to her. His dark eyes twinkled and Caroline's stomach flip-flopped. He was a man who, when he gave a woman his full attention, could turn her inside out. "I made the lumber store manager a deal. Trust me, you got more than a fair shake on the doors."

"How?"

"How'd I make the deal?" He seemed pleased with himself. "You'll do all your lumber business with him during the renovations and you'll give his kid free riding lessons."

"Free riding lessons?"

"Yep, you were planning on giving lessons, weren't you?"

She chuckled. "I am now."

Actually, aside from boarding and grooming the horses, Caroline had toyed with the idea of giving lessons after school and on weekends. Sam had just cemented the notion into reality.

He set the invoice for the cost of the lumber, doors included, onto the kitchen counter. Caroline leaned over to take a look. She couldn't fault him for being excessive since he had indeed gotten a fair price for the materials. She glanced up to meet his eyes. "Looks like I can afford you after all."

"So I'm hired?"

Caroline nodded. "For the month. Yes, I'll hire you. And I don't plan on starving my one and only employee. I brought dinner home from Patsy's Pantry. It's nothing fancy but the food's the best in five counties. Hungry?"

"I could eat," Sam admitted, "but I'd like to clean up first. Mind if I take a shower?"

A shower? Caroline's mind spun in a dozen directions, but it came back to earth quickly and focused on one final thought. Sam Beaumont, with his bronzed skin and strong body, *naked,* in her shower. The instant mind flash caused her a moment of doubt in hiring him.

He was good-looking to a fault. And sexy as sin.

Oh, Caroline, get a life.

"Sure, you can take a shower. Follow me."

Caroline grabbed a towel from the linen closet on her way toward the bathroom. "Sorry, all I have is this color."

Sam took the fluffy flamingo-pink towel. "Thanks. As long as it dries my bones, I'm happy."

"Take your time," she said once they reached the bathroom. "Dinner will keep." With that, Caroline headed for the kitchen, blocking out the image of hot steamy water running down Sam's bare body. Instead, she was grateful that Sam didn't have one of those macho, don't-give-me-anything-pink attitudes so many men share. A real man is secure enough in his own skin not to worry about trivial things like that. A real man knows who he is, and what he's made of.

It had taken Caroline twenty-nine years to realize what made a real man, and unfortunately, she just hadn't met too many of that breed in her lifetime.

She entered the kitchen, setting out paper plates and napkins, two glasses of lemonade and then... She remembered the fudge and caramel sundaes! "Oh, no!"

Quickly, she dug into the bag and came up with both ice cream concoctions. She sighed with relief. They weren't completely melted, so she set them into the freezer, hoping for the best.

Not ten minutes later, Sam reentered the kitchen. He'd dressed in his jeans again, but his chest was bare. Caroline blinked, opened her mouth to speak, but no words came out. Her naked-shower fantasy didn't compare to seeing the real thing. His jeans hung low, dipping under his navel and hugging a tight butt in the back. His chest, wasn't massive, wasn't muscle-man broad. No, it was simply the perfect amount of bronzed strength.

With hair slicked back, and tiny beads of moisture still caressing his skin, he headed straight for her in a slow sexy saunter. Sharp tingles coursed through her body as he came closer. Caroline held her breath, unable to move, staring.

"Excuse me," he said, passing her to reach for his shirt hanging on the back of the kitchen chair, the one he'd removed just before he began ripping out the damaged cabinets. He slipped his arms into the sleeves and turned to face her, buttoning up. "Smells good."

Her shoulders slumped ever so slightly "Oh, uh, yes. Let's eat."

Fantasy over.

And it was a good thing, too. Because if Sam Beaumont had reached for her hand, Caroline would have followed him.

Right into the bedroom.

* * *

"I'd like to seal the cabinets tonight, so I can get started tomorrow with the stables. The doors I can do outside, but I'm going to have to put the sealant on the existing cabinets where they are. Only problem is that the fumes will be too strong for you to sleep in the house."

Sam Beaumont collected his paper trash, helping Caroline clean up the kitchen after they'd eaten their meal. She wiped down the counter and table then turned to him. "Not a problem really. I can sleep in one of the stable stalls tonight."

"Are you sure?"

She shrugged. "The cabinets need to be finished. And I've got a sleeping bag. I've slept out there before."

"Oh, yeah? Have you lived here all of your life?"

"Most. When I married Gil, my parents retired and moved to Florida. They gave us the stables to run as a wedding present, along with the house I'd grown up in. They weren't crazy about changing the name of the stables to Portman, but they'd agreed. Gil had a thing about that. Status was everything to him. I should have known better, but I agreed, too. After all, I'd married into that name. At least when the place went to the dogs, my parents' name wasn't associated with the stables any longer. They'd worked hard most of their life to build up what Gil ruined in just four short years."

Caroline didn't want sympathy. And Lord knows, she'd agonized about this for too long. She wasn't looking back any longer. She had a future now, with the life insurance money that she'd received. And she was

determined to create a good life for Annabelle in the
process. One day, her daughter would have everything.

"Well, sounds like we've got a lot of work ahead of us.
It'll take me an hour or two to get these cabinets sealed.
And I can guarantee that you won't want to be in here."

Us? Caroline hadn't been one half of "us" in a long
time. She'd been the one making all the decisions, doing
all the planning and *hoping*. She sorta liked the sound
of it, even as she reminded herself that the sexy drifter
she'd hired would only be here for one month.

Caroline knew she to had take complete control—relinquishing her part in the ranch had been a mistake she
would never make again. She had too much to lose now.
She'd barely squeaked by these past few years, boarding
a few horses and taking on odd jobs just to earn enough
to keep food on the table and the bankers from knocking
on her doors. She'd never risk her daughter's future
again. And she'd never lay her heart and her life on the
line for another man. So this one-month arrangement
with Sam Beaumont was a perfect solution.

"Okay, well, I'll just muck out some of the stables.
I've got to check on Dumpling, anyway. She misses me
if I don't spend time with her at night."

"Dumpling?"

"Our family mare. She's a sweetheart."

He nodded. "So, will I be sleeping in the stables too?"

Caroline's mind once again flashed a thrilling image
of Sam Beaumont waiting for her on a plush bed of hay.
Her heart danced for a moment and, inwardly, she
sighed. "No, there's a room at the back of one of the

stables. Used to be a tack room, but I recently converted it into a guest room. I wouldn't expect much, but there's a comfortable bed, a dresser and electricity."

"Sounds fine."

But Sam Beaumont had already dismissed Caroline, focusing his attention on the cabinets. He worked his hands over the wood, looking for rough spots, surveying the job ahead.

Chuck from the Tie-One-On had been right in vouching for Sam Beaumont. He seemed intent on getting the job done and oddly enough, despite the way they'd met, Caroline felt she just might be able to work with him.

She reminded herself to ask Chuck how he'd come to know so much about Sam, and why he seemed so eager for her to hire him.

Sam Beaumont still was a mystery to her, the handsome drifter who seemed far too capable a man to be scrounging around for work, traveling from town to town like a vagabond.

The smell of wood and hay, of horse dung and leather brought back memories of happier times in Sam's youth. Sam stepped into the room he'd be staying in, breathing deeply, glancing around the small twelve-by-twelve room. He'd frequented the best five-star hotels in the country, but this room with its blue-checkered curtains, rough wood-framed landscapes and mismatched furniture, appealed to him in ways those elegant suites never had.

He and his younger brother, Wade, had been shoved

off to live with their Uncle Lee and Aunt Dottie on their working cattle ranch near El Paso. They'd had a small herd, earned a decent living and Sam would like to think he and Wade had brought some joy into their lives. His aunt and uncle couldn't have children of their own, and Sam's father thought it fitting to get the boys out of his hair while he built his new company from the ground up. Uncle Lee and Aunt Dottie had been the only true parents he and Wade had ever known.

Sam set his duffel bag on the bed then plopped down to test the mattress. Comfortable, he assessed, lying down and stretching out his legs. He laced his hands behind his head and rested on a navy corduroy pillow. He stared up at the ceiling, looking for a kind of peace that always seemed to elude him.

Sam had seen action in the Persian Gulf War, he'd battled the toughest opponents in the business world, but he had never known the kind of fear he experienced each night when he closed his eyes.

Thoughts of Tess would surface. But his mind denied Sam the sweet memories of his daughter. He didn't deserve them, not yet. Not ever. Sam had lost so much that day, his daughter, a wife who had blamed him, and the better part of his soul. "I'm sorry, Tess," he whispered quietly. "So sorry, sweetheart."

Sam rose from the mattress and paced the floor. He had no intention of sleeping on this comfortable bed tonight. He grabbed the doorknob and yanked open the door.

Caroline Portman stood on the other end, balancing a tray, ready to knock.

"Uh, hi," she said, "I almost forgot about dessert." She lifted the tray to his eyes. "Ice cream sundaes, slightly melted, but delicious all the same." She walked past him, stepping into the room. "Are you settled in for the night?"

"Not really. I won't sleep here tonight," he announced, "while you're sleeping on a bale of hay."

She grinned and those twin dimples peeked out. "I don't mind."

"I do. You get this bed tonight, or the deal's off."

"Really?"

"Yeah, really. The lady always gets the bed."

Caroline tilted her head to one side and smiled. "That's really not necessary."

Sam stared, standing still in silent argument, his expression set in stone.

Caroline sent him a look of genuine appreciation. "Okay, and thank you. That's very…very sweet." Sam got the distinct feeling she hadn't been treated with regard too often.

He wouldn't belabor the point. Instead, he glanced at the sundaes. "Those look good."

"Let's sit outside and eat them," she said, "before they melt even more."

They opted for a bale of hay just outside the barn. The night was warm, the sky overhead twinkling with bright stars. Sam enjoyed the serenity. He took a deep breath, and Caroline's fresh fruity scent invaded his brief peace. He glanced at her as she ate with gusto, devouring her ice cream. Sam found little enjoyment in life, but watching someone eat with such obvious glee made him smile.

"What's funny?" she asked, catching him.

Sam shook his head and pointed to her empty dish. "You ate that like there's no tomorrow."

His observation didn't rattle her; she grinned. "I know. I don't indulge often, but when I do, *watch out.*"

Good Lord, she looked pretty, sitting under the stars with moonlight streaming down. She had the softest features, a sweet smile and beautiful blue eyes. And Sam wondered about her comment. What other things did she indulge in? Her "watch out" statement intrigued the hell out of him. No, he wouldn't allow his mind to go there.

"You saved the day, Sam. I want to thank you for coming to my rescue today." Again, the sincerity in her tone made him think this woman, who deserved more, hadn't been treated with much regard in the past.

"I'm far from a hero, Caroline."

Caroline set the empty plastic ice cream dish on her lap and with head downcast, she admitted, "Still, I'm glad you're here."

"Because the stables mean everything to you."

She nodded. "My heart's been broken, Sam. I can't ever let that happen again."

Sam knew how she felt. Her sentiments echoed his own. Losses of any kind were hard to take—there was no way to measure the amount of pain they caused. Sam didn't think he had an exclusive on heartache. Obviously, Caroline had had a bad marriage and had almost lost her precious ranch. "We've got a lot of work to do starting tomorrow. Let's get some sleep."

Caroline agreed. She stood up abruptly, dropping the

dish and napkin that had been on her lap. Both went down to retrieve the items. They reached for the dish at the same time and bumped heads.

Sam's hand covered hers and an electric shock traveled through his system. Her sweet laughter rang out, tempting his senses. His body instantly reacted. Not just a little slight jab, but a full-fledged, piercing arrow that angled straight to his groin.

He went thick and hard below the waist. He summoned all his willpower to contain his massive erection. Wasn't happening. Instead, white-hot desire bulleted through his body. He ached from the fullness, something he hadn't experienced in a long time. That dead part of his body came alive and no matter how hard he tried to bring the numbness back, he couldn't.

Sam released Caroline's hand and backed off, staring into her eyes. Had he lied to himself last night when he'd kissed her? Had he persuaded himself that he was immune to her soft lips and warm womanly body? Had he fooled himself into thinking that Caroline Portman hadn't intrigued him from the very start, approaching him with her I-need-a-man, comment?

Sam didn't have answers. What he had was a hard-on that was killing him.

"Sam?" Caroline looked at him with curious eyes.

"It's nothing, Caroline. I'll see you in the morning." Stiffly, Sam rose and headed for the stable stall where he'd be sleeping tonight.

And he was hoping that when he woke, this momentary lapse would disappear in the morning's light.

Three

"You are a beauty," Sam admitted, stroking her female body, closing his eyes for a moment, relishing the feel of such a lovely creature. It gladdened his heart to see that she responded in kind.

"I see you've met Dumpling," Caroline said, walking up to the mare's stall. "And it appears you've made a new friend."

Sam patted the mare with affection. "She's a sweetheart, just like you said."

Caroline approached, rubbing her cheek against the mare's snout. The animal responded with a soft whinny. "Yeah, Dumpling and I go back a long way."

She eyed the horse with tenderness; her face glowing and Sam figured she saved that look for only those who'd earned it—only those she trusted.

"How'd you sleep?" she asked. When she turned her attention and her baby blues on him, Sam inwardly flinched, the blow taking him by surprise. Those sparks, those damned unwelcome fireworks hadn't disappeared as he'd hoped. They were alive and well and residing uninvited and unwelcome, flaming up his body. At least his anatomy below the waist hadn't betrayed him. Yet.

"Fine."

She narrowed her eyes. "Really? Were you comfortable in the sleeping bag?"

Last night Sam had had visions of lying with Caroline in the sleeping bag, counting stars and making love. He'd willed the sensation away, but the powerful urge only grew stronger. Unable to fight it off, he'd wanted to get up and run for the hills, but Sam had had enough of letting people down in his life. This time, he would keep his promise to work here for the month. He'd given his word, and he wouldn't back out now.

Caroline believed he wasn't interested in anything but an honest day's work and that's how he would keep it, as difficult as that would be.

"I slept just fine."

"Me, too." She sighed breathlessly. "Best sleep I've had in a long while, even though I miss Annabelle something fierce."

Sam turned away at the mention of the little girl's name. He had yet to come to terms with the death of his daughter. He didn't begrudge Caroline's love for her little girl, but the ache inside him burned deep and tore at him with raw agonizing pain. He couldn't hear talk of her little Annabelle without reliving the horrible day that young Tess had died.

Sam blamed himself.

And he always would.

He peered out over the yard and the other buildings they'd be working on and quickly changed the subject. "Do you have a plan of action?"

Caroline sidled up next to him. "After breakfast, I was hoping we could go over what needs doing. We could make a list of repairs. As you can see, the yard itself is pretty run down."

Sam glanced her way, seeing so much in her eyes, her hopes and expectations and her dream of a successful stable coming alive again. "I think that's a good plan. But I'm not one for breakfast."

She smiled. "Coffee then?"

"Sounds good."

"Well then, I'll go get it brewing and bring you out a cup. Sound fair?"

"You're the boss."

She lifted her lips in a soft smile. "I am, aren't I?"

Her scent lingered as he watched her walk into the house, her perfect derriere catching his eye. She moved with grace, the unintentional sway of her hips purely natural. She wore a plaid work shirt and ripped jeans. Work clothes. Yet Sam eyed her with more enthusiasm than he would an exotic dancer working a dance pole.

His body reacted, tightening up.

He cursed and grabbed a steel rake. He'd just burn off

his extra energy with good hard work. He wasn't above mucking out a stall, and from what he could tell there would be plenty of stalls to muck in the very near future.

Later that day, Caroline cooked spaghetti and meatballs and they ate dinner together in the kitchen, each absorbed in their own thoughts, or so it seemed. The radio, set on low, played down-home country tunes, easing the quiet. All in all, Caroline was pleased with the day's work they'd put in. Sam had proven himself a hard worker and a man of his word. So far.

But Sam didn't divulge too much about himself. And Caroline wasn't into prying. She knew what she needed to know about Sam Beaumont for now.

"So do you think we can finish everything on our list before the month is up?" Caroline asked, stringing a wad of spaghetti around her fork. She'd posed this question to Sam in different ways today and each time his reassurance had helped calm her nerves.

"I think so. There're major repairs to be done to the roofs and stable stalls, some painting and shoring up of your fences. The yard will need a complete overhaul. You'll need new supplies of feed and hay. But I think we can do it."

Caroline nodded. "Yes, I'm hoping so. I'd like to have everything done before school starts. Annabelle will be starting first grade. She'll be gone most of the day. I'll be able to run things, along with some part-time help."

"Do you have anyone in mind?"

She shrugged, not worried in the least. "There's

always high-school students ready to earn some extra cash. I know because I used to be one of them." She chuckled, recalling her days as a part-time employee. "I worked at Curly's Ice Cream Parlor, making root beer floats and banana splits after school."

Even though they spoke of nothing specific, Caroline enjoyed conversing with another grown-up. And this particular grown-up happened to make her heart stop every now and then when she least expected it. Sam Beaumont had a style all his own. His quiet demeanor, his work ethic and his incredible good looks blended into a man who had, to put it quite simply, entered into Caroline's fantasies.

Caroline set her fork down, her spaghetti plate empty. "What about you? Did you ever have a part-time job?"

Sam took a moment then nodded his head. "I worked for my uncle. He had a small ranch outside of El Paso."

"Ah, so you do know something about this life."

"Well, we had a herd of cattle, but ranching cattle isn't too different. And we had a healthy string of horses, too. Uncle Lee used an old army helicopter he'd salvaged to oversee his ranch. I'd go up in that bird every chance I got."

Caroline could only imagine a young Sam Beaumont completely addicted to flying, watching his uncle fly over the ranch and wishing he was the one behind the controls. "I'm surprised you didn't fly it yourself."

Sam stared down at his plate for a moment, then admitted. "I did. Got my pilot's license when I was twenty."

"You're a pilot?" Stunned, Caroline stared at Sam. Everything she knew in her heart about this man, contradicted his presence here in Hope Wells. Early on, she'd pegged him for a drifter, a man with no ties, no connections to anyone or anyplace, but the man she was coming to know didn't quite fit that bill.

"I was. I don't fly anymore."

"May I ask why?"

Sam glanced at her and for a moment she thought she might get an answer, but then the phone rang. "Oh, excuse me."

Sam watched Caroline answer the phone, twirling the cord on her finger as she leaned against the refrigerator. She smiled as she recognized the caller.

"Hey, Joanie. It's good to hear from you. Yes, yes, I know. I've been busy."

Sam rose from the table and took his plate to the sink.

"A girls' night out? Oh, that's sounds like fun, but I can't. Yes, I know how long it's been since I went out. But you know I've got only the month to get the stables running again. I'm working every day."

Sam put the iced-tea pitcher in the refrigerator, along with the container of Parmesan cheese and Caroline mouthed him a "thank you" as she slid out of his way.

"Yes, I know. I can't use Annabelle as an excuse right now. I do know that, Joanie, but oh—darn. I forgot it's Lucille's birthday. All the girls are going?"

He finished clearing the table, wondering if he should leave rather than eavesdrop on Caroline's phone conversation, but when he looked her way, she put up her index finger asking for one minute.

He leaned against the sink with arms folded and ankles crossed and waited, watching Caroline's eyes dance with delight, her blond ponytail bouncing as she bobbed her head in conversation. He enjoyed looking at her—way too much.

"Okay, Saturday night. You'll pick me up? Great. See you then."

Caroline hung up the phone and walked over to him. "Thanks for helping with clean up."

Sam nodded. "Dinner was good."

"I'm not the greatest cook, but I try."

"You're better than you think."

She appreciated the polite compliment for what it was. "Thank you. Oh, and I guess we're not working all day Saturday like I'd planned. You heard that conversation. I tried, but my friends won't let me off the hook. I'm going out for the first time since…well, doesn't matter. We'll just catch up on Monday."

"I can still work the weekend."

She shook her head. "No, that wouldn't be fair. We'll put in half a day on Saturday and Sunday we'll rest. Remember, we'd agreed on those terms?"

Sam didn't need a day off but Caroline did, whether she knew it or not. He'd agreed to her terms only to seal the deal. He'd worked seven days a week for so long that he really didn't think it a hardship. Although others had, and that's where he'd gone wrong in his life. His priorities had been way off.

He wouldn't make that mistake again.

"Sunday, we rest," Sam agreed.

"Good."

Caroline smiled with warmth in her eyes and she glanced up at the cabinets he'd replaced. "You wouldn't know that these had burned up yesterday. They're so much nicer now with the new doors. You did an amazing job. Have I thanked you properly?"

Sam could think of a dozen ways she might thank him but nothing *proper* entered into his mind. "Twice. You thanked me twice, Caroline," he said, his voice a husky whisper.

"Oh, I did?" She stared into his eyes, her gaze lingering, then she turned and reached up on her tiptoes to put a clean plate onto the shelf. She fumbled, the dish teetering on the edge. Sam moved quickly, sandwiching her between his body and the counter and caught the dish before it crashed. He set the dish on the shelf, fully aware of Caroline's body pressed to his.

He groaned, the sound a hoarse cry of need. He stood rooted to the spot, unable to move away, as his body heated up to a quick sizzle.

"Sam?"

"Shh, don't turn around, Caroline."

But Caroline did just that. She wiggled around, so that she faced him, trapped between his rigid erection and the counter.

Sam closed his eyes.

But her soft voice snapped his eyes open, real quick. "Maybe I need a test of my own."

Caroline leaned in, crushing her breasts against his chest and brought her mouth to his. She kissed him softly, the tender onslaught touching him deep inside. Sam kissed her back with urgency, his body sparked by desire, his mind on complete shutdown.

He swept his tongue in her mouth, his erection grinding into her at the sweet junction of her thighs. She moaned and wrapped her arms around his neck, their lips frantic, their bodies overheated. The steamy kiss lasted a long time, until, breathlessly, both came up for air.

Caroline pulled away slightly, breaking the heated connection. "Wow," she whispered. "I guess I have my answer."

Yeah. *Wow.*

Sam hadn't felt this alive in months, but he wouldn't rejoice. He didn't want the feeling. He didn't welcome the pulsating in his body and the racing of his heart. He stepped away from her, rubbing the back of his neck.

Leaning against the counter, Caroline folded her arms, pushing up breasts that Sam ached to touch as she stared into his eyes. Sam recalled her I-need-a-man statement and wondered if that hadn't been a Freudian slip. A shudder coursed through his body. Caroline was a widow with a small daughter to raise. Sam had had a taste of that life once and had failed miserably. He wasn't the man for Caroline Portman.

"Honey, the way I see it," Sam began gently, "we have one month to get your place up and running. We can work or we can…*play*. Either way, in one month's time, I'm gone."

Caroline's baby-blue eyes grew wide. She blinked back her surprise. Sam had shocked her. Hell, he'd shocked himself. But he had to lay his cards on the table, knowing what was most important to both of them.

Quietly, she confessed. "You're right. I've already had one man run out on me. And it took me a long time to recover. I'm not willing to chance it again. Renovating Belle Star is all that matters now." She smiled and her eyes softened with appreciation. "Thank you for your honesty."

Honesty? Hell, if he'd been truly up-front with her, he would have told her how he wanted to lift her up on that counter and drive his body into hers until they were breathless and sapped of energy.

That would have been the honest truth.

"I'd better go." Sam headed for the door and at the last minute he turned to face her squarely. "Just for the record, don't think it's easy for me to walk out this door."

Caroline bit down on her lip and nodded then she called out just before he stepped out the door, "Sam?"

She had his attention.

"Tomorrow, we'll start over. No more tests. Deal?"

He nodded. "Deal."

Sam exited the kitchen, walking out into the night but even the fresh crisp air couldn't obliterate Caroline's sweet scent from his mind. Or the feel of her soft body pressed to his against that counter.

Sam headed for his room and the bed that Caroline had slept in last night.

Suddenly, one month seemed like an eternity.

Caroline donned her one and only party dress, the black lace-trimmed satin that draped low in the back and hugged her hips tightly. She put on matching strappy heels that felt foreign on feet used to work boots. Foreign but so attractive that it made up for the lack of comfort. By the end of the evening, she could be certain her feet would ache like the dickens.

"The price of beauty," she said, repeating her mama's favorite saying, as Caroline stared at her image in her bedroom mirror. She applied a coat of Candy Apple Red lipstick to her lips then blotted.

Just like her mama taught her.

Caroline shouldn't feel guilty about going out with her friends tonight, but she did. After that night in the kitchen, she and Sam had settled down and gotten to business. She couldn't be happier with the results so far. They'd made good progress all week long. While Sam worked on repairing the stables, bolstering up the stalls and reinforcing the exterior, Caroline had tilled the yard, pulling up weeds that had taken firm root.

Both had worked long hours each day, sharing a quiet meal together in the evenings, speaking little. Caroline would catch Sam watching her from time to time, his dark gaze following her every movement. Her heart rang out from the way he looked at her at times, but even through all that she believed they'd developed a good working relationship.

And even though she felt a sense of accomplishment for the week's work, she still experienced deep-rooted guilt for going out tonight. She missed Annabelle something fierce for one thing and she hadn't forgotten the heat of Sam's kisses the other night.

Her best friend, Maddie Walker, newly married to one of Hope Wells's last remaining bachelors had sized her up perfectly with one wise statement, "Caroline, you've simply forgotten how to have fun."

Well, Caroline decided she did need a little fun in her life. And as Maddie had pointed out, *she deserved it.*

So she set her mind on forgetting about Sam Beaumont and chucking her guilt, at least for one night.

Because tonight, Caroline Portman was doing the town.

Saturday night at Tie-One-On wasn't the place to go for peace and quiet. Sam should have known better, but after a hard day of work, despite Caroline's efforts to curtail him, then catching a good long glimpse of her sliding into her friend's car for a night on the town, Sam had needed a drink.

While he sat at a corner table, three women had approached him on separate occasions, no doubt hoping to lend comfort to a lonely man. Sam politely refused, not being interested. So he'd gotten up to stand against the wall. With beer in hand, he faced the dance floor, blending in with a boisterous crowd.

Past midnight, he was on his third and final beer,

when a group of five young women walked in, laughing and having a good old time. But only one stood out. Only one held his attention.

Caroline.

She wore a knockout black dress that exposed long shapely legs. Her hair was a mass of blond waves and her baby blues, dancing with laughter, were the prettiest he'd ever seen.

She was a knockout and the only woman on earth who appealed to him.

She was his boss, he told himself. The woman was strictly off limits. They'd already settled that. Only trouble was, he wasn't sure he believed it anymore.

He stood, gripping his beer bottle tightly as he watched her dance with some duded-up guy wearing a Stetson. They danced three times, before Caroline begged off and headed back to her friends standing by the bar.

She laughed at something one of her friends said, then turned her head his way. That's when she spotted him. Through the crowd, their eyes met.

An electrifying jolt shot straight through him, his body tightened up, his heart did somersaults. She looked so pretty standing there with dim smoky light casting shadows on her golden hair, wearing a dimpled smile that appeared wholesome and tempting all at the same time. He stared straight into her eyes, the magnetic pull drawing him in.

And she stared back. Slowly, and with what appeared to be a shaky hand, she set the glass she held down onto the bar, keeping her eyes trained on him. He read so much in those pretty blue eyes, a hunger that matched his own, the hot sizzling promise of what was to come.

The attraction was real, sharp and potent.

Mesmerized, he focused his full attention on her and his body reacted, growing hard and tight quickly. With his gaze locked to hers, he took a step away from the wall. The Stetson guy approached her again and she broke their connection. He witnessed her shake her head no, but the guy didn't get the message. Instead, he grabbed her hand and tugged, attempting to get her back onto the dance floor.

Sam was there instantly, gripping the guy's hand, removing it from hers. Sam looked into Caroline's eyes. "The lady's with me."

"I don't think so, pal," the guy said without hesitation. He yanked his arm free of Sam's grip.

Sam ignored him, and faced his new boss, giving her the option. "Caroline?"

Caroline glanced at the other man and confirmed his pronouncement with no apology. "I'm with him."

The guy shoved his Stetson low on his head, cast Sam an angry look then took off mumbling curse words under his breath.

Sam took both of Caroline's hands in his. Leaning in, he whispered in her ear, "Let's get outta here."

Caroline nodded, her gaze never leaving his. She made a quick stop to whisper something to one of her friends, grabbed her purse, then waved farewell to them all. "Bye, ladies."

Sam didn't wait around to hear their stunned

comments. He led Caroline outside and swung around to the back of the building. Leaning his back to the wall, he pulled her against him. Caroline flowed into his arms.

He kissed her immediately, sweeping his tongue into her mouth, tasting her, open-mouthed and frenzied, the fire inside him burning with white-hot intensity.

She moaned and he pulled her in tighter, pressing her into his erection. "You've got me wound up real tight, honey. It's not my usual style, but the Cactus Inn's just next door. It's a nice place and I've got protect—"

Caroline silenced him with a quick kiss. Then she smiled. "Yes."

Sam kissed her back then took her hand leading her to the Cactus Inn Motel. He blocked out all the reasons they shouldn't be doing this, shoved aside all of his misgivings, but he wasn't fooling himself.

Sam knew they were heading for trouble.

And there wasn't one damn thing he could do about it.

Four

Caroline stood inside the neat and tidy motel room, her heart beating like mad. She peered at the no-nonsense furniture before casting her gaze on the queen-sized bed looming before her. She heard the decided click of the door as Sam came up from behind, wrapping his arms around her belly, gently pulling her against him. She leaned back, relishing his heady scent, the maleness of it all and the way their bodies seemed to fit together so perfectly, even in this position. "Why do you still have this room?" she asked as it suddenly dawned on her that Sam had been living in her makeshift guest room for several days now.

"I'm paid up for the month," he whispered, his breath warm against her cheek. "Didn't think I'd see this room again though."

"I didn't think I'd be here either," she said, turning

in his arms to face him. "I don't do…I mean this isn't me. I'm not good at—"

Sam shushed her with a deep lingering kiss that nearly buckled her knees. "I know what kind of woman you are, Caroline, and that's why I'm giving you a way out. Things got pretty hot and heavy back there. You need time to take a step back and think about this because, no matter what happens here tonight, I'm leaving Hope Wells in one month's time. Once the job is finished, I'm moving on."

Caroline understood that. She wouldn't ask for anything more. For too many years now, she'd kept herself in a safe cocoon, wrapped up in making a happy home for her daughter, unwilling to break loose to take a chance on anyone, or on life. She was a single mother who'd been granted this one opportunity, this one time, when she answered to no one but herself. And if Caroline had to indulge in her fantasies, who better to do it with but the only man she'd met in years who stopped her heart? Sam was that man. Though she had questions about him, the why and how of his drifting from town to town, she wouldn't dwell on that now.

Now, all she wanted was to feel womanly again. To be held and loved by a man who seemed to appreciate her. The fact that he'd just offered her a way out when she witnessed desire burning in his eyes, felt it in the way his stiff body pressed against hers, told her more than she needed to know about him.

She slipped the thin black straps off her shoulders in answer. "One month, Sam. You've made yourself clear."

"And you're okay with this…with us?" Sam asked,

and the hope registering in his eyes was enough to boost Caroline's fragile ego.

She nodded. And smiled. Then proceeded to wiggle the rest of the way out of her slinky, special-occasion dress. As long as she was indulging in her fantasies…

She stood before him in a lacy black bra and panties feeling self-conscious and more than a little brazen in her two-inch strappy heels.

Sam took half a step back, his eyes darkening to coal as they scoured every inch of her.

He reached up to stroke through her golden hair, bringing the waves forward to rest over her shoulders and the groan that escaped his throat went deep and guttural. "This is going to happen fast," he said, slowly removing his shirt, button by button, his eyes never leaving her body. His well-paced actions seem to belie his words. "The first time, I mean."

Caroline gulped, staring at the broad expanse of his chest. "The first time?"

Sam grinned and stepped closer. "We have all night."

Rapid hot tremors passed through her body. She breathed out, "Yes. Yes, we do." Oh, she thought, if only he was half as good as he looked, her fantasy would be unrivaled.

"Put your hands on me, darlin'," he said, and before Caroline could react, Sam reached for her hands, placing them to his chest. She laid her palms full out on the solid wall of muscle, feeling every bit of him she could reach. The contact made him groan and pull her into a tight embrace. He crushed his lips to hers, dipped his tongue into her mouth and stroked her with precision.

Caroline reacted in kind, making little throaty sounds as their tongues wreaked havoc on each other. Sam reached around and cupped her buttocks, drawing her closer, so that her softness crushed into his rock-hard shaft.

From there, Caroline lost all sense of time and space. Clothes flew off as the pair landed with a thud onto the bed and rolled until both were satisfied with the position. Sam guided her hands once again, this time to his waist and she toyed with his edge of his jeans until he grunted a complaint, then with a bedeviled smile, she lowered his zipper. He kicked off his boots, and tossed his jeans off in rapid succession, replacing her hands, right where they'd been.

Under Sam's guidance, she stroked him, sliding over the slick surface of his manhood and he moved in her rhythm, their bodies in line and fully tuned to each other. The need was urgent, their mouths hungry, their bodies hungrier. For Caroline, it had been too many years of abstinence. Too long for a young woman with a lot to give. So she gave to Sam, heartily and hungrily and soon, it was his turn to give. He rolled her over onto her back, his legs positioning her with firm command and when he slid his fingers between her thighs, stroking fast, she went slick and wet immediately.

"You ready for me, darlin'? Cause I'm about to implode."

Caroline nodded, too wrapped up in the heady sensations to speak. Heart beating wildly, she slithered up higher on the bed and welcomed him. Within moments, condom in place, he entered her, his full thick shaft filling her body. She ached a little, in a good way, in a way she'd never ached before, and when he began to move, Caroline threw her head back, giving him full access.

His movements were those of a man with need. Fast, precise, controlled, but oh, so incredibly, painstakingly gentle. Caroline moved with him, rocking with his rhythm, their desire seeming equal, what both wanted and needed at the moment. The motel room echoed with their quick, spontaneous, unabashed cries of release.

Sated in a way she'd never been before, Caroline sighed silently inside, a deep purr of satisfaction. Sam lay beside her and when both had caught their breath, he took her hand, entwined their fingers and leaned over to kiss her tenderly. "You're a beautiful woman, Caroline Portman."

Caroline looked up into Sam's deep dark eyes and saw something there that touched her heart. Gratitude. She heard it in the tone and timbre of his whispered words as well and she knew she wasn't mistaken.

She reached up to touch his face, the day-old stubble feeling rough against her fingers. Already, in just a few days, she'd gotten accustomed to him, his face, his rare smile and, now, his body.

If Sam had been grateful, then Caroline experienced that emotion doubly for the act of intimacy they'd just shared. Caroline had never felt more like a woman. She'd never been so aroused, so caught up in the moment. She'd never been so bold, either. She should be covering her face in shame for the audacious way she'd behaved, but she didn't feel anything remotely shameful. How could she when gorgeous, sexy Sam Beaumont was staring at her as though she was a gift he wanted to unwrap again and again?

"Sam," she began, but couldn't bring herself to thank him in words. "It was wonderful."

Sam chuckled, bringing her closer and folding her into his arms. "Not gonna deny that, but like I said, next time we'll take it slow. That's if you want a next time?"

Sam stroked her arms, sliding his hands up and down, then cupped her breast, feeling the weight, his fingers smoothing over her skin like a silken glove. "Please tell me you want a next time," he whispered in her ear.

"I'm ready when you are," she whispered back, already aroused again by Sam's caresses.

He let out a small hoarse cough. "Give me a minute, darlin'" he said, with good humor. "I need some time to regroup."

"Oh, I didn't mean right now. I mean, I did, but not if you're not—"

"Shh," Sam said, "let's just close our eyes a while. It's late and we have the rest of the night."

Caroline mentally chastised herself for not having a clue about any of this. But when Sam tugged her closer, resting her head on his chest, all of Caroline's doubts vanished. She let go of her insecurities and relished just being here with him. And when she closed her eyes she found precious peace in Sam Beaumont's arms.

* * *

Caroline woke from a deep sleep and for a moment, she became slightly disoriented. Where was she? The room didn't appear at all familiar. The bed, the walls, everything seemed strange.

And then she remembered.

It hadn't taken long for the sweet memories of making love to Sam Beaumont in his motel room to resurface. She smiled, stretched her arms full out then let them fall with a contented sigh. Dawn had yet to break through the darkness. She lay beside Sam, his body lending warmth and comfort. Caroline was in bed with Sam having her very first…what? *Affair* seemed too crude a word for what they'd shared. And this wasn't permanent. It was a…fling? Caroline shook her head, no. She wasn't a woman to have flings. Whatever it was, she decided simply to enjoy her time with Sam. No regrets. No repercussions. She faced facts. Once Belle Star was up and running, they'd go their separate ways. And that was okay with Caroline.

So, if she weren't having an affair, or a fling, she'd just have to label this as widow-gone-wild. She chuckled and decided that going wild felt real good. And if she were lucky enough to have Sam's full attention for one month's time, then she'd take it.

She'd indulge in her fantasy. "It's about time," she spoke aloud, forgetting that there was anyone else in the room. Old widow habits dying hard.

Sam cradled her from behind and wrapped his arm around her waist. His touch sparked immediate desire. "You waiting up for me, darlin'?"

Yes. "No, just thinking out loud. Sorry if I woke you."

"You didn't."

Caroline liked the intimacy of being held by Sam, having his whispered words caress her ears, so she didn't turn to face him to respond. She simply relished waking up in his embrace. "Good."

"I'm all rested now," he said in a slow languid drawl that would surely melt ice.

"Are you?" Caroline bit down on her lip to keep from chuckling. She liked playing Sam's game.

"Yeah, I'm feeling pretty…healthy."

"That's good, Sam."

"Yeah, and just so you know…I don't do this…I mean it's been a long time for me."

Caroline found that hard to believe. Sam was too sexy and virile a man not to have ample experience with women. A drifter, a man alone, looking as fine as any one man could get? It seemed to Caroline that women would flock to him. "Well, you certainly haven't forgotten anything."

Sam stroked her hip, making tiny circles with his fingers. "No complaints then?"

"Oh," she gasped as his fingers moved upwards on her torso. "None." She shook her head. "None at all."

Sam lifted her hair, moving it off her neck and planted tiny kisses there, his lips gentle, like a soft breeze blowing by. "Good."

"What…um, what about you?"

"You're kidding, right?" he responded immediately. His fingers found the hollow just under her breast.

He moved with soft caresses until the skin there prickled. Caroline sucked in oxygen. Shivers crept up her belly while heat flowed below. "I'm not fishing for compliments, but I want to know."

Sam stroked her nipple with his thumb, making her ache deep down inside. His body against hers went tight and his shaft hard. "Caroline, a man couldn't ask for anything more."

His admission helped heal past hurts and Caroline secretly thanked heaven for bringing this man into her life for the time being. Maybe that had been the plan all along. Maybe Caroline had been waiting for someone like Sam Beaumont to come along to put a salve on her open wounds.

No more words were spoken that night. And as Sam had promised when they made love again, it was long and slow and as delicious as steaming hot fudge melting over vanilla ice cream.

"I thought Sundays were meant for rest," Caroline cooed softly, her warm naked body pressed against him. Sam kissed her lips, stroking his hands up and down her arms, her creamy skin coming alive under his palms.

They'd left the motel at 6:00 a.m., Caroline keeping a low profile. Sam wanted it that way. He knew how judgmental small towns could be, and he wasn't sure how many people had noticed them striding out of Tie-One-On last night, barely able to keep their hands off each other, but he had to try to protect her. He wanted to leave Caroline with her reputation intact and her stables workable again.

But as soon as they reached her home, they'd reached for each other again and wound up horizontal on her bed. Sam hadn't experienced lust like this before. Not even as a young military recruit in his early twenties, or when he'd first married his wife, Lydia, had he felt this kind of raw elemental need. He chalked it up to self-imposed celibacy and the lonely months of drifting. But he knew one thing for sure—at this rate, they'd never get any work done.

"That's what we're doing. Resting."

"*Now,* we're resting," Caroline said with a dimpled smile. "But what happened a few minutes ago I would label as an intense workout."

"You made the rules, boss lady. Sundays we rest. Seems we've defined *resting* in new terms, though."

Caroline moved away from him enough to look into his eyes. She looked so beautiful right now, all soft and dewy-eyed, like a woman who'd been sexually sated. Sam wanted her again. Seemed he couldn't quite get enough. It took a great deal of self-control to keep from pulling her into his arms again and staking claim to her body.

"Sam, do you think that if we don't work, we'll end up doing this all day?"

Sam chuckled. "All day? Now, that's a tall order, but I think I'm up for the challenge."

Caroline's pretty mouth dropped open. "That's not what I meant. I guess…I don't know what I mean. It's just that, I've never…oh, you know. It's never been so—"

"Hot?"

She nodded.

"Good?"

She nodded.

"Amazing?"

Caroline shoved at Sam's chest, pulling away from him. "Don't tease me."

"I'm not. If you put your hand below my waist, you'll see that I'm serious as hell."

Caroline swallowed. And to his amazement, she did just that. She touched him under the sheets. The heat of his arousal sizzled in her palm. A groan escaped from deep inside his throat.

"Oh, Sam. What's gotten into us?"

"You might want to amend your 'Sundays we rest' policy, darlin'."

"Yeah, I think you're right. Shall we get up? I'll fix coffee, and we'll get some work done today."

Sam covered her hand with his, so that her grip on him intensified. "Don't think I can just now. Coffee can wait."

Sam encouraged her with gentle kisses and softly spoken words, until she moved once again with heat and passion beneath him. He needed her one more time, before he could concentrate on any work today. Caroline seemed to be in tune with him, generously offering what Sam so desperately craved. He came up over her, their eyes connecting, their bodies already familiar with each other, and as he entered her once again, thrusting gently, taking her with him, he marveled at Caroline's giving nature, the way she trusted him so completely.

He stroked her breasts, palming the deeply darkened circles as they peaked pebble-hard. Gasps of pleasure sprang from her lips, her face awash with such intense satisfaction that Sam's body reacted in kind. He brought them to the brink quickly then, showering her with escalating thrusts that lifted them higher and higher.

The release called to them both, each in their own worlds, then they came together in their fall back down to earth.

Sam lay sated and complete upon the bed, his face turned up, staring at the ceiling. "Can I say I think you're amazing, without you thinking I'm teasing?"

Caroline purred beside him.

"And beautiful." He turned to face her. "So beautiful, Caroline."

She smiled at the compliment, then stroked his chest, her fingers playing with the curling hairs there. "I think I could stay here all day, after all."

Sam grasped her hand and, bringing it up to his lips, he kissed her knuckles. "Yeah, a tempting offer, boss lady, but we have work to do."

He'd promised to help Caroline refurbish her stables so that she could have that grand opening she'd spoken about with such excitement. She had a deadline, and so did he. He wouldn't stay in Hope Wells longer than one month, so he might as well get cracking. There were stables to rebuild, a yard that needed tender, loving care and fences to mend. He kicked off the sheets and got out of bed. And when he turned to find Caroline's pretty blue eyes on him, her blond hair spread across the pillow, her sheet-clad body partially exposed, he knew he'd never seen a more stunning woman in his life.

But as his gaze wandered off slightly to the night-stand beside the bed, a photo he hadn't yet noticed caught his attention. A cherubic face, with blue eyes and curly locks, stared up at him, the child's face full of joy and expectation. Sam's heart slammed hard with regret and gut-wrenching pain. He'd almost forgotten. For the past twelve hours, Caroline had consumed him, mind, body and soul. But along with Caroline, came a beauty of a child, so much like his own Tess, that he couldn't bear to look any longer.

"Sam, what's wrong?" Caroline asked.

Sam smiled, transforming his grief-stricken face. He shook off her question. "Nothing. I'm going to take a shower."

He left Caroline's room as old and wearisome grief reminded him of why he was drifting, why he could never go back to the life he'd once led. Of why he'd leave Hope Wells in his dust in a few short weeks.

Five

Maddie Brooks Walker stared out Caroline's kitchen window, her gaze following the movements of the man upon the roof of the larger of the two stables on the property. "You say Chuck at Tie-One-On vouched for him?"

Caroline nodded and sipped from the tall glass of lemonade she was enjoying with her best and newly pregnant friend. "Yep. Chuck said they spent time together in the military, years ago."

Maddie frowned. "He doesn't look…I don't know. I hate to judge, but he's not your typical handyman."

Caroline grinned, thinking back on the last ten days and nights she'd spent with Sam. He wasn't 'typical' in any way, shape or form. From the way he worked with his hands, so expertly, so precisely that he seemed to craft the stables, fixing and repairing with the smallest amount of effort and the greatest amount of knowledge, to the way he worked his hands on her, so magically with gentle touches and hungry caresses that calmed her and heated her all at the same time. "All I know is that he's good at everything he does."

Maddie turned sharply to stare into her eyes. It must have been the tone of her voice, the way she spoke of Sam that put suspicion in her best friend's eyes. "*Everything* he does?"

Caroline smiled, turning away to pour more lemonade into both of their glasses.

Maddie walked over to the kitchen table, her gaze never leaving Caroline's. "Tell me."

Caroline sat down. Maddie did the same. A just-missed car accident on the main street of town a few years back had the two women bonding a friendship that would last until both were grandmothers. The pretty young veterinarian had fallen in love with the most stubborn, hard-nosed, best-looking bachelor in Hope Wells, and with a little help from Caroline and others, Trey Walker had finally realized that Maddie had been meant for him all along.

Caroline cherished their friendship. She wouldn't lie to Maddie. But these past ten days with Sam had been heaven, so private, so intimate. During the day, they'd work their fingers to the bone on Belle Star and at night, they'd fall into bed together and make love. And on those nights when one or both were too exhausted, they simply lay in each other's arms until sleep claimed them.

For Caroline, it was her fantasy come true.

She was living her dream, rebuilding her stables and sharing her nights with an incredible lover.

No regrets.

No repercussions.

Caroline granted herself these blissful weeks before motherhood and her professional life would once again claim her. "He's…very good."

Maddie leaned in, her green eyes rounding on her. "So you've said. How good?"

Caroline sipped lemonade. She'd never make the same mistakes she'd made with Gil. Her judgment and objectivity had been way off the charts then, but Caroline knew what she was getting into with Sam. She had no qualms about what she was doing, but she didn't want Maddie to worry about her. "He's very—"

"If you say *good* one more time—"

"Gentle, Maddie. Caring. And passionate. Just what I need, right now." She didn't add "sexy as sin." She guessed that Maddie had figured that out.

"Okay," Maddie said with a little pause, "got it. I would never judge you, honey, but are you sure you know what you're doing?"

"I've never been more sure. Sam's here to help out with Belle Star. He's hired for one month and he's been a godsend to me."

"Oh, dear. That's what I was afraid of. What if he decides to move on?"

Caroline smiled and with a shake of her head, she said, "That's exactly what will happen. And I'm okay with that. I won't fool myself into thinking he'll stick around. He's a drifter and I know that. Once the stables are done and Annabelle comes back, he'll be gone. I won't ever allow myself to get so caught up with emotion that I'm blinded again. Gil's negligence nearly destroyed Annabelle's legacy. He nearly destroyed me. My heart's well-protected now. I have no illusions."

Caroline stared out the window, watching Sam hammer the roofing material onto the top of the stables, his hair slicked back, his T-shirt sticking to his skin, exposing a strong and vital physique. "This time, I'm in control of my own destiny. And *you,* my dear pregnant friend, have nothing to worry about. Just concentrate on that new little baby growing inside you. How's Trey doing with all this?"

Maddie took one last glance out the window, looking at Sam, seeming unsure whether to let the subject drop. Then, with a sigh, she focused on Caroline, one hand placed on her still-flat belly. "Well, Trey's nervous, excited, crazed and thrilled. We both are. We can't wait. And he's looking at me differently now. Like he's afraid I'm going to break or something. It's really kinda sweet."

Caroline chuckled. "I can just picture that. Trey—the confirmed bachelor, happily married now and entering into fatherhood. Who would have guessed that ever happening a few years ago? Good thing you came to town when you did. Trey's life would have been much different if he hadn't fallen for you."

"Yes, it's amazing how fate works, isn't it?"

"Yes, in your case, amazing." Caroline maintained her smile for her best friend. She wouldn't relay her own disappointment when fate hadn't turned a kind hand toward her. She'd never been granted that wonderful kind of doting attention when she'd been pregnant with Annabelle. Gil hadn't been thrilled. He hadn't done anything to make her feel special. His indifference to the joyous occasion of their conceiving a child should have been a clue. There had been so many clues. And she'd labeled herself a fool for not recognizing all the signs earlier. No, fate hadn't been kind to her in that regard. But she had hit the lottery in bearing a beautiful daughter. Everything she did now was for her daughter's sake.

"How's our little Annabelle doing in Florida?" Maddie asked.

The mention of Annabelle always brought a smile. "I miss her terribly. I have to hear her voice at least once before I can get to sleep at night. So, Mom and Dad make sure we talk every day. She's being spoiled, I'm sure. But I can't even work up any real worry over it. That little girl deserves all the attention she gets. Lord knows, she didn't get much from her own father."

Caroline closed her eyes momentarily then shook her head. "I'm sorry. I shouldn't have said that."

"It's okay, Caroline. You can speak the truth with me." With that, Maddie rose from the table. She glanced out the window once again. Caroline followed the direction of her gaze and both viewed Sam Beaumont, shirtless now, at the base of the ladder, gulping water from a liter bottle. "I'm not going to judge you in any way," she added, with a little wink. "I'm glad you're making progress here."

Caroline appreciated Maddie's undoubting support

and loyalty. She knew she could trust her friend and loved her all the more for it. "Thanks. Things are going really well. I'm hopeful that I'll have my grand opening as planned." Caroline glanced at Sam again, before reassuring her friend. "I've got my eyes wide open this time."

Maddie gave her a hug. "Good thing, too. Because he's an eyeful."

"Maddie!"

Maddie grinned. "I'm pregnant, not blind. Oh, and don't exhaust yourself with all the *work*."

"The work isn't what's exhausting me," she said and both women laughed. Caroline walked Maddie outside. "I still have my maternity clothes. You're welcome to all of them, if you'd like. Just let me know when and I'll gather them up for you."

"Thanks," Maddie said, getting into her truck and starting the engine. "That's one offer I can't refuse."

Caroline waved until Maddie was out of sight on the road. She turned and bumped right into Sam. Moist with sweat, sun-baked to a golden brown, his body glistened. "What if I make an offer *you* can't refuse?"

Caroline smiled into his hungry eyes, her heartbeats racing. "What would that be?"

"Take a shower with me."

Water rained down, the steam rising up and over the shower door, bringing with it the fresh scent of soap. Caroline hesitated just outside the fogged-up pane, watching the silhouette of Sam Beamount as he lathered up his body, a body she'd come to know intimately.

She'd never showered with a man before. This was a first. Sam had introduced her to many firsts.

She stood there naked, biting her lip, wondering, with a sexy man waiting for her, why she hesitated. And a fleeting thought burned through her mind, a thought that frightened her. She was becoming accustomed to having Sam around. She liked seeing him in her kitchen in the morning. She liked sharing a cup of coffee and the day's work with him.

She liked him. Period.

And now, seeing him in her shower and enjoying the sight of him there…meant something. She recalled her words to Maddie earlier, words spoken from the heart. Sam was here only temporarily and Caroline had no illusions about him staying on. But now she wondered at her own bravado. Had she'd fooled herself into believing that Sam could leave here, leave her and then she'd go about her daily business, safely tucking away the memories of the times they've shared? Could she bank all recollection of her *first* shower with a sexy, passionate man and move on with her life?

"Hey," Sam said, opening the shower door slightly, granting her a peek at his wet slick body, "you coming in, darlin'?" He reached for her hand.

Caroline sighed before taking his hand. She shoved those niggling thoughts aside and accepted his hand. "I'm coming in."

"Good, 'cause it was getting lonely in here." Sam moved her to the back of the tiled shower wall, pressing his body to hers. Without a moment's notice, his lips were on hers, his tongue going deep into her mouth. Her breasts crushed into his chest, her thighs rubbed with his, their legs, rough to smooth, entwined. Though he protected her from the stream of hot water, his moisture became hers and soon she was as slick and wet as Sam.

"I should dock your pay for this," she murmured, after the long passionate kiss ended.

Sam stroked her breasts with one hand, while the other found a different playground, down past her waist. "Fine by me, but I think after this, you'll be wanting to give me a raise."

"No way…oh!" Caroline gasped as he cupped her between the thighs, stroking that sensitive spot until her body moved on its own accord. The sensations ripped through her as she gyrated to the rhythm of his stroking. He kissed away her tiny moans then went on bended knee to replace his fingers with his mouth.

Caroline rocked back from the jolt of pleasure. He gripped her hips to steady her and continued his assault. She closed her eyes. Water rained down on both of them, bathing them with steam and heat. She moved faster now, locking her fingers in Sam's hair, holding him to her as she lifted higher and higher, the cold wet tile from behind her brace. Sweet sensations gripped her, electrifying jolts that spiraled her into a world all her own.

"So…good, Sam." Caroline barely heard her own murmurs.

"Stay with me, darlin'. There's more."

Caroline hung on tightly, her body wracked with pleasure.

Sam lifted up then, kissing her gently, allowing her time to come down slightly. Then he spun her around. She faced the stream of water now and he moved her closer so that her face was protected from the onslaught. The shower of heat and spray paraded down her hair and back. Sam wove his fingers in her hair, toying with the tresses, kissing her throat, her shoulders and back from behind.

His shaft nudged her thighs and she felt the thick massive erection readying for her. With slick moist hands, Sam positioned her, guiding her hands above the faucets and bending her slightly at the hips. He braced his hands there and moved with her, teasing her with thrusts and caresses that touched and tempted her womanhood.

Sam's breaths came faster now, his thrusts harder.

The new position created sizzling tingles that spiraled into hot tremors. She wanted Sam with a desire she'd never known before. But before they'd really even begun, Sam spun her around again and turned the shower off.

Caroline stared at him, her mind whirling, her body humming.

"We need protection," he whispered with regret, "before this gets out of control."

Caroline had forgotten all about protecting herself. She'd forgotten everything but the man standing before her and the passion he'd elicited from her, a passion that could easily spin out without restraint. Good thing Sam hadn't forgotten.

No, of course he wouldn't forget. For whatever his reasons, he had an agenda and nothing would deter him from that. She knew him to be honorable enough not to leave her high and dry and pregnant. No, Sam, her temporary lover, wouldn't want the complication of a child.

He towel-wrapped her quickly and lifted her into his arms. "We're not quite done," he said, carrying her out of the shower.

Caroline had a momentary lapse. They seemed to be coming more often now. Her fantasy man was taking up too much space in her head. She found herself thinking about what life would be like if Sam Beaumont decided to stay in Hope Wells permanently. The rational part of her brain warned her not to fall for Sam; she had a mission in life and he was only the means to the end. Building Belle Star was all that mattered. Still, a small part of Caroline wished that he wouldn't leave at all.

But once he laid her down on the bed, all thoughts flew out of her head. Sam bent to her, kissing her lips, stroking her body and, now fully protected, he rose above her and entered her. The familiar warmth healed what hurt Caroline deep inside, obliterating all thoughts but the here and now.

Caroline moved with him, his thick shaft filling her, absorbing her heat as they climbed, thrust after thrust to the ultimate peak. Caroline's release came fast and urgently and she felt her body's completion from her head down to her toes. Sam wasn't far behind. And when they both lay sated and spent on the bed, she turned to look at him.

He smiled then touched a finger to her cheek.

Caroline smiled back. "I guess I won't dock your pay after all," she said.

Sam's expression changed, his eyes downcast. He glanced away from her for a moment, then when he turned back to look at her he opened his mouth to speak. "Caroline…" was all he managed.

She sensed what he had to tell her was somewhat important, urgent maybe. "What is it, Sam?"

Sam glanced above her head, seeming to focus on Annabelle's picture on her nightstand for a brief second before turning away. "It's nothing."

Caroline held her breath. "I think it might be something."

Sam rose from the bed granting her a great view of his powerful body. "I plan on working into the night."

"Sam, I was just kidding about docking your pay."

Sam shook his head. "Damn it, Caroline. I know that. But there's a helluva lot more work to be done and I have less than three weeks."

Nineteen days to be exact. "We're on schedule."

"You have to be ahead of schedule. In case something comes up that you hadn't planned."

"Like what?"

"Like, I don't know…anything." He lifted his arms in frustration. "A storm that will delay our work. Or an injury. Or someone not coming through with supplies."

Caroline sat up on the rumpled bed, looking at Sam now with deep interest. "Who are you, Sam?"

Sam glanced at Annabelle's picture one more time then turned his attention to her. "Just a man who's trying to keep his promise."

Three afternoons later, Sam flipped open his cell phone on the first ring and sidestepped into the stable, out of Caroline's range of vision. Only one person knew the number. Only one person would call him. And Sam hadn't spoken with his brother since before coming to Hope Wells. "Hey, Wade," he said.

"It's been more than a month."

Wade wasn't happy. Sam couldn't help that. He'd always been close to his younger brother. He cared about him and loved him. He was probably the only living breathing person that Sam did love.

"You promised to call once a month."

"I lost track of time."

"What the hell are you doing?"

Sam smiled as he glanced out of the stable to find Caroline admiring the new sign she'd had specially made for Belle Star, complete with burned-out wood lettering and a long length of golden stars outlining the perimeter. Sam had lent a hand in the design, but all in all, it was Caroline's baby. She'd known exactly what she wanted, and now that the deliveryman had deposited the large gate sign near her front steps, she stared at it in awe.

Sam's smile broadened. He admired her drive and gumption. Hell, in truth, there wasn't a darn thing about Caroline Portman he didn't admire.

"You still there?"

Wade's irritation came through loud and clear. "I'm here. I'm fine, Wade. Sorry I missed our deadline."

"Yeah, well, that's exactly what I need to know. That you're not lying *dead* somewhere. You took off eight months ago, big brother. Our father's fit to be tied. He's got men out looking for you."

"You've told him that I'm okay, right? And I don't want to be found."

"About a hundred times. But the old man doesn't like being left in the lurch."

"I should have left the company years ago." Sam couldn't say the words that remained stuck in his head. Words that he lived by. Words that he couldn't forget.

If I'd left the Triple B, Tess would still be alive today.

Gnawing guilt ate at him every time he allowed himself to think about the driving force that had led him astray. He'd wanted to prove his worth, to earn his father's love. It wasn't until Tess died that he'd realized his father was incapable of real love. The old man had only one true passion in his life—the Triple B. The construction company that he'd nurtured and fed with all his heart was Blake Beaumont's only love.

When he'd been too *busy* to attend his granddaughter's funeral, showing up hours later at the house, Sam had finally figured it out. He'd wasted his entire life trying to gain the love and respect of a man who had no heart. Sam had thrown him out of the house that day. And then he'd taken off shortly after, relinquishing all of his responsibilities, all of his duties at the Triple B.

He wanted no part of Blake Beaumont. He feared he'd become just like him. For Sam, there'd been no other way. He'd had to leave. To run away.

But Sam didn't think he'd ever really recover.

The running was what he needed to stay sane.

"You gonna tell me where you are?" Wade asked. Sam had expected this. Wade asked the same question every time they spoke.

"Nope. Not necessary."

"You don't trust me?"

"It's not a matter of trust." Sam couldn't explain that he needed the anonymity; he needed a complete, one-hundred-percent break from his old life. Not even Wade would understand that entirely.

"I'll call you in a few weeks. There's no need to worry."

"Don't miss your deadline again, big brother."

Sam chuckled. Wade acted like an old mother hen. He hadn't seen this side of his carefree brother before. He knew Wade missed him. Sam felt the same. But he couldn't face coming home. Not even to see his brother. "I promise. I'll call early this time. Hey, I miss you."

Wade hesitated before answering with heavy emotion. "Yeah, same here. Take care of yourself, Sam."

Sam flipped off the phone and glanced outside the stable, his gaze darting around the perimeter of the grounds until he located Caroline. He locked on to her image as immediate fear coursed through his system. "Ah, hell!"

He took off running, hoping to get to Caroline before disaster struck.

Six

Caroline had promised Sam that she'd wait for him to hang the sign but from the moment she'd seen it, with carved-out lettering and brilliant golden stars, she knew she had to be the one, the *only* one to place the sign where it rightfully belonged. It was fitting somehow.

Belle Star Stables was hers. And Annabelle's.

And the sign signified all that she'd accomplished so far. It signified what was to come. It held promise to the future. Maybe Caroline was being a bit melodramatic, but she didn't care. In her heart, she knew that she had to hook that sign above the gate to Belle Star all by herself.

By sheer determination and stubborn will, she managed to drag the heavy sign to its place beneath the gate. Then with all her might, she managed to heave the sign up the ladder, pulling it up from behind as she climbed the rungs. When she reached as far as she needed to go, she turned, trying to maneuver the heavy plank. She wobbled, the ladder shook, but she managed to lift the sign over her head, hooking the left side. She lost her balance then and the sign swung down like a swiftly moving pendulum. Caroline reached for the swinging sign, grabbing it just before it knocked into the ladder. "Whoa, that was close," she murmured.

With one side hooked firmly, Caroline reached way over, stretched as far as she could and somehow managed to hook the right side. The sign hung proudly now, but she'd reached just a tad too far over and the ladder swayed. Caroline did the same trying to keep her balance, but all she managed to do was to kick out from the ladder's rungs.

Luck wasn't with her.

The ladder fell one way and Caroline toppled the other.

"Caroline!" Sam's urgent voice resonated in her head.

She fell to the ground with a hard thump.

Sam hadn't reached her in time.

He caught the ladder instead, the wooden rungs trapping him to the ground beside her.

He stared at her with concern.

She gazed up at the sign, swinging slightly in the breeze. She'd done it. She'd hung the sign all on her own. There was something uniquely significant in that.

She smiled and murmured, "Isn't it beautiful?"

Sunlight faded to black, the gate sign the last image Caroline viewed before her eyes closed.

* * *

Sam paced and paced, his mind reeling. It had been three hours since Caroline's fall from the ladder and he still couldn't quite resign himself to the notion that she'd be okay. He'd stood outside her bedroom for a long time, peering in from the hallway on occasion, allowing the doctor and a set of friends who'd heard about her mishap to lend her comfort. It never ceased to amaze him how quickly word traveled in a small town.

Sam had acted quickly, dialing for help, refusing to move Caroline into the house until the paramedics showed up on the property. He didn't know the extent of her injuries and wouldn't chance moving her. But she'd woken up minutes later, demanding to get up and continue with her chores. It was all he could do to keep her down and calm enough until help arrived. She'd absolutely refused to be taken to the hospital. Sam figured both her pride and her lack of decent health insurance had caused that reaction.

So the town doctor had come out and examined her. No serious injuries. None. Thank God. But she did suffer a mild concussion from the fall.

Sam paced some more.

He didn't like the feelings emerging in his gut. Anger boiled over at her stupidity. Why in hell had she decided to hang that sign without his help? And the panic he'd felt once he'd realized he couldn't get to her in time brought out old and painful wounds of his own.

He'd been damn scared seeing her topple from the

ladder, but the fear inside him was nothing compared to his overwhelming concern. He cared about Caroline.

Perhaps too much.

A nasty buzzing in his head wouldn't relent.

He didn't want to care about anyone. Not ever again. And here he was, worried about Caroline Portman as if she had a place in his life.

She didn't.

Sam wouldn't go down that road again. Not ever.

"You can go in to check on her now," a uniformed man who had previously introduced himself as Sheriff Jack Walker announced. "She's feeling better," he said with relief.

Sam studied the man who had proclaimed a long-term friendship with Caroline. He'd spent the past half hour inside her room, holding her hand, making her laugh. Sam hadn't liked the sharp fleeting pangs he'd encountered seeing her smiling at the tall good-looking sheriff.

"That's good," Sam said.

"Yeah, Caroline's a keeper. I wouldn't want to see her get hurt again." Sheriff Walker spoke kindly enough, but the rise of one eyebrow told him the man might have meant something entirely different.

"I'll make sure she rests."

Walker eyed him thoughtfully. "Maddie's going to come out to stay with her tonight. My cousin's new wife won't have it any other way. Seems Caroline needs to stay awake throughout the night."

"That's a good idea." Though Sam's initial instincts were to stay by Caroline's side tonight, it would be better this way. Distancing himself from her a little would help get his feelings in check. The last thing he needed was to fall for Caroline. And he was absolutely certain Caroline would be better off without him. He had no place in her life. He wasn't a family kind of man.

"Sam, are you out there?" Caroline's soft sweet voice called to him.

"Seems he's been pacing off the design in your rug," Sheriff Walker announced, sticking his head inside the door, "waiting to see you."

Sam pushed past the sheriff. He strode into the room and his heart stopped for a moment, seeing Caroline looking exhausted, her face so pale that her beautiful blue eyes looked like deep dark troubled waters. She lay propped up in her bed with two pillows beneath her head. "I should wring your neck."

Sheriff Jack strode into the room, taking a place beside him. "Now that's what I call real tender loving care. You want I should toss him out?" He winked at Caroline, making her smile again.

Sam wasn't in a good mood, and the tall lawman was beginning to gnaw at his nerves.

"It's okay, Jack. I can handle Sam."

The sheriff chuckled. "No doubt about it. See you on Saturday night, then?"

Caroline glanced at Sam with what appeared to be guilt. "Maybe. No promises."

Sam glared at the sheriff. He'd definitely overstayed his welcome and when the lawman finally took his leave, it wasn't soon enough for Sam.

Caroline watched her friend exit the room before turning her full attention on him. "I think you mentioned something about wringing my neck?"

Sam crossed the distance to her bed. He sat down carefully and chose his words with extra thought. There was no sense upsetting her now. Her head must ache like the devil. "We were going to hang that sign together. What made you change your mind?"

"It was something I needed to do myself." She shrugged it off. "I'm not sorry I did it. But I'm sorry that I caused all this trouble."

Sam nodded. Oddly, he understood that need. Hanging that gate sign was symbolic, speaking of Caroline's much-coveted independence and her sheer determination to restore the stables to their rightful place. But he wouldn't condone Caroline putting herself in danger. "Seems you've got a core of friends who worry about you. I've met at least five of them today."

"Yes, well, that's a small town for you."

"I'd say you're one lucky woman."

Caroline stared into his eyes, her lips lifting ever so slightly. He wanted to plant tiny gentle kisses there until both needed more. He'd miss sleeping with her tonight, even though he knew that they wouldn't make love. He had a need to hold her to reassure himself that she was safe and unharmed.

"I'm lucky because I have friends, or because the fall didn't take me out?"

"Neither. You're one lucky woman because I decided not to wring your neck after all."

Sam bent over, kissed her quickly on the lips and exited the room. Her friend would be here soon and Sam had double the chores to do now. But he didn't mind. Working kept his mind off Caroline and the subtle ways in which she was beginning to break down all of his defenses.

Sam spent the rest of the afternoon working on the stables, priming the outside of the wood siding for paint. He'd replaced many of the old planks, where weather, age and neglect had damaged a good percentage of the outside walls. He'd spoken with Caroline about saving time and money by simply using a protective coat of varnish for the outer walls, but she'd insisted on painting the stables the same creamy light-beige color that matched the house, complete with chocolate-brown trim. The appearance of the grounds had to be impeccable. It was something she wouldn't negotiate. Which meant more time and energy spent on the exterior.

There was still a good deal of work to do on the interior of the stalls and Sam had a good handle on improvements inside that would save Caroline and her helpers a lot of work, once the stables were up and running.

As it was now, at full capacity, both buildings could house twenty horses. The monthly revenue provided by boarders would ensure Caroline a steady income, and any added features, such as supplying riding lessons and opening up a small tack store could definitely increase her profits. But it was hard work for a woman alone with just some part-time help.

Sam intended to make her job as easy as possible before he left Belle Star. He slapped on the primer, watching the color absorb into the wood, as rambling thoughts filtered into his head.

Who the hell was Sheriff Jack Walker anyway? And had he asked Caroline on a date?

See you Saturday night then?

Sam knew he had no claim on Caroline. It shouldn't matter that she'd been asked out for Saturday night. The cocky sheriff made no bones in showing interest in her. And Sam wouldn't do anything to embarrass Caroline or himself in front of her friend Jack.

Sam couldn't name what his relationship with Caroline was, exactly. He honestly didn't know. In the beginning it had seemed like a good idea. They'd been up-front with each other. There seemed to be an undeniable attraction that they both wanted to satisfy. Sam hadn't deceived her. She knew he'd leave in a month. Caroline seemed fine with that.

All of his instincts told him that Caroline Portman wasn't the dallying kind of woman. She didn't have much experience with men, or in having affairs. Sam had known that about her the minute she'd walked up to him at the bar with her proposition.

So, why had it bothered him so much that Jack Walker could make her smile?

Sam continued slapping on the primer with a vengeance. He worked fast, making his way around the corner of the building. He had turned to work the back of the structure, when something in the distance caught his eye.

He set down the paint and brush and walked over to a small tricycle in obvious need of repair. The handle was tweaked in such a way that it couldn't be ridden anymore.

Sam bent down, his heart hammering in his chest. He placed his hand on the small triangular seat, caressing it and imagining the young excited rider. Though he knew the tricycle to be Annabelle's, another image popped into his head.

"Watch me, Daddy! Watch me ride." Tess looked up at him with eager eyes, so proud of her accomplishments on her new trike. Sam sat down on the front lawn of his Houston house as his three-year-old daughter began to pedal, her little legs working hard, her hair blowing in the breeze, her face alight with joy. "See me, Daddy."

"I see you, Tess," he called out, right before his cell phone rang.

The call had come in due to an emergency on site. The foreman at the Triple B had been injured and Blake Beaumont insisted Sam take over the project. "We need you there, boy. Right now."

Sam took one last look at his daughter riding down the sidewalk before taking off for that high-rise building project. He hadn't returned until late that night and he entered Tess's room immediately.

She opened her eyes, looking so terribly sad. "You didn't see me, Daddy. You didn't."

"I did, Tess. I saw you ride your new trike, sweetheart."

But Tess had turned away then, closing her eyes, pretending sleep.

Sam stared at the broken tricycle for long moments, his heart aching. He'd been such a fool. He'd lost the most precious gift a man could ever hope to have, and for what, to gain the respect and love of a man incapable of either emotion?

Sam's wife had left him shortly after that, taking Tess along. But for their daughter's sake, they'd made allowances, pretending to be one big happy family whenever they were together. Sam missed Tess in his daily life, but by that time, he didn't know how to fix things. He'd neglected his wife and child for the sake of the company one too many times.

And the last time he'd let them down they'd paid dearly, with their lives.

"Sam?"

A pleasant-sounding voice interrupted his thoughts. He lifted up from the tricycle and turned to find a pretty red-headed woman smiling at him.

"I found you," she said. "Hope you weren't hiding from me."

"Ah, no. I didn't know you were looking for me."

"Caroline sent me out on a mission. Hi. I'm Maddie Walker." She put out her small delicate hand. "The town veterinarian and Caroline's good friend."

Sam shook her hand. "Sam Beaumont. Is anything wrong? How's Caroline feeling?" Sam moved away from her then to peer around the building, glancing toward the house. "Does she need anything?"

Maddie shook her head. "Nope, not a thing. She's doing fine. Talking my ear off about Belle Star."

Sam nodded, hiding his relief.

"But she's worried about you."

"Me?"

"Have you eaten anything?"

"No, but I won't starve. There's nothing for her to worry about."

"It's past eight. The sun's almost gone. Why don't you come inside? I brought over a tamale casserole. It sure would ease her mind if you had some dinner."

Maddie looked at him and he instantly knew that she'd been informed about his relationship with Caroline. But there was no judgment in her eyes, only concern.

"She cares about you, Sam."

He muttered a soft curse. He didn't want this…this caring. He'd spent the better part of the year blocking out those feelings.

Maddie turned and walked away. "I'll tell her you'll be in after you clean up."

"Right," he said to her back.

Sam walked over to the tricycle, taking one last look before picking up his paint supplies. After stowing them away, he headed to check on Dumpling. Soon the horse would have loads of company, but right now, the gentle mare had only him.

And tonight, all Sam had was the mare.

He found comfort in that.

And later that night, Sam retired to the guest room in the back of the stables unable to work up an appetite. He had some thinking to do and tamale casserole inside Caroline's cozy kitchen didn't fit into his plans.

* * *

"Should you be up?" Sam asked, as Caroline walked toward the stable Sam had been priming last night. She brought out a steaming cup of coffee as morning sun worked its way through low-lying gray clouds. The air was hot and humid and she wondered if she should have forgotten the coffee in favor of something cold and refreshing.

"I'm feeling better. Maddie took great care of me. She left about half an hour ago."

"Yeah, I saw her take off in her truck."

"She had an emergency across the county. A stray dog was hit by a car."

Sam winced. "Bad?"

Caroline lifted a shoulder. "I'm not sure, but if anyone can fix the injured, it's my friend, Maddie."

Sam took the offered coffee from her hand. "Well, then it's a good thing that she stayed with you last night."

Caroline smiled then looked at the work he'd done on the stable. "Maddie said you were up before dawn, painting." Caroline admired his work. "You've gotten a lot accomplished already. I'll change into my painting clothes and join you. We should finish this building by the end of the day."

"No."

"No?" Caroline looked into Sam's dark brooding eyes. His jaw set, he didn't move a muscle. "You don't think we can finish or—"

"Or, I think you need to take it easy today. I can finish this on my own."

"I have work to do, Sam. I'm not going to let a little setback stop me."

"Caroline, how much sleep did you get last night?"

She rolled her eyes. "You know the answer to that. Maddie stayed over so that I wouldn't sleep much. She roused me every few hours. But I'm feeling fine. Great actually. And I'm anxious to get back to work."

"Fine, then, why don't you go inside and work out the budget for the supplies we're going to need. I'll make a trip into town tomorrow once you've worked it all out."

"Sam." Caroline didn't want to pull rank. In her heart she knew that Sam was only trying to help. But she'd been run roughshod over by the best of them, and she'd vowed never again. No man, not even sexy Sam Beaumont was going to tell her what to do. "I'm perfectly capable of taking care of myself. The budget is all done anyway, and it looks like if we don't get cracking soon, a summer shower might just take the chance from us. I promise to stop when I get tired."

Sam grunted, taking a sip of his coffee then setting it down to give her a sideways glance. "You're the boss."

Damn straight, she wanted to say, but she smiled instead and within minutes she was painting the lower half of the stable, while Sam worked up on a ladder, painting the upper half.

By the end of the day, they'd nearly finished the entire building. Only the trim remained.

"Not too shabby for amateurs," she said, once they'd cleaned up their paintbrushes and put everything away. Satisfied with the progress they'd made, she leaned against the corral post adjacent to the stable, working the kinks out of her shoulders and neck. Everything ached, including her bones. She was totally wiped out, but couldn't confess as much to Sam. He had an I-told-you-so look about him right now as he studied her, with his hands planted on his hips. Even through paint smudges on his face and clothes, the man looked like heaven and if she weren't totally exhausted, she might have wanted to do something about it.

"You need a hot bath," he said. And just as she was about protest that he wasn't looking all too clean either, he finished with, "and a massage."

Caroline closed her eyes at the thought. Was that a legitimate offer? Because she would surely accept. Nothing sounded more perfect. "Mmm."

"No extra charge for the service, ma'am. Then a quick supper and I'm tucking you into bed."

"Sounds…interesting." She raised her brows.

"Alone." Sam's expression didn't change. He appeared dead serious. "You need a good night's sleep."

Caroline surmised that Sam Beaumont was accustomed to barking orders. She'd certainly seen it firsthand. Ever since she'd taken that fall from the ladder, he'd somehow taken control. Caroline had more experience now and she knew that she would pick her battles wisely.

On the one hand she was touched by his concern, but more importantly, she wouldn't have another man telling her how she felt and what she should do about it. Caroline had grown up through hard knocks and harder lessons. She'd learned to trust her own instincts, so if Sam wanted to dictate orders then he had a stubborn opponent on his hands. She had a few surprises of her own. If all went well, her man Friday wouldn't know what hit him.

She smiled at his comment about sleeping alone tonight. Softly, she added, "We'll see."

His plan was to let Caroline get the rest she needed tonight. No way had Sam expected to sleep with her. She'd been injured and had hardly slept the night before, then she'd stubbornly insisted on working alongside him until fatigue took the sparkle from her pretty blue eyes. Offering her a massage hadn't been in his plans, either. It would be much harder to say goodnight and retire to his guest room that way. But he'd seen how her body stiffened up after they'd finished work for the day. He'd imagined the soreness settling into her bones and the weariness she must have felt.

Hell, massaging her tired body seemed like a real good idea at the time.

But as he stood outside her bathroom, listening to her contented sighs with each little splash of water, Sam knew it would be a test of his willpower to keep from making love to her tonight. He wanted her. That was a given. But he wanted her to rest even more. And a part of him wanted to make sure he wasn't getting in too deep. For both their sakes, Sam had to keep it simple so that when the job was finished here, he could walk away without looking back.

Caroline opened the door wearing a smile and not

much else but a fluffy towel that barely covered her female assets. "I'm ready for my massage now." Her smile was bright, the sparkle returning to her eyes. "Where do you want me?"

Sam took a swallow. *Where did he want her?* On a soft cushion of straw out in the stable. Out in the tall green pasture as the sun began its decline. On the kitchen table. "How about on your bed?"

Caroline smiled. "I'm looking forward to this." She brushed past him, heading to her room. The soft scents of flowers and freshness followed her. Sam did, too.

He cleared his throat. "Yeah, well, I'm not an expert at this, so don't expect much, okay?"

She turned her head, her eyes full of mischief. "Anything you do to me will be just fine, Sam. I've never had a massage before."

Sam opened his mouth to debate the issue, but clamped his lips shut instead. His body kicked into overdrive and he had a hard-on developing that only Caroline Portman seemed capable of inspiring.

Out of nowhere it seemed Caroline handed him a bottle of body oil. Then she lay down on her belly, and wiggled her toes. "I'm ready when you are."

Sam stared at her back, the towel dipping low now, barely covering her sweet little derriere. Sam had seen the woman naked before, but this time, it was different somehow. More exciting. Definitely sexier than anything they'd yet encountered. And the open trusting way in which she offered herself up to him gave him pause.

"I read once that massaging the body releases endorphins. They called them the happy hormones. Well, Sam, honey. I'm ready to get happy."

Sam chuckled. He poured oil onto his hands, rubbed it in then came down gently on her shoulders.

"Ohhh," she cooed with pleasure as his fingers worked deeply into her skin. He felt the knots unwind slowly as her body released pent-up tension. He surmised the release wasn't just from a hard day's work today, but maybe from months and months of doubt and worry about her future. She'd taken on a whole lot lately and as he worked kinks and tightness from her smooth skin, he hoped to erase past pressures and concerns as well. "Feel good?"

"Mmm, you don't know how good."

But Sam knew. She might be the recipient of the massage, but Sam's body was feeling good right about now, too. He closed his eyes and absorbed her softness. His hands slid over her shoulders and with each little moan of pleasure she murmured, Sam's body reacted in kind. Giving her pleasure brought him pleasure.

And pain.

He worked lower on her back, pressing his palms firmly onto the triangular area just above her derriere. His fingers fumbled when he got too close, causing Caroline to giggle. "It's okay. I'm sore there, too."

Sam sucked in a breath. "Hell, darlin', a man can only take so much."

For his own sanity, he skipped over those two lovely mounds of flesh, still covered by the towel he noted thankfully, and began working on her upper thighs. He slipped his hands up and down, taking in the creamy firmness, rubbing oil in and working the tension out.

He moved down past the backs of her knees, caressing the lower legs, stroking his palms up the long length and down again. With every delighted sound Caroline made, Sam's body grew tighter. Her flowery clean scent invaded his nostrils and the dewy softness of her skin under his palms caused his undeniable hard-on to strain against the material of his jeans.

But he pressed on, back up to knead her shoulders then he worked his hands up and down her arms, emitting happy hormones along the way. When he entwined his fingers with hers, sliding them in and out, for just one moment, Caroline grasped his hands still. They remained locked for several beats, both bodies frozen momentarily as unspoken words traveled between them.

Sam's heart ached, but his wounds still ran deep and he couldn't allow Caroline in. Not in that way.

God, not ever.

Sam leaned over her, whispering in her ear. "I'll go heat up the tamales. You must be hungry."

Caroline rolled over, the towel now unfastened and exposing the most beautiful woman Sam had ever seen. "I'm not hungry for tamales, Sam."

She handed him the body oil. "There's more to do."

Sam hadn't an ounce of willpower left. He'd commended himself on keeping his sanity during that rubdown, but he wasn't immune to Caroline, as he'd once hoped. Hell, he'd rather cut off his right arm than leave this bedroom now.

"I need you, Sam," Caroline whispered.

Sam needed her, too. And that's what scared him. He didn't just want Caroline Portman. He *needed* her.

And that need churned inside him. She was an ache that wouldn't go away. A pain that seared his gut and wrecked his mind.

Sam hadn't intended to make love to Caroline tonight. He'd wanted to keep things simple. It was essential to his survival. But right now, taking her in his arms seemed more essential and he couldn't fight his desire for her another second.

He dripped oil onto her breasts, each little drop hitting its mark, until Caroline's eyelids lowered and tiny gasps escaped her throat. "Oh, Sam," she whimpered.

Sam massaged the oil in, caressing her full round globes until heat nearly sizzled from her skin. Then he bent his head and licked the tips with his tongue until her gasps grew louder. He dripped oil everywhere and the massage took on new meaning as she gyrated to his every touch, moved to each of his caresses.

Sam stripped off his clothes and returned to her, fisting her long blond locks in his hand while he crushed his lips to hers in a long passionate kiss. "We're both gonna get happy now, darlin'."

And when Sam entered her with one powerful thrust, her eyes rounded. She breathed in deeply and accepted him fully. He moved inside her with almost violent need and Caroline didn't rebel, but caught up to his rhythm, racing with him now, and when their explosion came both rocked for long lingering moments, the release something shattering and all-consuming.

Sam stayed inside Caroline a long time, their bodies meshed, their arms and legs tangled. Both needed the comfort, the connection. When their breathing finally steadied, Caroline whispered, "You're good for me, Sam Beaumont."

Sam rolled off her then and stared up at the ceiling.

He couldn't respond, and if that hurt Caroline, he was painfully sorry.

Because he knew he wasn't good for Caroline.

She was dead wrong.

Seven

The scent of brewing coffee woke Caroline from her sleep, the aroma teasing her nostrils and tempting her to get out of bed. She opened her eyes as daylight poured into the room. Caroline smiled. Her body rejuvenated from Sam's expert hands, she couldn't remember a time when she'd felt so contented and so incredibly free.

She rose and showered quickly, putting on a pair of jeans and a white tank top. When she entered the kitchen, Sam looked up from sipping coffee at the table, his eyes noting her appearance and lingering on the silver writing stretching across her top: Cowgirl Up.

"Nice," he said and her temperature shot straight up. Sam had a way of looking at her that told her just what he was thinking. And sometimes, those hot hungry looks made her blush. Then he added with curiosity, "Too nice for painting."

Caroline poured herself a cup of coffee and stood across the table from him. "That's because I don't intend on painting until later in the day. I've got to make a trip into town and run some errands. I'll pick up the rest of the supplies we need at the lumberyard. We're down to our last ounce of coffee beans and there's not a thing in the house to eat."

"I'll finish up the painting. We got a lot accomplished yesterday. I should have it done by the time you get back."

"Actually, I have a favor to ask of you."

Sam sipped his coffee and watched her over the rim of the cup he held. "Another massage?"

Once again he'd made her blush. That sensual massage would be in her head for years to come. And the way he'd taken her last night, as though his life depended on it, wasn't going anywhere either, that memory was imprinted for all eternity.

"No, nothing like that."

Sam smiled. "Too bad."

"I'll take a rain check though."

"Any time, darlin'. What's the favor?"

"I need a ride into Midland on Saturday."

"What's in Midland?"

"The Lone Star Horse Rescue. I'm hoping to adopt a pony for Annabelle. I want it to be a surprise when she comes home."

"She's a little young, don't you think?"

Caroline sat down on the chair facing Sam. She settled in, tucking one leg under the other. "I know. But I think it would be good for her. When we open the stables, I'll be busy with all the horses and I don't want her to feel neglected. This way, with a pony of her own, she won't feel left out. I'll make sure I spend time with her, teaching her how to care for it."

Sam studied her a moment, his eyes unreadable. "You're a great mother, Caroline."

Caroline leaned way back in the chair. Almost speechless, she managed, "Thank you."

It was probably the kindest, most generous compliment he could have given her. Caroline tried, but she wasn't perfect. She knew she'd made mistakes in the past, but being a good mother to Annabelle was her number-one top priority. Such easy words, but somehow coming from Sam, they meant a great deal.

"So we're off to Midland tomorrow," he said.

"It's just a preliminary interview. These adoptions can get pretty intense. They'll go over all my applications to make the final determination. I won't know for some time if I'm accepted or not. But it's worth the trouble to adopt a good animal in need of a home."

"I can't imagine them not approving you."

"Maddie will vouch for me and they'll go over my resources and the facility to make sure I'm capable of caring properly for the animal. I'm hoping to be approved." She shrugged. "I could drive into Midland myself, but I guess I need the moral support."

"You've got it. We'll get an early start in the morning.

I'll have to get you back in time for your date with the bumbling sheriff."

"The bumbling sheriff?" Caroline laughed. "Oh, you mean Jack? Good lord, Sam. I'm not dating Jack. How can you think that?"

"He asked you out right in front of me the other day."

"Yes, and you think that I'd date someone, after…after what we've—"

"Caroline, no. I didn't think that. But I wasn't sure what to think."

"Sam, I've known Jack Walker since I was a kid—a really little kid. Our parents were good friends and he's like a brother to me now. He offered me a ride to Maddie and Trey's monthly poker game. The game is sort of a tradition in the Walker household and since Maddie came on the scene they include the ladies once in a while. I told Jack I'm not going."

"You could go. I mean…you and I…we're keeping it simple, right?"

Caroline planted her feet on the ground, pushed out her chair until it squeaked against the wood floor and stood up. "Right. *Simple.*" Caroline cocked her head to one side, her thoughts in turmoil. "Maybe I will go after all. And maybe I'll call Jack back and ask him to pick me up."

Sam pushed out from the table too and rose abruptly. "Okay, never mind. So, it's not simple. Truth is, I don't want you anywhere near that guy. And I have no right to feel that way and even less of a right demanding that of you."

Caroline looked into his eyes. Again, Sam had surprised her with his open, honest admission. She'd known the stakes when she'd slept with him.

One month.

And then he'd be gone.

She forced herself to realize that Sam had no claim on her. And she had no claim on him. She didn't fully understand why he had to leave in one month or why he'd put himself on such a deadline. She figured it was better that she didn't know. His leaving was inevitable. But he was here now and she wanted to make the best of it. "You don't have to demand anything of me, Sam. I don't want to go out with Jack. That's *simple* enough, isn't it?"

Sam nodded, but his gaze held hers. "Simple and a whole lot of complicated."

Caroline dropped the subject before she said something she'd regret. She wanted no regrets with Sam. Neither could she afford them. "I'd better get going. I want to get back in time to get some work done."

Sam looked her squarely in the eyes. "I want to take you to dinner tomorrow night, Caroline."

Stunned, she asked, "Like a real date?"

He nodded.

"You think that's wise?"

"Hell, no. But you deserve to be taken out. Saturday night is date night, isn't it?"

With a slow nod, she agreed.

"I'm asking, and I'm hoping you'll accept."

Caroline sent him a smile. "I accept."

Her heart ached for what could never be, but she

vowed to make the best of this situation. And she couldn't think of a better way to spend her Saturday night.

"Good then," Sam said. "It's an official date."

And there was nothing *simple* about it.

Sam finished painting the stable in the early afternoon, the second coat going on faster than the first. He had to admit that Caroline had been right. The difference between the freshly painted stable and the one yet to be painted was incredible. No amount of varnish would have made the stable look so elegant. The clean fresh look of the stable would certainly instill confidence and entice serious boarders. There was no doubt in his mind that Caroline would take the best care of the horses left in her charge.

After he'd cleaned and tucked away all the equipment, he took a long hot shower, scouring off all remnants of paint, then dressed in a clean pair of jeans and a chambray work shirt. He thought he'd saddle up the gentle mare and take Dumpling for a ride to inspect the fences surrounding Caroline's property.

He knew there were repairs to be made, but he wanted to mark the damaged areas so that he could estimate the cost and supplies needed first. And he had to speak with Caroline about ways to make the inside of the stables more durable. He had a few ideas on the subject.

Sam exited the bathroom and looked across the hall. The door to Annabelle's room was open and bright little-girl colors caught his eye. He'd never ventured down the hall before, wanting to keep his distance, which wasn't hard to do since Caroline tended to keep the door closed most of the time.

But today, the vivid colors drew him closer and as he approached, a copper-haired doll with big blue eyes and a wide smile beckoned him.

He recognized the doll; it was named Patsy Pumpkin.

He'd given one just like it to Tess.

And though he knew better, he continued on down the hall until he found himself inside the room surrounded by soft fluffy animals, crayon drawings and the sweet angelic scents of childhood.

Pinks and lavenders, brilliant yellows and neon greens colored the walls and small furniture. Sam leaned over the bed, picking up the doll from her perch atop a purple chenille pillow. He held the doll away from him, clutching her tight as memories rushed in.

Tess, hugging the doll to her chest.

Tess, playing in a room not at all so different from this one.

Tess, falling asleep without a kiss from her daddy.

How many nights had he missed tucking her into bed?

"I'm sorry, honey," he whispered, shaking his head slowly. Tears that he'd never allowed welled up in his eyes now. Emotions he usually tucked within the confines of his mind surfaced with unyielding bitter clarity. Sam welcomed them. He deserved the heartfelt anguish. He'd been a terrible, neglectful father. "I'll never forgive myself, Tess. Not ever."

"Sam?"

Caroline's curious voice startled him. He remained where he stood, holding Annabelle's doll.

And when Caroline moved into the room to look at him, Sam couldn't meet her eyes. He spoke softly, "I've never come in here before. Didn't think I could face it."

"Sam?" Caroline said again. He couldn't miss the concern in her voice. "What is it?"

Sam sank down on the bed, staring at the doll he held. "I had a daughter once. She would have been Annabelle's age, had she lived."

Caroline's soft gasp didn't surprise him. Parents weren't supposed to bury their children. "Oh, Sam."

She lowered down beside him on the bed. "I'm so sorry. How did it happen?"

Sam continued to stare into the eyes of the doll as the confession rolled off his tongue. "A helicopter crash. It was my fault."

"Oh." Again, he heard Caroline's soft intake of breath. Most people weren't used to hearing these kinds of confessions. Sam knew he'd staggered her.

"It's not what you're thinking. I didn't fly the helicopter that day. I should have. I should have been there to fly my daughter to her grandparents' house. My wife's...my wife's family adored her. It was Tess's birthday and she was so excited to be visiting them. But I was too busy. An emergency came up at work. I had to postpone the trip. Tess had been heartbroken and my wife had had it with me disappointing our daughter. I can't say that I blame her. I let Tess down time and again. And this was her birthday celebration.

"Lydia had already left me by then. But we held it together for Tess's sake whenever we could. She was so angry with me she hired a pilot and took Tess on that helicopter with her. The weather turned bad and the pilot was inexperienced. They all died in that crash."

Caroline touched his arm. "Sam, I'm so sorry. But it wasn't your fault. You didn't cause that crash."

Sam turned to her, unable to hide his pain. "Don't, Caroline. Don't try to make it easy for me. I'm to blame. I neglected my daughter countless times. I should have piloted that chopper that day. I know they'd all be alive today if I had."

"You don't know that for sure, Sam," she said softly.

She'd repeated his brother Wade's words exactly. But he'd tell her what he'd told Wade and everyone else who'd tried to ease his guilt. He'd tell her what he knew in his heart to be true. "I know, Caroline. That pilot made mistakes only a rookie would make. If I'd been flying that day, the crash wouldn't have happened. I should have been there."

"So, now you don't fly anymore?"

"Not once since then."

"Oh, Sam."

Sam rose from the bed. "I shouldn't have come in here."

Caroline stood to face him. "You need time to heal, Sam. And to forgive yourself."

Sam shook his head, the pain inside burning raw and deep. He'd never spoken of this before today. He'd held it all inside. But with Caroline...he felt she would understand. And although he unleashed the burden of his guilt to her, he didn't feel any differently. Nothing could change his self-loathing. No one would ever know the depth of his own self-contempt. "I'll never forgive myself, Caroline."

Caroline stood frozen to the spot, shocked by what she'd just heard. The pain in Sam's voice, the anguish on his face, the grief he couldn't let go tore at her heart. She loved Annabelle with her very soul. She couldn't imagine losing her. Any parent would feel the same. So Caroline understood Sam's agony. She understood his guilt.

Of all of her wild imaginings about the mysterious, quiet-spoken drifter, this wasn't what she'd expected. His admission had certainly answered some of her questions, but the brief glimpse he'd given her into his life had also provoked even more questions. He'd been married. He'd had a wife and child once. Where had they lived? And who was Sam Beaumont, exactly?

Caroline saw the depth of pain in his eyes, heard it in the defeated huskiness of his voice. She knew she'd never ask those questions, but she hoped that maybe Sam would open up to her more about himself one day.

Self-protective devices told her to let it be. Not knowing about Sam would save her heartache when he left. But Caroline wasn't made that way. She'd never protected herself to the point of not caring about another human being. She hadn't built up that tall a wall of defense.

She took Patsy Pumpkin with her and closed Annabelle's door. Caroline walked into the kitchen, peering outside the window in time to see Sam saddle up

Dumpling then mount her. With a black Stetson on his head, his body rigid, his face a mask of stone, he headed out on the mare. She watched until he became a faded silhouette on the horizon.

Caroline clutched the doll to her chest. Her stomach ached. Her heart broke in two. Her eyes filled with tears. She knew Sam's pain. It matched her own.

Because Caroline realized in that one moment that she'd fallen in love.

Eight

The drive to Midland was quiet, Sam making only light conversation. Caroline sat in the passenger seat of his truck with a file folder on her lap containing all the pertinent papers required by the Lone Star Horse Rescue for the pony Caroline hoped to adopt. She realized how this might affect Sam. Up until yesterday, she had no reason to worry or concern herself about Sam's feelings regarding doing anything for her child.

But now that she knew, she wondered how hard this must be for him, helping her surprise Annabelle when she returned from Florida. He hadn't flinched when she'd asked, Sam had always given her his full support.

He'd been unselfish with his time and had worked so hard at Belle Star that Caroline loved him even more for his sacrifice.

That she loved him at all had come as a shocking revelation. She'd thought herself immune to love, thinking her failed marriage to Gil had destroyed all hope for a happily ever after. Not that she'd hope for that with Sam. She had a better understanding of him now. She suspected his reason for drifting from town to town had to do with his daughter's death. Perhaps he was punishing himself. Perhaps he wanted no ties to anyone or any place. Moving on from month to month would afford him that luxury. Perhaps he needed that to survive. To not care. To not feel.

Caroline ached for him. And she wanted him. But she wouldn't delude herself. Sam didn't love her. He might never be capable of the emotion again. Certainly, Caroline hadn't thought she could ever experience love again.

And the shock of it all remained with her.

"It's up ahead, just a few miles. Are you nervous?" Sam asked.

"A little. But I'm excited, too."

Sam reached out to her side of the seat and took her hand in his. He squeezed gently. "They'd be foolish not to approve you."

"Thank you, Sam. It means a lot."

Sam nodded and spoke again, this time more softly as he continued to hold her hand. "About yesterday. I want to thank you for the things you said. It meant a lot to me. But let's move on from there. You don't have to walk on eggshells around me."

"Does that mean you're willing to talk to me about your life?"

He shook his head. "It won't change anything, Caroline. So no, I'm not going to dredge up the past."

Caroline sighed. The pain was still too deep for Sam to open up to her. She understood that. When Gil had abandoned her, it had taken her weeks to admit it to anyone. She'd just "pretend" it away and make excuses for why Gil wasn't home. That only lasted a short time before her friends and neighbors got suspicious.

But Caroline recalled the pain as if it were yesterday. She'd hated Gil for what he'd done to Annabelle. She felt betrayed for herself, but she'd also felt humiliated— a complete failure as a wife.

It had taken her a long time to come to terms with that. And still she wondered about the role she might have played in his abandonment. Still, in a corner of her mind, she'd wondered about her own character flaws that might have sent him packing.

In her heart, she knew that Gil hadn't been right for her. He hadn't been the love of her life. She'd recognized that immediately after they'd wed, but she had loved him in the beginning. She had tried to be a good wife and mother. She'd finally come to the conclusion that Gil was the one with the character flaws. Gil hadn't known how to commit. He hadn't known how to care about anyone but himself.

Caroline had matured enough to realize that now. And she understood Sam better because of it.

"Okay. No dredging up the past."

Sam sent her a charming smile. The first one she'd seen from him since she'd found him in Annabelle's room yesterday. "Thanks."

The smile and gratitude sent her heart into flip-flop mode so she was glad when Sam pulled the truck into the rescue site. "Would you like me to wait or go with you?"

"Oh, I'd love your input on the horses. Maybe we'll find a filly here."

"You got it."

Sam strode beside her and within minutes, Caroline was meeting with the facilitators who explained everything once again in person. She'd already done most of her research by phone calls and the Internet, so what she learned now about the rescue organization wasn't entirely new to her.

She turned in the remainder of her paperwork. Some of her applications were already on file, so she had a little head start there. "Now, that the papers are in order, would you like to see our horses?" Betty Manning, the director asked.

"Yes, please. As you know, I'm looking for a filly or colt. It's for my daughter. And it would be best if they both grow up together."

"Well, we have two to chose from now. One of each gender. Both came to us as foals."

As they walked outside, Caroline caught sight of more than a dozen animals in corrals, grazing peacefully. Some of the horses had obvious physical problems, but for the most part they looked healthy enough and well-cared for.

"It's a misconception that we only rescue and adopt out horses that nobody wants or that aren't healthy enough to sell. Many of our horses are worth thousands of dollars, but their owners would rather see them adopted out to a good home with our strict policies on protection than to put their horse on the selling market. As you know, we take pride in keeping track of the adoptions, and we make sure the horse goes to a loving home."

"Yes, I know. That's one reason I decided on a rescue. Believe me, if I'm approved, the horse will have all the love we have to give."

Betty smiled and nodded. "That's all we want. Ah, here they are." She stopped at a smaller corral, where the two animals were nuzzling and playing with each other. "Striker is our colt. He's the bay. And Princess is our filly. She's the chestnut. Both have come here under different circumstances. Striker's owner died and the family is selling the farm, but decided to send him here since they didn't know enough about the animals to sell them. Princess, well, she's a whole story in itself, but the bottom line is that she survived a horrible mudslide. I won't go into details, but she was a wreck when we first got her. She's healthy now and a great little gal."

Caroline stepped over to the corral fence and called to the animals. Both shied away at first, but then with more coaxing, Princess wandered over. Caroline spoke softly, "That's a girl. You're a survivor, aren't you, girl?"

Sam walked over to where Striker stood. The colt took one look at him then dashed around the corral, snorting and prancing, showing off his talents. Sam chuckled. "This one's feisty. I'd take him in a minute if I could, Caroline. But I think the filly might be better for Annabelle."

"Princess is definitely the more sedate of the two, but neither are going to roll over and play dead. They both have spirit," Betty said.

Just then Princess backed up and pranced off, running circles around the colt.

"Oh, this is so hard. I wish I could adopt them both. They look like standardbreds."

"They are. You know your horses, don't you?" The director said with a hint of admiration. "They're bred to have great ground manners and they adapt to any tack you have available."

"They don't grow too large, do they?"

"About fourteen to sixteen hands. They have longer bodies and shorter legs. Which is perfect for a child."

Caroline nodded and smiled. "Well, I've made up my mind. Princess it is. She'd be perfect for my little girl. Now that my applications are in, how long before I get word?"

"Well, since you've sent some of the work in earlier, I'd say we'd have a decision in a few weeks. We'll give you a call."

"She won't be adopted by anyone else, will she?" Caroline bit her lip. She'd pretty much attached herself to this filly already. She wouldn't want to lose the chance to adopt her.

"Not much chance of that. No one else has filed paperwork for her yet. So, you'd have first consideration."

"Great," she said.

They all shook hands and Betty said her farewell.

Caroline stared at Princess, wanting this so much for

Annabelle. She could only imagine her daughter's face when she laid eyes on Princess and learned that she had her own pony.

Sam sidled up next to her. "You made a good choice, Caroline."

Caroline feigned a shudder. "Now, all I have to do is go home and wait by the phone."

Sam wrapped his arm around both her shoulders and pulled her away from the corral. "C'mon. Let's go into town. I'm starving. And there's some things I want to discuss with you about improving the stables."

"So," Sam said, "what do you think? If you invest the money now, you'll get a lifetime of wear from the stable stalls. The horses you boarded before chewed them down and destroyed a good deal of the wood. With re-inforced stalls, they won't get their teeth into the wood as easily."

"I didn't know how badly Gil neglected the horses." Caroline couldn't hide her remorse. She loved animals and hated that she'd been so caught up in keeping the household going when Annabelle was a baby that she hadn't paid enough attention. She should have guessed that Gil would cut corners. He did very little to preserve the stables and the Portman good name. "Many of them turned to cribbing to ease their boredom and frustration and as a result, they ate through a good deal of their stalls," Caroline said, setting her fork down.

She and Sam sat in the shade at an outside café, opting for the peace of outdoor dining and fresh air instead of the noise inside the busy eatery. Sam tackled a grilled cheeseburger, while Caroline chose a chicken salad. A case of nerves had her insides churning and her appetite waning. The past twenty-four hours had made mush of her mind and hammered her stomach to pieces. She'd fallen in love and planned on adopting an animal, and now Sam proposed she spend the bulk of her remaining budget on the interior stalls at Belle Star.

"The horses need exercise every day. And they'll need to be turned out. You have enough grazing land for that right now, but it doesn't mean that when you do stable them, you won't end up with all the same problems."

"I know, Sam. But it's expensive. And right now, I can only afford to repair the broken stalls. Once the stables turn a profit, I can look into rebuilding the stalls."

Sam looked doubtful, his jaw set stubbornly. "What if I—" he began, but then clamped his mouth shut. He stared into her eyes and shook his head. "You're…the…boss."

He seemed reluctant to lose this battle and even more reluctant to speak those last words. He'd held something back, she assumed, something that warred within his mind. Caroline knew he had a good head for business, but she knew precious little else about him.

When the meal was over, they headed to the hardware store to pick up a few supplies before heading back to Hope Wells. Caroline made her purchases quickly and Sam carried everything to the truck, loading the supplies into the back.

"Oh, look at the sweet pup," Caroline said, striding over to a tiny Jack Russell on the street. She was a sucker for animals anyway, but she'd once had her own Jack Russell so the pull was magnetic. Before she knew it, she was speaking to the owner, petting the pup.

Sam leaned against his truck, smiling at her. Caroline was a remarkable woman. He'd always thought so, but the more he'd come to know her, the more he admired her.

It was all he could do to stop from convincing her to let him purchase the new reinforced stalls for her today. In his estimation, he felt she vitally needed them to ensure the success of her stables. And Sam had almost made the offer. But good sense had followed. First, he'd have to tell her who he was and he wasn't ready to do that. He could barely face it himself much less speak of it. He'd already shed part of his soul to her yesterday, and he'd spent the night tossing and turning as old memories crept into his mind.

Secondly, and probably more importantly, she'd never accept his monetary help. She had more pride and guts and determination than most men he knew. He wouldn't insult her. He wouldn't offer something he knew she needed, because she'd have to refuse.

So Sam held back. It would be better for both of them that she not know his real identity. Better, because Sam was getting too close to her, getting too deeply involved.

Knowing that he would leave in less than two weeks was killing him, while at the same time, it was a balm to his soul. It was necessary to leave. He banked on it. But he'd miss her terribly. Still, spending time with a drifter whom she'd never see again and creating wonderful memories was better than messing up both their lives with the truth.

"Sam, isn't he adorable?" Caroline came toward him.

Just then, Sam noted two men slowing down their black SUV on the street near Caroline. The license plate read: 3B HSTN.

Caroline glanced their way, but to his knowledge, they hadn't seen him. He waited for them to pass, then grabbed Caroline's arm and spun her back into the hardware store. He pressed her against the wall and watched through the window as the car moved on down the street.

"Sam?"

Sam blinked and refocused on Caroline.

"What are you do—?"

He kissed her.

His lips claimed hers in a sweeping long kiss that probably shocked most of the patrons entering the store.

When he ended the kiss, Caroline's brows furrowed. Out of breath, she asked. "What was that all about?"

"You looked so cute with the puppy. I couldn't resist."

Caroline's mouth twisted. She shoved his chest. "You're lying through your teeth." She glanced out the window, searching. "Who were they? And why don't you want them to see you?"

Sam sighed and kept silent.

"Well?"

Caroline was no fool. Sam had to reassure her. But first he wanted to get out of town. "C'mon. Let's get going."

Caroline shook her head and crossed her arms over

her middle. She set her chin stubbornly. "No. I'm not going anywhere until you give me some answers."

"What do you want to know?"

"Who are they?"

"I don't honestly know." He didn't know who the men were, but he'd noticed their license plate and it was a Triple B car. He didn't know if they were here on legitimate business or if his father hadn't given up his search for him. Sam had made it clear that he didn't want to be found. But true to his father's style, that didn't seem to matter. Even this, his father had to try to control.

"Then why are you hiding from them?"

"There's a difference between hiding and not wanting to be found."

"No, there's not."

"In my case there is."

She looked at him suspiciously. Sam had to wipe that look from her face. The last thing he wanted was Caroline's mistrust. "I'm not a criminal."

"You're not?"

"No! Of course not."

"Do you owe money?"

Sam chuckled. "No. I don't owe a soul anything."

He could see Caroline's mind working overtime. She wanted the truth. Sam couldn't give it to her. He wasn't ready. "Then why—"

Sam took both of her hands in his. He looked deep into her pretty blue eyes and spoke from his heart. "I need your trust on this. Do you trust me?"

She hesitated. "I did."

"Past tense?"

Caroline searched his eyes, looking for and finding what she seemed to need. She sighed. "No, not past tense. I do trust you."

"Good. Know this, I haven't committed any crime and I'd never hurt you in any way. I know you have questions, but I can't tell you anything more than I have already. Do you think you can live with that?"

"I, uh," She nibbled on her lower lip. Then, she shrugged. "If I have to."

It was asking a lot of her, he knew. But the wall of anonymity he'd created around himself was his only protection. He needed that. And yes, perhaps he was hiding, hoping not to be found out. But he'd give Caroline one last parting bit of information, to help her understand the trust she'd placed in him. "Let's just say it's a family matter."

Under the circumstances Caroline thought it best to cancel her date with Sam tonight, but the man was adamant and wouldn't take no for an answer. She'd been wary and suspicious all afternoon and the debate going on in her head all but wore her out. The very last thing Sam had said to her surrounding the events of this afternoon was that it was a family matter. That eased her mind quite a bit. She'd come to the conclusion that if it was truly just a personal matter between family members then she could live with that. She had to. Sam wouldn't share anything more of his life with her. But that didn't mean she wasn't completely and utterly curious about his family and what had happened that kept him from wanting to be found. She surmised that it was none of her business and left it alone.

So she put the finishing touches on her appearance tonight. Instead of the black dress she'd worn that night at Tie-One-On when Sam had swept her off her feet, she wore a clingy crimson dress that still dangled the price tag, a pair of matching red heeled sandals, chandelier earrings that nearly touched her shoulders and a thin silver necklace that dipped into the hollow between her breasts.

Sam had said to dress up, and this was the best she had. She smiled at herself in the mirror then scooped up her long blond hair, rounding it into a knot at the back of her head and pinning it in place with a shimmering rhinestone clip. Some tendrils escaped, falling loosely around her face and shoulders.

Caroline liked the look and had gone for broke. She knew that Sam would leave soon, her precious Annabelle would return home and the stables would open, with a flourish she hoped, putting her life back into a tailspin. She'd be swamped with everyday chores and life would return to normal. She wanted to embrace tonight's memory, holding nothing back.

When the knock came sharply at seven, Caroline moved to the front door. Usually Sam just wandered in through the back so she wasn't entirely sure what to expect. She opened the door with a quick tug and she could barely keep her mouth from dropping open.

Sam stood there wearing a pair of black pleated

trousers, a gray silk shirt and a matching tie with his suit jacket slung over his shoulder. Groomed to perfection without a hint of a beard and every lock of hair in place, he looked like a million dollars and then some.

Caroline's stomach dipped. She berated herself for agreeing to this date. She should have known better. Sam wouldn't be in her life much longer and seeing him like this only intensified the pain. But she was sick and tired of living her life in fear of feeling something for someone again. She told herself to buck up. To have fun tonight and forget everything but what happened in the moment. And in those fleeting seconds, that's exactly what Caroline decided to do. She put aside her fear and buried her pain. This was her time alone with Sam. She wouldn't think past tonight. Hadn't Sam said that she deserved a night out?

"Wow," she said, stepping back from the door.

Sam walked in and handed her a bouquet of yellow roses. She'd been so floored at seeing him all cleaned up that she hadn't even noticed the flowers that he held. "Thank you," she said, "they're gorgeous."

"No," Sam said, taking her into his arms and planting a light kiss on her lips, crushing the bouquet between them, "*you're* gorgeous, Caroline. The most beautiful woman I've ever known."

Caroline could have melted in a puddle then, her heart singing with joy. "Thank you," she said looking into Sam's serious dark eyes. From the look about him tonight, she knew she wasn't in for a casual date. Sam had *dangerous* written all over him.

"I'll…I'll just put these in water," she said, heading to the kitchen, fumbling with the bouquet like a love-struck teen.

Sam followed, and, as soon as the flowers were standing in a clear cut-glass vase, Sam wrapped his arms around her, nuzzling her neck from behind. "I hate to rush you," he whispered, "but if we don't get out of here now, there's no telling what might happen."

He was close, so close that his body pressed against hers, leaving no room for doubt what he was thinking.

"Sam," she breathed out.

"Shh," he said, nuzzling her neck again. "Mmm, you smell good."

"It's… Sinful."

He groaned. "What's *sinful* is that that kitchen table is looking real good to me right now. But then I'd ruin your pretty red dress, wouldn't I?"

Sweet heat spread through her body. "Wouldn't want to rip my new dress."

Sam contemplated.

"You might scuff my shoes too," she said, deciding to play his game. "When you tossed them off."

He sucked in oxygen. "Right."

"And my hair might come down in a mess of tangles," she said softly.

Sam chuckled and whipped her around to face him. Hot hungry eyes stared back at her. "You're a cruel woman, Caroline Portman." He took her hand and dragged her from the kitchen and away from temptation. "Let's get going."

Nine

Sam pulled up to the home snuggled up against Clear Lake, about fifty miles outside of Hope Wells. It had been a long drive and after today's excursion to Midland, he wondered if Caroline would mind. But she hadn't complained or asked too many questions. She'd just sat there next to him in his truck, making light conversation, looking more beautiful than a woman had a right to look.

He smiled at her sleeping form, her head resting sweetly against the windowpane. She'd dozed off about ten minutes ago. He watched her a moment until she sensed that they had stopped. She lifted up and fidgeted with her dress and hair, then gazed out the window.

"We're here," he said quietly.

"Here?" Caroline shot him a puzzled look. She glanced again at the house. "It's magnificent."

And it was. The lakeside manor had been built in the early days of the Triple B and the architectural design, along with the use of only premium materials, made this home one of their company's finest accomplishments. Sam had known the owners, now in their early seventies, for years. And when he'd placed a call to them yesterday, they'd offered up their home without question or qualm. They no longer lived here full-time and luckily for Sam, they were out of town for the entire month.

Sam exited the truck and opened the door for Caroline. She stepped out and, as if Cinderella was heading to the ball, she stood for a moment in awe. Then she turned to him. "I don't understand."

Lights shining from the perfectly groomed lawn illuminated her pretty puzzlement. Sam took her hand. "I did some work for the owners a while back. They let me use this place from time to time."

Caroline took a moment to let that sink in. Sam guided her to the side of the house. They entered through a tall decorative iron gate and proceeded toward the grounds in back. Moonlight shimmered on the lake and a boat dock appeared. Soft music seemed to drift by, out of nowhere. And then he led her toward the patio area where a round glass table dressed with linens and china appeared.

Dinner.

Sam had to commend the management company who worked for the Pattersons. They'd done everything according to his specifications. It'd been the only time since leaving Houston that Sam had used his name and position to get what he needed. The irony struck him. Here he'd spent most of his time convincing Caroline that he was a drifter, a loner with no ties and no roots, yet she was the one and *only* person for whom he'd been willing to compromise his rigid self-proclaimed rules.

Pulling rank to make the night special for Caroline was a no-brainer. But Sam hadn't enjoyed going back to his old ways to do it. The one-time CEO of a powerful company no longer thrived on getting what he wanted at any cost.

And Sam figured that was good thing.

"Sam," she said breathlessly, "this is…this is lovely. How did you—"

Sam kissed away her question. "Cinderella, enjoy the ball. Tomorrow we turn into pumpkins again."

Caroline chuckled, the warm rich sound of her laughter filling his head. And his heart. Sam fought the feeling. Fought the joy he felt just being with Caroline. He wanted to give her a special night, but he had to remind himself that this fairy tale would end differently. There would be no happily ever after. He had less than two weeks left at Belle Star before Annabelle returned. Sam had to be gone by then.

Sam led Caroline to the table and pulled out her chair. She tucked her bottom down and smiled her thank-you. "Hungry?" he asked.

"Famished."

Sam removed the lids that kept their meals warm and they gazed at a plate of scallops, shrimp and lobster baked in a lemon wine sauce over steaming hot angel-hair pasta. Bread and wine accompanied the meal.

"Not usual Texas fare. I hope you like it."

"It looks delicious, Sam, but I still don't know how you managed all this."

Sam smiled. "First dates should always leave an impression."

Caroline shook her head at him. "This one's going to be hard to beat."

That's what Sam secretly hoped. Though he would leave her one day soon, he wanted her to remember this night. He wanted her to know he felt her worthy of making an extra effort. She'd been through a bad marriage and she hadn't been treated right. If Sam could change that, he would. So he did the next best thing by showing her that she deserved nothing but the best.

They dug into the gourmet meal with gusto, each saying very little, but their eyes made contact often and the magnetic pull seemed to energize the warm air. When they were through, Sam rose and put out his hand. "Dance?"

"I'd love to."

And since the only music that had played all night had been slow sexy ballads, Sam took her into his arms, drawing her close. He breathed in her scent, memorizing the fragrance that he'd remember as Caroline's alone.

Sinful.

Caroline rested her head on his chest, their bodies pressed to one another's and they danced that way, with soft moonlight and music lulling them into the sort of peace that Sam had only known in her arms. And after three more ballads, Sam looked down into her eyes. "Want to see the lake?"

She nodded and together, hand-in-hand, they walked out onto the small wooden dock that jutted out into Clear Lake. They stood gazing at the water, the night air bringing a slight breeze. Sam wrapped his arm around her shoulder.

"Hmmm, it's so peaceful here." As Caroline gazed out, her blue eyes caught the light of the moon, the sparkle a sight to behold.

"It's quiet and secluded. A good place to think."

"Or not think."

"Right. Not thinking is good too," Sam said, meaning every word. He'd done his share of overthinking everything in his life and he'd just recently learned that not thinking was sometimes the better choice. "How'd you get so smart?"

Caroline chuckled. "Flattery will get you everywhere."

"Oh, yeah? What if where I want to go isn't appropriate on a first date?"

She looked into his eyes. God, she was so beautiful, so intelligent and so incredibly sexy. "You're doing great so far. I'd say, take your best shot."

He took her hand and led her off the dock. They walked along a darkened path where the moonlight touched the lake's surface, casting slight shades of light. Sam stopped amid a cluster of tall oak trees, leaning up against one, pulling Caroline in close. He lifted the hem of her dress, inching it up her legs. He stroked her thighs up and down, her soft creamy skin under his palms heating him instantly. Then he inched his fingers up and played with the lace of her panties. "I've wanted to do this all night," he whispered, kissing her lips roughly.

Caroline moaned.

He tugged her panties down and worked them off slowly, letting her step out of them. "And this." He cupped her between the thighs, spreading her legs, his palm open, skimming the soft folds there. She bucked and moved against his hand.

"Feels so good, Sam," she whispered urgently.

"Damn it, Caroline, I'm gonna die a happy man." Sam moved with her now, stroking her until he needed more. With his other hand, he lowered the top of her clingy red dress, exposing a tiny red-lace bra barely keeping her full breasts from exploding out. Sam maneuvered that undergarment off in seconds, and lowered his mouth to one globe, taking her into his mouth. She gasped and threw her head back, her blond hair tumbling out of its confinement. Sam moistened her with his tongue, making wide sweeping circles until the very tip of her breast pebbled hard and erect.

Caroline moaned again, softer now, more intensely. "That's it, sweetheart," he said and he felt the pressure building. She rode his hand now, bucking against him, and when he'd reached his limit he set her aside, unzipped his pants, taking out a condom quickly and then twirled her around. The wall of the oak braced her back and he impaled her with one swift efficient thrust.

Their groans met and lingered. Sam held her tightly

and allowed the initial mind-blowing union between their bodies to take hold. Caroline opened her eyes and met his gaze as he began to thrust into the sweetly familiar cove that welcomed him.

Sam lifted her then and she wrapped her legs around him. They moved as one until they succumbed to the heat, the force and the power developing between them. They climaxed together and gasped out their intoxicating release.

Caroline lowered her feet to the ground and they clung to each other. It was the best sex of his life, but it was more than that. And as Sam held her, he knew that he'd been a fool. A stupid, crazy fool—because how on earth could he believe that he could make love to this beautiful, gutsy, intelligent woman every night and not fall for her?

"Sam, I love it here," she said with a deep sigh, "but it's getting late. Shouldn't we get going?"

Grateful for the interruption of his thoughts, he answered, "Only if you want to, sweetheart."

"We have a long drive."

"We could stay here. The Pattersons wouldn't mind at all."

"Really? But I didn't bring anything with me."

Sam chuckled. "I managed to snag both of our toothbrushes before we left."

Caroline shook her head, looking at him with a twinkle in her eyes.

"They have five bedrooms here," he said.

"It is a *long* drive home, isn't it?" Caroline didn't

want the night to end any more than he did. "We'd have to be up and gone by the crack of dawn. Tomorrow's a work day."

They'd both agreed that if they'd played on Saturday, then they'd turn Sunday into a workday. And they had played. Sam loved playtime with Caroline. "If the boss lady says we work, then we work. So what do you say? Want to stay the night?"

Caroline smiled and nodded. "Well, since you went to the trouble of bringing our toothbrushes."

Sam picked up her bra and panties, stuffing them into his pocket. Caroline adjusted her dress, shifting it back into place as Sam looked on. Just knowing she wore that dress now without benefit of underwear shook him to the core. The material hung on every curve, every hollow and her pebble-hard nipples jutting out, defining the rounded shapes of her breasts and keeping the dress in place, worked on making a spent man hot and ready again. He took her hand. "Let's try out one of their bedrooms, darlin'."

Or with the way he'd begun to feel about Caroline, maybe they'd try out all five.

On Monday morning, Caroline sat down at her computer thanking high heaven for online banking. She'd saved a ton of work and many trips to town by setting up this new method of bill-paying.

She'd been on fire lately, eager to start advertising the grand opening of Belle Star in two weeks. She'd already contacted local newspapers and had flyers made up, along with commissioning a huge banner that she'd designed to welcome the visitors to her new stables. She planned a huge Texas-size barbecue with Maddie and several other friends offering to lend a hand. In her mind, it would be the perfect celebration to bring back old customers and garner some new ones as well.

When the phone rang, Caroline's heart sped up. She lifted the receiver and answered, taking her eyes off the computer screen to give her full attention to the caller.

"Hi, Mommy."

"Annabelle, sweetheart. Good morning. How's my favorite girl?"

"'Kay. Grammy said I could call 'cause to tell you good morning. We're going to Anna Marie's birthday party today."

"Oh, that's so nice, sweetie. I know you'll have fun at Anna Marie's today. How old will she be?" Caroline asked, knowing that her mother's friend's grandchild was just a baby.

"She's gonna be one, Mommy. I get to change her diaper at the party."

"That's my big girl."

"And we get rainbow cake and pony rides."

"Mmm. Cake sounds yummy. You be careful on the pony. Remember what Mommy always says?"

She could sense her daughter nodding into the phone.

"What does Mommy say?" Caroline asked again.

"Mommy says hold tight and re-spect the pony."

"That's right. And what does *respect* mean?"

"Means to be nice, right Mommy?"

Caroline laughed. "That's right, sweetheart. You did remember, you smart girl."

Annabelle giggled, the sound sheer pleasure to Caroline's ears. She missed her daughter terribly. But keeping busy had helped ease some of her loneliness.

"I love you, sweetheart."

"Love you too, Mommy. Here's Grammy. She wants to talk."

"Okay, have fun at the party."

Caroline finished her conversation with her mother and hung up the phone. She always needed a minute after one of Annabelle's phone calls to reassemble her thoughts. She couldn't wait to hold her daughter in her arms again. And tuck her into bed. She even missed waking up in the middle of the night just to check on her, to make sure she was sleeping peacefully.

Lord, motherhood was wonderful. And trying. And blessed. And every other emotion she could imagine wrapped into one tight, almost-five-year-old bundle.

"Coffee's ready," Sam called out from the kitchen.

Caroline smiled. She'd gotten used to having Sam here. Still on a high from their first "date," Caroline had daydreamed all of yesterday, barely able to keep up with Sam's relentless quest to finish painting the second stable. They'd worked their fingers to the bone and then fallen into bed exhausted last night.

Caroline couldn't have asked for a better worker. Sam did the work of two men, never stopping until he was satisfied. And at night, the same held true, except he managed to satisfy them both. "I'll be right there."

Caroline checked her bank statement, ready to click off the computer, when something odd struck her. Neither of the checks she'd given to Sam for his weekly salary had been cashed.

She thought back on the lavish dinner and beautiful surroundings he'd supplied for their Saturday night date. She figured he'd used some of his earnings. So she couldn't imagine why Sam hadn't bothered to cash his checks. After all, he was a drifter with no roots and no great source of income. Or was he?

Caroline wandered into the kitchen ready to ask Sam about the uncashed checks. "Sam, I have a question."

But Sam wasn't in the kitchen. She found him standing on the back porch, looking skyward. Caroline followed the direction of his gaze, watching a helicopter hovering overhead, the flapping sounds becoming louder and louder as it zeroed in.

To her surprise, the helicopter set down on her property. Caroline bounded out the back door and shouted to compete with the roar of the powerful machine. "Sam, did you see that?"

Sam winced, then ran a hand down his jaw, but no surprise registered. He remained calm and nodded.

"Sam!"

"It's okay, Caroline," he shouted, then guided her back into the kitchen away from the deafening noise. He shut the back door and sighed with resignation. "I know who it is."

Angered and confused, Caroline's voice held no patience. "Well, *who's* landing a helicopter on my property for heaven's sake?"

Sam looked up at her like a child who'd been caught with both hands in the cookie jar. "My brother."

Caroline had a bad feeling about this. She stood just outside her back door with arms folded, waiting for Sam to return. He'd said to wait until he found out what was going on, and then he'd explain everything to her. Now, she watched him out in the south end of the property speaking adamantly with his brother. The two had been out there for quite some time. And from what she could see of the helicopter, it sported some sort of fancy emblem on the side, though she couldn't make out what it said.

Sam had a lot of explaining to do and she figured that she wouldn't like any of it.

Finally, the two men approached and Caroline immediately saw the resemblance. Sam's brother was younger, perhaps a little more lean, but those dark eyes and that crop of dark hair couldn't be missed. Both men wore a somber expression. When they finally reached her back porch, Sam spoke up. "Caroline Portman, I'd like you to meet my brother, Wade. Wade, this is Caroline."

Wade put out his hand. "Sorry about landing the chopper here. I had to find Sam immediately. There's been some bad news."

Caroline took Wade's hand in a brief handshake. She still didn't know what any of this meant. And the resemblance at close range was remarkable. Both men were gorgeous. "What kind of bad news?"

Wade stepped back. "I'll let Sam explain."

Sam shot him an impatient glare.

"Your stuff is in the tack room at the back of the stables, right?" Wade asked.

Sam closed his eyes for a second. "Most of it, yeah."

Wade smiled at Caroline. "It's a pleasure, ma'am. I'll let you two talk now."

Both of them watched Wade's back as he headed for the stables. "What's this all about?" Caroline asked with a sense of impending doom.

Sam took a deep breath, his chest heaving. "Let's go inside. Have that cup of coffee. There's a lot to tell."

Caroline's legs went weak from his tone, and only with Sam's guidance, a hand to her back, did she muster the steps necessary to go inside. There, she sat while Sam poured them both a fresh cup of coffee.

"I just found out that my father died last night. The heart attack took him quickly."

Caroline gasped. She hadn't expected this. "Oh, Sam. I'm so sorry."

Sam shook his head. "Don't waste your sympathy on him, Caroline. I'll explain about my father later, but first you have to know that I never meant to hurt anyone, especially not you."

Caroline's eyes rounded, her heart beating fast. "What will hurt me?"

"I'm hoping nothing, but then I'm a bit of a fool when it comes to you, darlin'. You see, my father owned and operated the biggest construction company in the Southwest, the Triple B, which stands for Blake Beaumont Building. And for the past nine years, I've been the CEO and my father's right-hand man. Well, up until eight months ago, that is."

"When you lost your daughter?"

Sam nodded. "Yes, about then. The long and the short of it is that I hated the man I'd become. I couldn't live with myself and I hated everything about my father's company. So I took off. I left the Triple B and my father, leaving behind my old way of life. I needed to do that for my sanity, Caroline. I couldn't live with myself another minute.

"As a young boy all I wanted was my father's love. I'd tried everything I could to be worthy in his eyes until I finally understood what I needed to do. The Triple B meant everything to him, so if I could make him an even bigger success, if I could earn his respect, I thought I'd also earn his love. But I realized far too late, that my father wasn't capable of loving anyone or anything but the Triple B. And I'd allowed him to suck me into his web quite easily.

"I'm a millionaire, Caroline. I have more money than any one person could ever need or want. But the price of my success was far too high. I was the worst kind of husband and father. I neglected everyone in favor of the company. In the end, I sacrificed my daughter's life. And now, it seems that I'm heir to my father's legacy."

Caroline listened, her heart breaking for Sam's loss, but her head spinning in anger and betrayal. Sam was a millionaire, doing what? Playing at being a lonely drifter with no money and no roots? He'd been deceitful and Caroline couldn't get past his duplicity.

"So, you decided lying to me was your best bet? You'd simply string the young widow along, giving me your one-month deadline. How many other women have you done this to? How many others have you lied to? I'm sorry for what you've gone through, Sam. Lord knows, I'd be a heartless mother not to recognize your grief, but you had no right to do this to me. You lied to me. You betrayed me."

"No, Caroline. I never betrayed you."

"I don't know you, Sam."

"You *do* know me. You can trust me."

Caroline didn't trust anyone at the moment. She glanced out the window, her nerves raw, her heart aching. "Your brother has packed your stuff up. He's waiting for you by the helicopter." Caroline realized that Sam would leave now, days before he'd intended. And all those old feelings of abandonment when Gil left came rushing back. The haunting memory of his betrayal was fresh again. She trembled, fighting off those old feelings of failure and turned away from Sam. "Go back to wherever you're really from, Sam."

"Houston. But it's not my home anymore, Caroline. That's what I'm trying to tell you. I never meant for any of this to touch you." He came to stand in front of her, so that she had to look into his eyes—eyes that had lied to her one too many times.

"Well, it has, hasn't it?"

"I'm sorry. Truly sorry. But I'm not Gil. I won't abandon you. And hell, Caroline, I've never felt this way about another woman. That's not what this was about. I never stayed in one place long enough to get involved with anyone. I didn't want to get involved with you, as you might remember."

"Oh, so now it's my fault? I was the desperate, needy woman who threw herself at you?" With arms folded, Caroline's face flamed. She recognized the truth in that, which made her even angrier.

Sam bit his lip. He shook his head. He let a beat pass, then another, as if he had to rein in his own anger. "No, you were the gorgeous, courageous woman I couldn't keep my hands off, if you want the truth. And I did get involved. Too involved. I don't know where it's going with us, but I do know that I'll be back to help you finish Belle Star, Caroline. But right now, I have to leave. I don't want to, but Wade needs me. He's a bit out of his element right now. There are papers to sign and a whole lot of red tape. I'll make it quick. I'll be back as soon as I can."

"That's what I thought when Gil left. That he'd come back."

Sam took her into his arms. She allowed him to, because she didn't have the strength to fight him. He pressed his face close to hers, making her look into his eyes. "I'm not Gil. Just give me a few days."

"That's up to you, Sam."

"So, you won't throw me out when I return?"

She shook her head. "No. We had a deal."

"Right, and I'll honor my part of the deal. I promise."

Wade started up the helicopter engine and from the corner of her eye she saw the blades beginning their rotation. "You'd better go."

Sam stared at her lips. Caroline pulled away.

"I'll be back," he said before walking out the door and if she hadn't been so heartbroken, she might have laughed at the cliché.

Ten

"It's not the end of the world that Sam's a millionaire with good looks to spare, my friend," Maddie said, pulling up a thick weed along the shady side of the house. Both women wore heavy gloves and were armed with small hand shovels. "I agree that he should have been honest with you."

Caroline yanked hard, pulling up a stubborn dead bush, the hard work easing her frustration. "He lost his daughter and blames himself, that much I get. But why lie to me? Why couldn't he tell me the truth? I would have understood."

Maddie stopped tugging long enough to meet Caroline's gaze. "Maybe because he could barely face the truth himself. Drifting from place to place, keeping his distance from everyone—maybe that was his way of coping with his loss. Maybe running was his only salvation."

Caroline shook her head. "He didn't have to lie to me. He knew about Gil and what I went through with him. I'd been open and honest, foolish me."

Maddie found a wilted plant from last year's garden and began to dig. "You're right. He's a creep. A scoundrel. Maybe you should toss him off the property when he comes back."

"*If* he comes back. I'm not holding my breath. And he's not a creep. A scoundrel maybe," Caroline said softly.

"For taking your heart?"

Caroline tossed the weeds in the garbage can she'd pulled up to the wall and began turning over the soil with her shovel. "There is that. I may have fallen for him, but I don't trust him. How could I? I thought I knew him."

"Maybe you do know him. Ever think about that? Maybe he's through being his father's man now. Maybe the Sam Beaumont you've come to know is really the man that he is."

Caroline thought she'd be a fool to hope. She'd learned hard lessons from Gil. She wouldn't give an inch this time. *This time,* she knew better. She dug deeper into the soil, lifting and tossing the dirt, making a nice bed for the hibiscus and gardenia bushes she planned to plant there.

"He's rich and the CEO of a giant construction company. Up until a few days ago I didn't know he'd been married or had a child. No, I don't really know Sam. None of this matters though, Maddie. He's got responsibilities in Houston now."

And what Caroline didn't add, but felt in her heart, was that Sam couldn't face seeing Annabelle. Thinking back now, he'd avoided all talk of her whenever possible. Caroline could only imagine his anguish at losing his daughter and ultimately feeling he'd caused her death. How hard it must have been for him to see Annabelle's things about. And now she understood why he'd avoided looking at the photos in her room—Annabelle's sunny face smiling into the camera was too hard to bear.

Caroline ached for Sam.

But she still felt betrayed.

"It's been three days," Maddie said. "Have you heard from him?"

"He's called every day and leaves a message."

"Because you won't pick up the phone?"

"Busted on that. I wouldn't know what to say to him. Besides, he only asks about Belle Star. How is the work going? How am I doing? He doesn't say anything about returning here."

"Sounds like the man cares about you."

Caroline shrugged and patted the soil down with her gloved hands. "If he comes back, it'll be all business. My personal time with Sam is over."

She almost said that she'd had her little fling, but it hadn't been that way with Sam. For her, it had been something special, so she wouldn't trivialize it. The memories wouldn't fade anytime soon. She knew that for certain.

She still loved him.

The scoundrel.

After lunch, Caroline bid farewell to Maddie, thanking her for the help. She finished up planting in the afternoon and worked into the evening on odds and ends. Tomorrow she'd try her hand working inside the stables.

She fell into bed just before ten o'clock, exhausted.

The next morning Caroline woke up feeling refreshed from a good night's sleep. She rose quickly, dressed in her work clothes, jeans and an old tank top that read Rhinestone Cowgirl with half of the pink sequins missing. The summer had heated up, and now gray clouds hovered overhead, causing the humidity in the air to rise considerably.

Caroline headed to the kitchen and brewed coffee. While she waited for the coffeemaker to fill the pot the sound of banging coming from the stables caught her attention. She listened carefully, and, no, she hadn't been mistaken. The hammering sound grew louder when she opened the back door.

Caroline poured herself a cup of coffee and strode purposely toward the sound. When she entered the stables she found herself face to face with Sam Beaumont. Barechested, wearing jeans and a studious expression, he was hammering a replacement plank onto one of the stalls.

Her heart in her throat, she remained speechless watching Sam's efficient movements as he continued to work.

"You still mad at me?" he asked, taking a moment to meet her eyes.

Her joy at seeing him, at his return, warred with the

sense of betrayal and disappointment she felt. But no, she no longer held on to her anger. How could she be angry with a man who'd looked bone-tired and weary, as though he hadn't gotten a wink of sleep, while he worked on her stables?

He'd come back, just like he said he would. But things had to be different between them now. She had to protect what was left of her heart.

"I have one question and I'd like an honest answer. The night we went…the night you took me to Clear Lake."

He nodded. "I remember."

As if either of them could forget that wonderful night.

"Do you own that house?"

Sam looked up from his stall, removing his heavy work gloves to look squarely into her eyes. "No. I don't own that house, Caroline, but I built it."

"Oh," Caroline muttered, "no wonder you knew your way around so well."

"I didn't lie to you about that."

"Didn't you?" She kept the accusation out of her tone, but felt it deep inside. There was so much to Sam Beaumont that she didn't know. So many facets to his life he hadn't wanted to share. And now, it seemed too late.

"I told you I'd done some work for the owners."

"It's a beautiful house," she said, lost in thoughts of his craftmanship and work ethic. She couldn't begrudge him that. But he had lied to her, over and over again, and he might think his explanation good enough, but Caroline, a woman who'd had the rug pulled out from under her one too many times, Caroline recognized that truth.

"It was one of the first ones we'd built together, my father and I. My design, his corrections." Sam smiled wistfully. "It had been my pride and joy, until…" He stopped and shrugged, and Caroline sensed that he'd been thinking of his daughter.

"I didn't think you'd come back."

"I would have been here sooner, but the funeral was yesterday and I couldn't get out of going. Family and friends expected me there."

"You look tired."

Sam inhaled sharply. "Haven't gotten much sleep lately."

Caroline handed him her mug of coffee. She hadn't yet touched a drop. "Here. Take a break."

The irony in what she'd just said struck Caroline with clarifying force. Offering Sam Beaumont, the CEO and heir to a multi-million-dollar company, a cup of coffee and allowing him break time seemed so odd.

Sam took the cup, his fingers brushing slightly over hers. The contact hit a nerve with her, and she backed away. She couldn't weaken. She had to keep to her resolve. Sam would leave sooner rather than later, and protecting herself would be crucial to her survival.

Sam leaned against the stall post and sipped his coffee, closing his eyes as if relishing the taste. "I missed…your coffee."

Caroline didn't respond. Lord, how she'd missed him.

"Looks like you've gotten some work done in here," he said, glancing around, seeing firsthand what had already been accomplished.

"Jack came by the other day. He spent his day off from the jail working with me."

Sam stopped the coffee mug, just before reaching his lips. "Jack, huh?"

"He got a lot done that day." She felt she had to defend Jack's efforts. "He never let up. He's been a good friend."

Sam listened, sipping his coffee, and nodded.

"Sam, I can't say I'm not surprised that you came back. Judging from the work you're used to doing, this must seem trivial to—"

"Not trivial, darlin'. If it's important to you, how can it be? It's your livelihood and your legacy to your daughter. No, I don't look at it as trivial at all."

"Thank you." She felt as though he really meant that. "But what I was about to say, is that things have changed between us now. If you want to stay and see this through with me, I would appreciate it. But you and I…well, it's over."

Sam pursed his lips and looked away for a moment. Then he met her eyes with softness and understanding. "I figured as much."

"And you still came back?"

"A deal's a deal. Besides, I've got something invested in this place, too. I want to see your success."

Caroline smiled for the first time in four days. Then she remembered that Sam would leave soon. She couldn't allow the warm tingling feelings surging up her body. She had to hang on to some of her misgivings. "Don't say nice things to me, Sam. Let's keep it all business."

Sam chuckled as if what she'd said had been ridiculous. "Don't know if I can do that, Caroline."

"You have to, Sam," she said vehemently.

"Why?" He looked genuinely puzzled as if he hadn't a clue.

"Because I really need your help."

"I know that, sweetheart. That's why I came back."

"And because…" she began but couldn't go on.

"Because?" he asked softly, his brows furrowed, his eyes probing.

"Because, I've fallen in love with you, you idiot!"

Sam braced himself against the stall, watching Caroline storm out of the building, her parting words a shock to his system.

Caroline loved him.

He hadn't expected it. Nor had he expected to be encased in the soft afterglow of those words. It surrounded him with warmth and goodness and everything Sam didn't deserve. Yet, the glow stayed, like energy circling his body, those sweet words reverberating in his ears.

I've fallen in love with you, you idiot!

For a moment Sam smiled, thinking he'd heard better declarations, but the smile faded soon enough.

And so did the afterglow. Sam felt cold inside now, a frigid wave passing over him. He hadn't wanted this. He hadn't wanted to hurt Caroline Portman. There was no hope for the two of them. There never had been.

Maybe if he'd told her the truth from the beginning, she might have realized she shouldn't have wasted time on a man who'd never win a husband-of-the-year award. He'd never be able to face little Annabelle, either. He should have told her everything up front and maybe they wouldn't have gotten so deeply involved.

But God, it was good to see her again. He'd missed her. Missed everything about her. And just seeing her walk into the stables, offering him a cup of coffee, her blond hair flowing and that tight faded tank top clinging to her body, had nearly sent him to his knees. She was the most beautiful, courageous woman he'd ever met. And he didn't deserve her.

He'd had to think twice about coming back, wondering if a clean break would have been easier. But Sam couldn't abandon her, not when she needed him. He'd given his word and that much about him *had* changed. He would rather have cut off his right arm than not return to finish what he'd started. He could do that much for Caroline. He could get the stables ready for her grand opening.

Sam took half a second debating what to do. He had to speak with Caroline, though he didn't know what he could say to make things better for her. Nothing had changed. He still had to leave when the work was done. But damn it, he had to try.

He strode into the yard and made it to the back door within seconds. The screen door slapped from behind when he entered, startling Caroline from her spot by the kitchen sink. She looked up and didn't give him a chance to speak.

"Don't say anything, Sam. Not one word. I said what

I said, and I meant it, but I would take those words back in a minute if I could. You're not obligated to me in any way. Go back and finish what you were doing. I'll call you when lunch is ready."

Caroline turned her back on him and continued rinsing out the coffeepot.

The tic in Sam's jaw worked overtime. He stood there gazing at her with both anger and pride. The woman always seemed to elicit conflicting emotions within him. Today was no exception. But damn, he couldn't just walk out of here and not have his say. She needed to hear some things, whether she wanted to or not.

Sam took the steps necessary to stand behind her. Both arms reached around to brace the kitchen counter, trapping her from moving.

"Caroline, I have some things to say to you. Some of them are *nice* and some are gonna be damn hard to hear, so just stand still and listen."

Sam stood close enough to breathe in her scent, a heady mix of soap and flowers and Caroline. In a weaker moment, he would have wrapped her into his arms by now, but that wouldn't happen today or any other day. She'd made her feelings clear. And Sam would respect that.

He spoke from behind, holding her to the spot. "Are you willing to listen?"

"Do I have a choice?"

"No."

Her stance relaxed then and Sam realized she'd been rigid and nervous before. "I'm listening."

"None of this was what I expected, Caroline. I never would have taken the job if it meant hurting you in the process. I've been drifting from town to town for months, trying to piece my life back together. Yes, I've been running away, but it's all I know to do. Up until I came here, I didn't know a peaceful night's sleep. I had hard times facing the days, but nights were the worst.

"Where others say I will heal in time, I don't think it's possible. The pain inside me goes deep. It's raw and gnaws at me every day. I was a worthless husband and a terrible father. I neglected everyone I cared about. And what's really pathetic is that I didn't even recognize what I had until it was too late.

"You're a beautiful woman, Caroline, inside and out. I admire everything you're doing here. You've had some rough times in your life as well, but you didn't give up. You've got a good plan and you won't let anything get in your way.

"Walking away from you is going to be harder on me than you might think. I didn't mean to, but I got involved. Deeply involved. And honey, I just can't afford that. I'm still running. Can you understand that?"

Caroline nodded and when Sam released his arms to come around to look at her, silent tears were rolling down her cheeks. The ache in the pit of his stomach intensified and only confirmed what he'd always recognized. He was no good for Caroline. He'd hurt her and would only continue to bring her pain.

"Ah, sweetheart," he said, unable to keep from touching

her. He wound his hand around her neck and brought her close, wiping her tears with the back of his thumb.

Caroline stepped away. "You're being nice again," she said on a shaky breath.

Sam dropped his arms. "Sorry."

She cast him half a smile. "I get it, Sam. I always have. I can't help how I feel any more than you can. I know you have to go. I know it in my head at least."

Sam nodded, understanding that what's in the heart is a whole lot more potent and a whole lot more dangerous. "I came back here to help you achieve your dream. I know that's important to you. I'm willing to stay until we're finished, if you still want me here."

"I still want you here, Sam."

"Then I'm staying."

Caroline nodded then smiled. "Okay."

And as Sam walked to the back door, she added, "Annabelle is coming home on Sunday night."

Sam strode out the door, his gut twisting into a knot. He had three days to finish the work here because come Sunday morning he had to be gone.

Eleven

Saturday morning dawned with clouds and a gloomy sky. A light drizzle moistened the ground and Caroline could only thank heaven that the stables were all but finished. Early this morning she and Sam had cleaned out all remnants of the old straw and bedding in each stall. They had worked like demons sweeping out the stalls and inserted what Caroline deemed her only real luxury, stall mats. The mats that had been custom-sized, would protect the ground beneath and would reduce the amount of straw and shavings she'd need inside each.

They'd eaten lunch late and, as usual these days, their conversation bordered on quiet and cordial, each one feeling their own sense of grief. Caroline's anticipation over seeing Annabelle tomorrow night had been weighted only by the thought of never seeing Sam

Beaumont again. She told herself that her dream of Belle Star Stables was finally coming true and she should be rejoicing instead of feeling the hours tick by like a woman walking toward her own execution.

Caroline sat at the kitchen table now, staring at the brochures and price lists from her competition in the area. She needed to make money, but she also had to be practical. First and foremost, she needed to garner some business which required her to post the most competitive prices she possibly could. When she opened her doors next week at her grand opening, she'd have brochures of her own along with a list of services and fees.

"You ready for me?" Sam asked, whipping off his hat and stepping into the kitchen. He tossed his hat in Frisbee fashion onto the kitchen counter, a gesture Caroline had come to think as his alone.

"Not a minute too soon. I've been going over these, but I could sure use your input. Any problems on the grounds?"

Sam had taken Dumpling on one last tour of the grounds to scour the fences and pasture to make sure there wasn't anything they'd overlooked. "Everything looks good out there. We didn't miss anything." Sam sat down next to her. "What smells so darn good?"

"Cookies. Chocolate chip," Caroline said absentmindedly. "Annabelle's favorites."

Sam nodded and glanced toward her range. It was just one more reminder that tomorrow their lives would change. For Caroline, hers would go back to normal, the way it had always been, but she wondered what life had in store for Sam.

"You sharing?"

She smiled. "I made a pan just for you."

"For me?"

She shoved the brochures his way. "It's a bribe. I need to figure out how to make this all work. And you're elected to help me."

Sam frowned. "You got milk to go with those cookies?" She nodded.

"Okay, then let's get to work."

Sam studied the figures and her set-up costs, working up a fee list that would compete with other stables while giving her enough of a profit to stay in business. After half an hour, he said, "These fees will keep you afloat, but the real profit to be made is in any extras you can include, such as riding lessons and selling small items and riding gear. You need strict rules and must make sure everyone who boards a horse pays on time. Do you have anyone lined up to help you?"

"I've spoken with one high-school boy who'll be available in the early mornings and after school. And there's a young girl who recently dropped out of college who used to babysit Annabelle once in a while. She loves horses and is willing to work full-time for the time being. I think I'm covered."

Sam slid the fee schedule over to her. "Take a look and make changes if you want. But this is what I feel would work for you."

Caroline rose from her seat and slid the cookies she'd

baked onto a large plate. She brought the plate to the table, setting it in front of Sam. On impulse, she picked up one warm cookie oozing soft chocolate and lifted it to Sam's mouth. "I trust your instincts, Sam."

Sam took a bite of the cookie and when she made a move to pull away, he grabbed her wrist. The connection heated her skin. She lifted her eyes to his and saw a hunger that matched her own. She hadn't touched him since he'd come back, and now her foolish maneuver sizzled between them. She wanted his touch, his hands on her, their bodies pressed together, but at that very moment Sam released her hand.

She backed up a step. "I'll, uh, get the milk." She turned to the refrigerator, ready to open the door.

"I don't want milk, Caroline."

Caroline spun around but was saved from Sam's heated stare. The phone rang.

She lifted the receiver immediately and when the brief phone call was over, she turned to Sam, overjoyed. "Sam, that was Lone Star. I was approved! I'm going to adopt Princess!"

Sam rose from his seat and opened his arms. Without thought to propriety or her guarded uncertainties Caroline flew into his arms, unable to contain her delight. His embrace felt so right, so real and they remained that way, holding on to each other for a long moment. He pulled back long enough to look into her eyes. "I knew you'd get approved, sweetheart. You're perfect." He brought her close again and hugged tight. "Absolutely perfect."

"This is going to make Annabelle so happy," she said, then caught her mistake. Since finding out about Sam's loss, she'd tried to be sensitive to his feelings. Losing a child had to be devastating enough, but with Sam, the pain of his guilt went deeper than she might imagine. "Sam, I'm sorry. I shouldn't have said—"

"Shh, it's okay." He put a finger to her lips, keeping her from finishing her apology. "You're happy. And I'm happy for you. You deserve nothing but the best."

He moved his hand to her cheek, spreading his palm and cradling her. She turned her head into his hand, absorbing his tenderness. "Oh, Sam."

"Don't think I won't miss you, darlin'. I'll be gone but you'll be in my thoughts every day."

Caroline wrapped her arms around Sam's neck. She looked deeply into his eyes, and his gentle expression was too much to bear. With a desperate need to have this man hold her one last time throughout the night, she spoke from her heart. "We have tonight, Sam. Let's not waste it."

Sam closed his eyes and nodded and when he opened them again, she witnessed his desire warring with self-restraint.

"I'm sure, Sam. It's what I want and you said it yourself. I deserve the best."

Sam smiled. "In that case." He lifted her into his arms and headed for her bedroom.

Caroline lay curled up on the bed, the cotton sheet in a tangle around her body as she watched Sam lift up from the mattress to open the window and part the curtains. Soft rain fell and the air that rushed inside filled the room with crisp dewy freshness.

Sam peered out the window and she continued to watch the shadows play against his form, bared to her, strong and powerful. They'd made love once already and her memory would be forever painted with vivid, sexy images.

Caroline rose from the bed and walked over to him. She stood beside him and he wrapped his arm around her shoulder. They both stood there watching the sky above, listening to the sound of rain hitting the ground. Gray clouds covered the stars, but Caroline imagined them, twinkling above, ready to spread light rays when the clouds dispersed.

They'd spent the better part of the afternoon and night in bed, holding each other, making love and dozing in peaceful sleep. Caroline remembered what Sam had said about not knowing a good night's sleep until he'd come here. For that, she was grateful and she wondered how either of them would sleep once he was gone. Time ticked by too quickly—they had only a few fragile hours left.

"It's a magical night, Sam."

Sam turned to face her, his eyes a shadow of sadness. He put a finger to her cheek and outlined her jaw then caressed her lips, his touch oh so tender. He brought his lips down on hers, kissing her softly with the utmost care. "I love you, Caroline. I know that now. But I can't stay."

Caroline rejoiced for a moment, glad to have Sam's love. She hadn't thought him capable of ever loving again, and just the fact that he'd admitted his love for her meant certain progress. She should be overjoyed. But in her heart, she wasn't entirely sure if he knew the emotion fully. She believed he loved her, but not enough to overcome his own fears and misgivings—and certainly not enough to conquer his guilt. The brutal reality never veered far from her thoughts. She knew Sam had to leave. She'd always known.

"It's okay, Sam," she said for his benefit. Inside, her heart tore in two.

"I want nothing but the best for you, sweetheart. Your stables will be a succ—"

"Shh," she said, stopping him from finishing his thoughts. She didn't want his admiration or his encouragement. Not tonight. Tonight, she only wanted his love. "Let's go back to bed, Sam."

He stared into her eyes, and nodded with understanding. He took her hand, leading her back to bed. She lay down and reached up for him. He came down on top of her, their bodies pressed to one another. "Make love to me, Sam. Once more."

They both knew it would be their last time together.

Sam cradled her in his arms and skimmed his lips over every inch of her, making her heart soar and her body hum. His touch created sensations that both aroused her and made her feel like a precious treasure. He kissed her gently, caressed her skin, rounding her breasts with his palms then sweeping his hands down lower until she became lost to everyone and everything but the heady, loving stirrings Sam created.

She melted into him and he into her. They moved as one, with cravings and yearnings that tore at her soul. She kissed him fervently, caressed his chest, skimmed his navel and lower yet, to feel his powerful erection in her hand. She stroked him soundly, memorizing the feel of him, his silky strength. She tasted him and he groaned, stroking her with his hands spread, their bodies entwined.

And when he nudged the tip of her womanhood, she ached for him. He entered her then, and she welcomed him, the movements new and familiar all at the same time.

He lifted up and gazed into her eyes. She met his eyes and they moved together with thrusts that peaked, tearing a gut-wrenching cry from her throat. He filled her and she took every last ounce he offered, until they reached as high as two souls could possibly go.

They shattered at the same time, both crying out each other's names with declarations of love and bittersweet longing.

And when their breaths steadied and their bodies relaxed, Caroline felt safe and secure in Sam's arms once again.

For the very last time.

Caroline woke to a murky day, the tumultuous clouds outside no match for her own sense of gloom. She reached out to touch the empty space beside her in the bed and knew that Sam had left her in the wee hours of the morning. She rose slowly, fighting off her tears, shoring up her courage and thinking of making it through one day at a time.

She showered and dressed in her usual work clothes although she didn't have too much work left to do. Amazingly, she and Sam had made a great team. They'd gotten everything done she'd hoped to and now the stables were ready for honest-to-goodness-paying customers.

The only bright spot in this dismal day was that Annabelle would return home. Caroline's parents would travel with her and they'd stay for a few days before heading back to Florida. Caroline had wanted them to stay for her grand opening, but her father's health wasn't what it had once been. It was enough that they would see Belle Star Stables the way she'd always envisioned it. Her dream of refurbishing the stables had come true.

Caroline entered the kitchen and set the coffeepot to brewing. A cloud of loneliness surrounded her. She would drink coffee alone this morning. There would be no more sharing of thoughts and dreams with Sam. There would be no more late-night dinners. There would be no more cuddling in his arms and lovemaking until dawn.

Caroline sat at the kitchen table, her head in her hands. When the front doorbell rang, she couldn't help but hope that Sam had returned, but as she glanced out the parlor window on her way to reach the door, those hopes all but shattered. A rain-splattered patrol car from the Hope Wells Sheriff's Department sat in her driveway.

She plastered on a big smile and opened the door. "Morning, Jack."

"Hey there," he said, entering without invitation. That's how it had always been with Jack. They'd been friends forever. He handed her a white bag. "I brought you doughnuts. Hey, cops don't have an exclusive on them, you know."

"So you've said about a…" she glanced into the bag loaded with maple, sugar, chocolate and lemon-filled doughnuts "…a *dozen* times. A dozen, Jack? Trying to fatten me up?"

"I thought you might need some nourishment."

She raised her eyebrows.

"Okay, I saw Sam driving out of town this morning. Thought you could use a friend."

"You're on a mission of mercy?"

He shrugged, then made his way into the kitchen. "Coffee ready?"

"Just about. Sit down. You're gonna help me eat some of these and the rest are going straight back to the sheriff's office. A girl's got to watch her figure, you know."

Jack sat down and dived into the bag, coming up with a maple bar. Before sliding it into his mouth, he took a slow leisurely tour of her body. If it were anyone else, she might have blushed. "You've got nothing to worry about." He winked. "Everything's in the right place."

She slumped into the chair and grabbed a chocolate doughnut. "Thanks."

"Really. All joking aside, how are you?"

Caroline set the doughnut down. "Annabelle's coming home today. Belle Star has never looked better. I'm good, Jack."

"You never were much good at lying." He took a giant bite of his doughnut and chewed thoughtfully. "Being honest to a fault has its drawbacks. Your friends can see right through you. And I don't like what I'm seeing."

"I'm afraid to ask."

"You fell for the guy. He lied to you and broke your heart."

"That's not true," she said, rushing to Sam's defense. "He didn't lie to me about leaving. He never gave me false hope."

"Ah, okay. So, you're…good."

"Yeah, I'm good."

Jack rose to lift the coffeepot from its cradle. He took two mugs out of the cabinet and poured, looking outside at the rain. "Hey, what's that?"

Caroline took another bite of her doughnut. "What's what?"

"Outside, on the back porch. Come take a look."

Caroline walked over the kitchen door and unlatched the lock, then opened the screen. A cool mist of rain surged forth as she stepped outside.

There, on the porch, shining with new red paint and rust-free straightened-out handlebars, sat Annabelle's tricycle—the one Caroline was sure had been ready for the garbage heap. Only Annabelle's pleas to keep the old thing had kept it from its true fate.

Her hands flew to her mouth. She gasped the moment realization dawned. "Sam."

And then tears she'd bravely held back all morning, flowed down her cheeks, rivaling the droplets pouring down from the darkened sky. Caroline knew what it must have cost Sam to fix Annabelle's dilapidated tricycle. The memories it must have stirred up, the heartache he must have felt. She understood his pain and how hard it was for him even to think of Annabelle without reliving his own loss. For Caroline, what he'd done was more than a kind gesture. It was an act of love.

Jack sidled up next to her and put his arms around her shoulders, bringing her close. "Maybe he's not such a jerk after all," he whispered into her ear.

She shook her head. Softly, she replied, "No, he's not a jerk." Then she turned into Jack's embrace and sobbed silently, the pain a physical ache to her heart.

"I'm such a damn jerk," Sam said, shoving aside a stack of papers on his desk. He glanced at the clock on the wall. He'd been at it all night—reviewing the ongoing projects at the Triple B, dealing with his father's attorneys and their requests, speaking with distraught friends and family members.

Old familiar pangs of what life had been like just a year ago plagued him. He'd worked through the dinner hour and now it was nearly midnight. Fool that he was, he hadn't stopped, but had kept up the pace, hating the obligation, but assuming it nonetheless.

His eyes stung, his head ached. The knot in the pit of his stomach burned deep. He hadn't eaten or slept well in three days.

He hated sitting at his desk.

At one time, being set up in the father's old corner office had meant everything to him. He'd come in that first day on the job, taken his seat on the finest brown-leather chair money could buy and swiveled it around, looking out the wall-to-wall glass window to view the magnificent Houston skyline and thought that he'd finally made it.

Now, he resented every piece of furniture, every honor and award displayed on the walls, every bit of opulence that at one time, had defined his success.

Too late, he'd learned the true meaning of success.

Caroline Portman had had a hand in that learning process, but he couldn't even begin to think about her. He hadn't, not consciously. He couldn't think about the amazing woman he'd left behind. But she stayed with him, buried deep, and unlike the other burdens he'd managed to stow away, she remained a vital part of him, unconsciously.

Sam stared down at the papers he had yet to review and cursed his fate. The life he'd run away from had come back to haunt him.

Wade strode into the office, his nose in a file. "We've got a problem with the Overton project."

Sam looked up. "What?"

Wade tossed the file on his desk. "Over budget, under-staffed. The folks in the community are kicking up a fuss. They're protesting at the site. Seems our fine citizens don't want the bar and grill going up."

"Why, is the food that bad?"

Wade chuckled. "What food? It's going to be a Coyote Ugly with dance poles."

Sam shoved the file aside. None of this mattered to him. He didn't want to be here. He didn't want any of the obligations that came with being Blake Beaumont's heir. He rubbed his eyes and yawned.

"Hey, when did you eat last?" Wade asked.

Sam shrugged. "Lunch, I think."

"Are you sleeping at all?"

Sam shrugged again. "Some."

"Liar. Go home, Sam. You look like crap."

"Thanks. Compliments will get you everywhere."

"I'm not joking. You look like you've been run over by a truck."

Sam glared at his brother.

Wade spread his arms out wide. "All of this can wait. The company isn't going to fall apart in a few days. Go home. Get some rest. We'll catch up on this stuff tomorrow. Better yet, I'll take you home and stay over at your place tonight."

"I don't need a babysitter, Wade."

"That's debatable. Come on, let's go." Wade gave him no option. He strode to the door and shut down the lights.

Later that night when Sam put his head to the pillow, he was glad that Wade had insisted on coming home with him. He'd missed his younger brother and the two had sat up for an hour, shooting the breeze, tossing back a few beers and reestablishing their relationship.

Sam closed his eyes and knew a minute of peace before images popped into his head. He thought of his daughter, Tess, her guileless innocence and the love she'd bestowed upon him even though he hadn't done anything much to earn that honor. Sam stored her sweet face away in his mind, holding on to the nuances that made her unique, and, only when he thought he could handle it did he upload those images to view and savor for a few precious moments.

Then his mind drifted to Caroline.

And a shallow gaping hole filled his heart. It seemed that Sam was destined to hurt the people he cared most about. But he could take some comfort that she should be happy now, having Annabelle home with her. He wondered if they'd picked up the filly, Princess, yet and could only imagine Caroline's joy at seeing her daughter's surprised face when she presented the pony to her.

After long restless minutes Sam finally slept, though fitfully, throughout the night.

The next day was more of the same. He sat in his large luxurious office, shuffling papers, trying to find a way to continue here. In truth, he hated the job, the company and everything that went along with it. No amount of money or accomplishment would change that.

But he stayed for Wade's sake. His younger brother had taken on the brunt of the work and the majority of their father's wrath when Sam had dropped the ball and taken off. He'd basically left Wade to hold down the fort. And Wade had worked doubly hard, never once complaining to Sam on those occasional phone calls they'd made to each other. No, Wade had been his sole source of emotional support. He'd let Sam go, had even encouraged it so that he could get a grip on his life.

Sam owed Wade.

He turned away from the desk and stared out the window. As much as he tried not to think of the woman he'd left behind, thoughts of Caroline entered his mind. He missed her terribly. He missed Belle Star and small-town life. He missed the simple things, like sharing a cup of coffee. Worrying over the price of feed and bedding. He even missed working long hours on the stables and the great sense of accomplishment that ensued once a project was finished.

But mostly, he missed Caroline's pretty blue eyes smiling at him.

"Go back to her."

Sam swiveled the chair around. Wade stood with his hands on his hips, shaking his head.

"What?"

"You're miserable here. Go back to Hope Wells. I figure Caroline wouldn't mind one bit."

Sam shook his head. "But I'd mind. I couldn't do that to her. I have the worst track record when it comes to marriage. And don't forget, she's got a daughter. It's a big responsibility. I don't think I'm capable, Wade. There have been too many failures in my life. Besides, I have a company to run. We've got ongoing projects and I can't ask you to do this all alone. You've already covered my butt countless times, as it is."

Wade braced both hands on Sam's desk and bent to look him in the eyes. "That's just it, Sam. Don't you get it? *You* are the heir to the Triple B. *You* can determine what happens to the company. *You* can sell it off. Break it up. Downsize. Hell, you can move a portion of it to, say, Hope Wells. The options are all yours. It's *your* company now."

Sam's eyes rounded in surprise. The company had

been a staple in the Beaumont family for years. He'd never thought of the possibility of selling, or moving or downsizing. It was obvious that Wade had been thinking with a clear mind, while Sam's head and heart had been muddled with confusion and doubt. "And what of you, little brother? It's your livelihood, too."

"Hell, we both have more money than we need now. I'm thinking that California sounds real good—the ocean breezes and all that. I could use a change of pace."

The phone in the outside office rang and Wade gestured for Sam to stay put. "Let me get it. Probably more complaints about the Overton project. I'll handle it. You sit back and think about what I just said."

Wade returned a minute later with a somber look. "Sam, that was one of Caroline's friends. There's been trouble at Belle Star."

Sam looked up. "What kind of trouble?"

"They've been having T-storms for days now. The land is flooded. And well, late last night, lightning struck down one of the trees on the property. It caught fire and spread to one of the stables. Seems there's a lot of destruction."

Sam rose to his feet. "Damn it."

"Wait, there's more. It seems that Caroline rushed into the stables to rescue her mare."

Sam's gut clenched. Dread and despair gripped him hard. "Don't tell me she's—"

"She's okay. She saved the mare and herself. But she's down with smoke inhalation."

Sam squeezed his eyes shut and cursed up a blue streak. "She's really okay, right?"

"Her friend said she should be fine in a few days."

"Was it Maddie?"

"No, some guy named Jack Walker."

Sam glared at his brother. "Did he say anything else?"

Wade scratched his head. "Yeah, uh, he did. He said that you shouldn't *screw* this up. And, bro, he didn't exactly use that word."

Sam nodded. He paced. He ran his hands through his hair. Frustrated and alarmed, he spoke quietly. "I wasn't there for her. I should have been there. She shouldn't have risked her life. Damn it."

"It's not your fault, Sam."

"Don't you see? I failed another person I care about. Caroline could have lost her life!"

"And *that* wouldn't have been your fault, either. But she's fine and you know what? I see this as a second chance for both of you. You might not have been there this time, but you can be there the next time. And the time after that. You can always be there for her. If you love this woman, you deserve to give it a chance."

There was no doubt in Sam's mind that he loved Caroline. Just thinking of her rushing into those burning stables to save her horse put a frightful scare into him. And the thought of her precious stables being destroyed by flood and fire made him sick inside. She must be devastated.

"Do me a favor. Get the *Raven II* ready," Sam said.

With a hopeful smile, Wade nodded. "You want me to chopper you over to her?"

Sam shook his head. He was ready to put his life back on track. "No, this is something I have to do myself. Besides, I have something more important for you to do right here." Sam made notes on a legal pad and handed them over to Wade. "Can you manage this?"

Wade glanced at the list of instructions. He grinned. "Sure can. The crew will be loaded and ready by tonight."

"Great." Sam looked at his brother and smiled. "You might be living with those ocean breezes faster than you think, Wade." With that, he hugged his brother. "Thanks for everything. I'll be in touch."

Sam strode out of his office quickly, never once looking back.

"Looks like someone is here to see you, Caroline. Are you up for more company?" Jack Walker asked, gazing out the front window.

Caroline lay resting quietly on the parlor sofa, her mind in turmoil. She had plans to make. She had to try to figure out how to repair the damage to Belle Star and she had Annabelle to think about. Weary and tired from the smoke inhalation and the problems facing her, she really didn't want any more company. "Who is it?"

"Don't know exactly, but a helicopter just landed on your property."

Caroline closed her eyes. "Jack, what did you do?"

"Me? I'm innocent." She popped her eyes open and he grinned before walking to the front door. "But you'll thank me one day."

Jack opened the door and Caroline thought she heard Jack issuing a quiet warning. "She's on the sofa. Don't screw this up."

"You're okay, for a bumbling sheriff."

Jack laughed. "I'm outta here."

But it wasn't Jack's laughter that caught Caroline's attention. It was the low sexy timbre of Sam's voice.

Sam.

Caroline's heart raced. He was here. He'd come back. But she wouldn't allow any hope to enter her thoughts. Not until she knew why Sam had returned to Belle Star.

Sam approached the sofa and knelt by her side. He looked better than heaven, but she couldn't miss the day-old beard, a face plagued with concern and eyes just as tired and weary as hers. Regardless, he was the most handsome man in her world.

"Sam," she said breathlessly.

He didn't mess with a verbal greeting. Instead he brought his lips down on hers gently and the sweet tender kiss they shared was like a balm to her soul.

"The way I see it, sweetheart, I owe you at least a week's worth of work. I've sent for my crew and they'll be here tomorrow. We'll work night and day if we have to. Belle Star will have her grand opening."

Caroline smiled sadly. "I don't know if I can afford you, Sam Beaumont."

She'd spoken those words to Sam when he'd first arrived here in Hope Wells. But both knew that she wasn't speaking of money this time.

Sam stroked her cheek. "There's no charge for my love, Caroline. That comes freely now."

"Oh, Sam," she said, letting that notion sink in. He loved her. He truly loved her. Then a thought struck. "Did Wade fly you here?"

He shook his head. "No, I took the *Raven* out myself. I figured it was time to begin living in the present and not dwelling in the past. Besides, I had to get here fast. Couldn't let old Jack horn in on my woman."

Caroline let that silly comment pass, as if any man would measure up to Sam Beaumont. But she realized how significant it was that Sam had piloted that helicopter to get to her. She loved him all the more because of it.

Sam continued, "I was on my way back to you before I heard about any of this. I'd pretty much decided that I couldn't live my life without you. And now we've been given a second chance. Like I said, I owe you one week, but I owe *us* a lifetime. You and me and little Annabelle. I want us to be a family."

Caroline smiled with tears of hope in her eyes. "Oh, Sam," she said quietly. "Annabelle's here. Would you like to meet her?"

Sam nodded, taking Caroline's hand in his. "But first I need to know if you'd consider marrying a drifter who has seen the last of his drifting days?"

"And what of the CEO?"

"The CEO? He's going to retire most of his duties, probably sell off some of the company and turn the rest over to his brother, Wade. This CEO plans on running

Belle Star with his wife and daughter. He'll even let you remain the boss."

Caroline chuckled and a warm glow filled her heart. With Sam's help she lifted up from her prone position to sit on the sofa. She gazed down at the man kneeling in front of her. "I love you, Sam Beaumont."

"I'll take that as a yes, sweetheart." Joy and hope Sam had believed he would never experience again spread throughout his body. He rejoiced at being given this second chance in life. He rose up to kiss Caroline soundly on the lips. This woman, who had shown him how to love again, would be his wife. Slowly, with her love, he would allow himself to heal past wounds.

He brought her to her feet, locking her in a passionate embrace. Sam had never known completion like this before. He'd never known such monumental success. He looked into her eyes and spoke with certainty now. "I want to meet Annabelle."

Caroline nodded, her eyes filling with blessed understanding. She reached for him and together, hand-in-hand, they headed toward Annabelle's room to meet the daughter Sam planned to adopt, and toward a future that he had once believed completely out of his grasp.

A future Sam Beaumont couldn't wait to begin.

* * * * *

HOLIDAY CONFESSIONS
by
Anne Marie Winston

Dear Reader,

Animals have been an important part of my life since my childhood. In 2001 my family and I began raising guide dogs for Guiding Eyes for the Blind and subsequently came to know many guide-dog users. Brendan's story is my tribute to these friends, who deal gracefully and intelligently with daily challenges that I cannot even fathom.

Puppy raising has been an adventure that changed my entire family. We have lived the excitement of receiving eight-week-old puppies, the daily delight, occasional frustration and frequent amusement that occurred throughout the puppies' lives with us, and the heartbreak that we felt when it was time to let them go.

I strongly urge the dog lovers among you to consider puppy raising. Yes, it is difficult to say goodbye, but the joy and satisfaction of knowing the part you have played in offering someone independence and safety is an extraordinary feeling.

Wishing you warm, wriggly puppy snuggles (and an enjoyable read)!

Anne Marie Winston

ANNE MARIE WINSTON

RITA® Award finalist and bestselling author Anne Marie Winston loves babies she can give back when they cry, animals in all shapes and sizes and just about anything that blooms. When she's not writing, she's managing a house full of animals and teenagers, reading anything she can find and trying not to eat chocolate. She will dance at the slightest provocation and weeds her garden when she can't see the sun for the weeds any more. You can learn more about Anne Marie's novels by visiting her website at www.annemariewinston.com.

With special thanks to my guide-dog-using friends
who patiently answered my questions, especially:
Sally Rosenthal and Boise,
Tony Edwards and Paragon,
And the whole Juno List gang.

And

in memory of every beloved guide
who will always live in his or her partner's heart.

One

Lynne DeVane was returning several more empty moving boxes from her new apartment to the hallway when she heard a loud crash and thud, followed by some very creative, vivid language. Whoa. She'd been a lot of places with a lot of jaded people but she'd never heard that particular combination of words before.

She dropped the boxes she was carrying and rushed through her open door into the hallway of the lovely old brick building in Gettysburg, Pennsylvania, where she'd just rented an apartment. Boxes were scattered everywhere around a man—a *large* man—she noted, who was just rising to his feet and dusting off his dark suit pants. A golden retriever stood close by, nosing at the man with apparent concern.

"Oh, Lord, I'm so sorry," she began.

"You should be." The man cut her off midsentence, his blue eyes on his dog rather than her. "The hallways aren't a repository for trash."

She was so stunned by his curt response that she didn't know what to say next. And before the right words came to her, the man groped for the frame of the open doorway directly opposite hers. "Feather, come." He didn't look back, but as she watched him fumble for a second with the doorknob, she felt concern rise.

"Hey, wait! Are you all right? Did you hit your head?"

Slowly, he turned to face her as the dog disappeared inside his home. "No, I did not hit my head. I banged the hell out of my knee and scraped my palm, but you don't have to worry about being sued."

"I—that wasn't it." She was taken aback by his abrupt manner. "You just looked as if you might be dizzy or disoriented and I was concerned."

"I'm fine." Now his voice sounded slightly weary. "Thank you for your concern."

He turned and found the doorknob again. But as he turned the knob and carefully moved forward, a realization struck her.

Her new neighbor was blind. Or, at the very least, significantly visually impaired.

The man vanished inside and the door closed with a definite *clunk*.

Well, cuss. That was hardly the way to get off on the right foot with your closest neighbor. She began to drag the offending boxes down the back stairs to the trash receptacles at the rear of the building, where she'd seen a cardboard recycling container. If she'd had any idea her neighbor couldn't see, she'd never have left boxes lying around in the hallway.

Even through her lingering chagrin, she remembered that he was extremely attractive, with dark, curly hair, a rough-hewn face with a square jaw and a deep cleft in his chin. The dog clearly had been anxious, and she wondered if it was a guide dog. But if it was, why hadn't it been guiding him? And if it wasn't, wouldn't he have been using a cane? Maybe she'd been wrong and he wasn't blind at all, just clumsy.

It didn't really matter. She owed him an apology. With cookies, she decided. Very few men could stay mad in the face of her grandmother's chocolate peanut-butter cookies, a family recipe bestowed on Lynne the day she graduated from high school. Neither of them could have guessed that it would be almost ten years before Lynne was able to eat those cookies again.

She hiked back up from the cardboard container and returned to her floor for a second trip. Maybe her neighbor would come out and she'd get another chance to apologize. But the door opposite hers was closed and it appeared that it was going to stay that way.

After the fourth trip she took a break and hung her grandmother's large mahogany-framed mirror above the sideboard in her dining area. She caught sight of her reflection as she stood back to admire it, and was momentarily taken aback by the stranger in the mirror.

The woman she saw was a slender, washed-out blonde with her hair twisted up in a messy knot. The woman she still subconsciously expected to see had a headful of layered, permed coppery hair and she was thin. Not just slender but really, really skinny. And she wouldn't be wearing ratty old jeans and a T-shirt. Instead she'd be in something unique from a top designer's fall collection.

More than a year had passed since she'd walked away from a major modeling career. Her timing was professional suicide. Even if she ever wanted to go back, she'd burned all her bridges completely. She'd just finished her first *Sports Illustrated* swimsuit edition when she'd made the decision. The only place to go from there had been up, but she'd opted out.

"But why?" her agent, Edwin, had asked in frustration. "You're the hottest thing since Elle MacPherson, honey. Your name could be bigger than anybody out there. Just think of it." He'd sketched a mock billboard in the air. "A'Lynne. Just a single name. The face of…Clinique, or Victoria's Secret, something major like that. How can you even consider quitting?"

"I'm not happy, Ed," she'd said quietly. And she wasn't. She was tired of hopping flights to God-knew-where for photo shoots in freezing-cold surf. She was tired of having to monitor every tiny bite she put in her mouth so that she didn't gain weight. She was sick of the casual hooking up and the partying that went on at so many of the functions she was required to attend.

But when one of the producers of the *SI* shoot had looked at her critically and said, "Girlie, you could stand to lose at least five pounds," something inside her had snapped. Enough was enough. She was already too thin for her almost six feet of height. And she wasn't even sure she remembered her real hair color. Like most of her co-workers, she sported a distinctive hairstyle and color as part of her public persona. Unlike many of them, though, she had yet to resort to bulimic strategies, binging and purging, to lose the necessary weight. Was she anorexic? She didn't think so. If she weren't modeling, she was pretty sure she wouldn't feel compelled to eat so very little.

But she wanted to find out.

"You might not be happy," Ed said, "but you're famous. And damned well paid. Who needs happiness when you're a millionaire?"

The thought that she might one day become that cynical was the scariest one of all. "I don't want to live like this anymore." Her voice grew stronger. "I *won't* live like this anymore. No more jobs. I'll finish what I'm contracted for, but then I'm done."

"But what in hell will you do?" Ed had asked, utterly perplexed. In his world, life was all about fame and wealth.

"Be happy," she'd said simply. "Be an everyday, ordinary person with everyday ordinary concerns and schedules. Eat what I like. Do volunteer work, go to church. Be someone who matters because of the good I do in the world, not someone who only matters because of how good the weirdest designs on the planet look on my body."

Yes, she'd definitely burned her bridges. She'd dropped the odd *A* that her mother had thought looked so sophisticated in front of plain old Lynne, and she'd begun using her real last name rather than her father's mother's maiden name. A'Lynne Frasier was dead, but Lynne DeVane was alive and well.

She'd moved back home to Virginia with her mother, gained back enough weight that she no longer looked as if she'd stepped out of a concentration camp and let her heavy mane of hair begin to grow back long and straight, although she wore it up and out of her face much of the time. With no makeup, her normal blond coloring made her forgettable enough that she'd managed, so far, to avoid recognition and the media harassment it would inevitably bring.

After a year, though, her sanity had demanded she find her own place to live. She'd decided on Gettysburg, just over an hour from her sister's home.

With luck, tucked away in a small town in the mountains of Pennsylvania, she would stay forgettable.

She crossed her fingers as she carried out yet another load of cardboard and stomped it flat before depositing it in the recycling container. If she didn't run into any hard-core *SI* fans, she thought she had a chance.

She was getting winded after the seventh trip so she walked around to the front and lowered herself to the front steps for a few minutes to enjoy the small-town atmosphere of her new home. Holy cow. She'd thought she was in decent shape, but those stairs seemed to be getting steeper with each climb. Lowering herself to the top step on the small brick porch outside the entryway, she took a couple of deep breaths. Under her breath she muttered, "Are those boxes cloning themselves? Surely I don't have that much junk."

"Am I going to fall over you or your stuff again?"

Startled by the deep voice, she whirled around. Her grumpy neighbor had just opened the entrance door. His left hand was gripping the handle of a leather harness now, but the dog in the harness wasn't the golden one she'd seen earlier. This dog was big and black and distinctly bulkier. The leather-covered metal handle, along with a leash attached to the dog's collar, was firmly gripped in his left hand. She'd been right when she'd suspected he was blind.

Jumping to her feet, she opened her mouth to apologize again. And then she noticed he was smiling. Belatedly she realized his tone hadn't been angry, but rather wryly amused.

"Sorry," she said. "Just taking a breather. Those stairs are starting to make me wish I'd added a few more miles to my morning run."

He chuckled. "Good thing it's not a high-rise."

She groaned. "Perish the thought. But if there was, there would be an elevator." She took a deep breath. "I really am sorry about the boxes earlier. I guess you noticed I moved them."

"I did." He smiled again, strong white teeth flashing, and she was mildly shocked by her instant reaction to the impish, bad-boy quality in the expression. It invited her to smile along with him, to share some unspoken joke. It also made him one of the sexiest men she'd ever met. And it was a heck of a contrast to his earlier behavior.

"I'm sorry, too," he said. "I'm usually not such a bad-tempered jerk. And I know better than to leave the apartment without my trusty eyes."

"Apology accepted," she said. She looked at his dog. "Did you dye your dog to match your clothes or something?"

His eyebrows rose and then he laughed. He inclined his head toward the dog standing patiently at his side. "This is Cedar, my guide. The dog with me at lunchtime was Feather, my retired guide. I was just going down for my mail."

"I thought if you weren't using a dog you needed

a cane." She didn't know what the protocol was for discussing a person's handicapping condition, but he'd already yelled at her once, so what was the worst that could happen?

He grinned sheepishly. "It's a hassle to harness the dog for such a short walk, so I don't usually bother. I should take my cane but the mailboxes are just at the bottom of the stairs and I have the wall and railing to hang on to the whole way, so I cheat." He extended his free right hand. "Brendan Reilly. I take it you're my new neighbor?"

"I am," she said. She placed her palm in his. "Lynne DeVane. It's nice to meet you." It was more than nice. His hand was large and warm and as his fingers closed firmly around hers, her breath caught for a moment at the leap of pleasure his touch produced deep within her. "And Cedar, too," she added belatedly.

Reluctantly, it seemed, he let her hand slide free. "Are you almost finished moving in?"

She nodded, then realized he couldn't see her. "Yes. Everything's in. And I only have about six more boxes to unpack."

"Only?" He shook his head, and she was struck by the naturalness of the movement. He hadn't been blind all his life; she'd bet on it. "That's six boxes too many for me."

"In a few more hours, they'll all be gone. And I can't wait!"

"If I were a really good guy, I'd offer to stay and help you unpack." He smiled again. "Sadly, I'm not that nice. I have to get back to work."

"Was this a lunch break?"

He nodded. "I came home to let Feather out and give her a little more attention. I'm an attorney with a law firm a few blocks from here."

"How convenient that it's so close."

"It's handy because I can get around without needing someone to drive me," he told her.

"I like it, too," she said. "I was looking for a place away from the city, but I wasn't quite ready to go totally rural, so this seemed just right."

"Which city?"

"New York. I used to live in a studio in Manhattan."

"Yikes. Those places aren't cheap."

"You sound as if you know that."

He nodded. "Columbia School of Law. I shared a place on the Upper West Side with three other law students and it was still pricey."

She nodded sympathetically, then remembered again that he couldn't see her. That was something she'd always taken for granted. It was a little shocking to realize how much of a role body language played in her interactions. "You can say that again. I didn't realize just how expensive it was until I started looking for something in Gettysburg. I like it much better here."

"It's a great little town," Brendan responded. "Any special reason you chose it?"

"Not really." She had no intention of telling anyone in her new life about her old one. "I came here in high school on a class trip and thought it was lovely, so I just decided to see if it was still as I remembered it. And it was, so I started hunting for a place."

"You're lucky to have found this. These apartments don't turn over often. The tenant before you was a bachelor who lived there for almost thirty years."

"Who knows?" she said lightly. "I might be here in thirty years myself." She cleared her throat. "Well, I won't keep you. It was nice to meet you."

"You, too," he responded. "Good luck with the rest of those boxes."

"I promise I won't leave them in the hallway," she said with a chuckle.

"If I'd had a guide with me like I should have, it wouldn't have mattered," he countered as he turned toward the street. "Have a good afternoon."

"Thanks." She almost lifted a hand before she caught herself.

"Cedar, forward." Brendan turned his attention from her to the dog.

She watched as he walked confidently away from her to the end of the block and headed toward the pretty little center square. She wondered how he'd lost his sight. He had an awful lot of the mannerisms of one who'd once been able to see, like the way he confidently extended his hand for a shake, or like the simple way he seemed to focus right on her face as he spoke. If she didn't know better, she'd have sworn he was looking right at her.

She thought again of the cookies she had planned to bake. She'd still make them, even though he seemed to have accepted her apology.

That evening Brendan was checking his e-mail when his doorbell rang. Feather and Cedar, lying on opposite sides of his chair in his study, both leaped to their feet, although neither of them barked. Cedar barreled toward the door, but Feather stayed with him, and he put a hand on her head as he stood, turned around and automatically negotiated his way across his office. "You're my good girl," he told her softly as they went down the hall and through the living room.

"Who is it?" he called as he reached the door. Cedar's broad tail thumped against the front of his right leg while Feather simply hovered near his left side.

"Lynne. Your neighbor."

She wouldn't have needed to add that. He'd remembered her name instantly. Not to mention the softness of her hand and her pleasantly husky voice.

Cut it out, Brendan. You're not interested.

It was a lot easier to tell himself that than it was to believe it. "Hi," he said, unlocking the dead bolt and pulling open the door. "I didn't expect to see you again today."

"I brought a peace offering."

He heard the sound of tinfoil rustling, and then an incredibly, amazingly wonderful smell assailed his nostrils.

"What is that?" he asked, inhaling deeply. "It smells heavenly."

"Chocolate peanut-butter cookies," she said. "My grandmother's recipe."

"You didn't need to do this," he said.

"I know." She paused for a moment and he'd bet his last nickel that she'd shrugged. "But I really am sorry for cluttering up the hallway, and besides, I needed a good excuse to make these."

He laughed. "If they taste as good as they smell, I can see why. Would you like to come in?"

"Oh, no, I—"

"Please," he said. "I fully intend to dig into these cookies right away and it would be nice to share them with someone who says something besides woof."

It was her turn to laugh. "In that case, I'd be delighted."

Brendan stepped aside and waited until he heard her pass through the doorway and move beyond it. Closing the door, he indicated the arrangement of easy chairs, couch and tables in his living room. "Please, sit down. Would you like a drink?"

"Do you have water or milk?" she asked. "Either of those would be fine."

"No milk," he said. "Are you an ice or no-ice person?"

"Ice, please."

What in the world had possessed him to invite her in? As he got a glass of water for each of them as well as a handful of napkins and returned to the living room, he decided it was the voice. He'd already decided that getting tight with the new neighbor could get sticky, but something about that sexy, low-pitched voice had completely overruled his better judgment. Setting his glass down, he reached for the coasters he kept on his coffee table and slipped one under each glass. "There."

Tinfoil rustled again and he realized she was removing the wrapping from the cookies. "Your dogs certainly are well behaved," she said. "When I was a child, we had a cocker spaniel who would eat anything left unattended."

"At least he wasn't a big dog."

She laughed, and the sound was a warm peal of music that made him smile in return. "Oh, high places didn't faze Ethel. That dog climbed onto chairs—and tables—and could leap right up onto the counter. Drove my mother wild."

He was used to hearing unusual names for dogs. But…"Ethel?"

"We had Lucy, too. But Ethel was the problem child."

He chuckled. "That's a polite way to phrase it."

"You have no idea," she said in a dry tone. "Are all guide dogs this well behaved?"

"For the most part." He nodded. "They're still only dogs, though. Just about the time I get to thinking my dog is perfect, he or she reminds me that there is no such animal."

"You spend a lot of time training them, though."

"We mostly just brush up on obedience on a regular basis and work on any specific commands we want to use. The puppy raisers are the ones who get the credit for the pleasant behavior."

"Puppy raisers?"

"The people who get them when they're little pups. They teach them basic obedience, they socialize them around lots of people and other animals, and they teach them good house manners."

"Like not getting food off the table."

"Or out of the trash, or anywhere else they see it, which can be a real challenge, especially for a Labrador retriever. The dog learns not to chase cats around the house, not to jump up on people, not to get on the furniture—"

She cleared her throat. "Ah, I hate to tell you this, but there appears to be a large black dog lying smack in the middle of your love seat."

He laughed. "Don't ever tell anybody, please, or I'll get fifty lashes with a wet noodle."

"You wouldn't get in trouble for that?"

"No. Once we are partnered with a dog, that dog becomes ours. The only time a school might step in and remove a dog from a handler is if they suspect abuse. And I personally am not aware of anyone ever doing anything to warrant something like that."

"Feather doesn't get on the furniture?"

"Feather," he said, "is not about to leave my side. She's never been interested in sleeping on the couch or the bed."

"I noticed she went into the kitchen with you and came right back out when you did."

"Feather's having a hard time adjusting to retirement."

"Do they have to retire at a certain age? She still looks pretty chipper."

"She is pretty chipper," he said, "for a family pet. But she's almost ten and she's getting arthritis. She was starting to have trouble walking as much as I needed her to. And she was starting to hesitate."

"Hesitate?"

"Lose her confidence. She didn't want to cross the street, even when it was clear. One day she stopped in the middle of a crosswalk and wouldn't move. I still don't know if it was fear, if she was in pain or if she just lost focus. But that was the day I realized I was going to have to get a new guide."

"That must have been hard."

"Very." He still found it difficult to talk about, and he had to clear his throat. "We were partners for more than eight years. I hated it. Felt like I was pushing her aside. I'm sure that it felt that way to her." He sighed. "Some people keep their retired dogs, some let them go back to the person who raised them. Some are adopted by a family member or friend or someone approved by the training school. I thought it would be too hard to let her go. But now…now I'm not so sure." He cleared his throat. "Sorry. TMI, I'm sure."

"It's not too much information at all. I find it very interesting."

He heard the ice clink in her glass as she took a sip. "Have a cookie," she said after a moment, when he didn't go on. "They're always best when they're still warm."

"Twist my arm. Where are they?"

"On the coffee table. Ah, sort of to your right—"

"Think of the hands on a clock," he said. "If I am facing twelve, where would the plate be?"

"Are you in the middle of the clock or at the six?"

He had to grin. It was a legitimate question. "The middle."

"Two o'clock," she said promptly.

He reached out, gauging the distance down to the coffee table, and was gratified when his fingers encountered the edge of a plate. It had little ridges around the edge, and…there. He picked up a cookie and brought it to his nose. "I'm not sure I can bring myself to eat this. I might just sniff it for the rest of my life."

"I can give you the recipe," she pointed out. "It's not like you'll never see them again."

Instantly he could tell that she realized what she'd said. There was a short, horrified silence.

"Oh, cuss," she said with feeling. "I am so sorry. What a thoughtless comment."

"Cuss?" He was struggling not to laugh aloud. Most of the people he knew didn't bother to censor their language.

Again he suspected that she shrugged. Then she said, "It's a nice satisfying mix of consonants to mutter when I'm mad. I don't like to use—or hear—strong language."

"Cuss." He said it again. Kendra hadn't liked foul language, either. It was one of the little things he'd loved about her. "Works for me."

Thinking of his former fiancée made him realize that he hadn't thought of her in a long time.

"Anyway," Lynne said, "I was in the middle of a major apology."

"Unnecessary apology. It's just an expression like 'I see.' You don't have to censor your vocabulary."

He made a show of taking another bite of his cookie and miming pleasure, hoping to get past the awkward moment. Since he'd lost his sight, the only woman he'd gone out with was Kendra. And after they'd broken up, he'd stayed as far away from the dating scene as possible for a while. In recent years, he'd dated some, but it had never seemed right; something within him just hadn't been interested enough to pursue a relationship.

"I'm glad you like the cookies," she said. "Would you like to come over for dinner tomorrow night? There are more where these came from."

"Thank you, but no." His refusal was automatic. He might have almost mastered the art of eating without seeing his food, but he had a serious dread of making a fool of himself. "I have the dogs and—"

"You're welcome to bring them. A little dog hair is not going to ruin my home."

"You really don't have to do that." She felt obligated because she'd tripped him up in the hallway; he already could tell she was the kind of person who would take something like that to heart.

"I want to," she said. "I know virtually no one here. You can tell me about the town."

Well, hell. He could think it, even if he wasn't going to say it aloud. Without telling her an outright lie, there was no graceful way to get out of it. "All right. What time?"

"Is six-thirty okay?"

"Yes."

"Any special requests?"

"No spaghetti, please."

He could tell he'd startled her. Then she laughed. "I guess that is a bit of a problem food, isn't it? Okay. No spaghetti, I promise."

He couldn't place her accent. The way she'd said, "a bit of a problem" had sounded almost British. But every once in a while he thought he detected in her drawled syllables a hint of the South as well. Maybe tomorrow night he could steer the conversation in her direction. It would be a nice change from his usual routine of answering questions about his vision issues and his dog.

Lynne finally got the last packing box out of her new home. In just two days, after the furniture had arrived yesterday, she'd gotten most things in their proper places. Not many pictures on the walls or other personal decor, but that was something that would happen eventually.

The whole place needed a good vacuuming after she was done, and then she made another batch of cookies. She decided to make a chicken and bake some potatoes, and mixed up some honey-and-wheat bread dough. After she got it rising in the bread machine, she rinsed broccoli to steam later.

Cooking and baking still felt vaguely like forbidden fun. She'd spent almost ten years modeling, worrying about every extra ounce she gained, keeping her body at a weight far thinner than she would be naturally. Since she'd stopped, she'd gained nearly fifteen pounds. But she'd done it carefully and when she'd felt as if she looked more like a normal human being than a scarecrow in stilettos, she'd stopped and concentrated on maintaining that weight. It was ridiculously easy compared to the rigid diet she'd adhered to in the past.

As she soaked her aching body in a gloriously hot, soothing bath, she worked a cramp out of her calf, wincing as she kneaded the knotted muscle. She had to admit, even to herself, that she'd gotten a little carried away with the unpacking, cleaning and baking today. It would be pretty mortifying if she yawned in Brendan's face. Or even worse, if she fell asleep!

With that thought in mind, she drank a soda loaded with caffeine as she set the table a few minutes before six-thirty, then rushed into her bedroom to put her hair up again.

Her hand stilled as she realized what she was doing. Brendan couldn't see what she looked like! The realization was a surprisingly freeing thought. Tonight she would be judged solely on her character and conversation, on what she was like as a person. Her looks would never even enter into the mix.

It might be freeing, but it also was terrifying, she decided. What if she wasn't an interesting person?

Two

Brendan finished washing up the bowls from the dogs' dinner. He'd already taken each one out, but as he listened to the time, he realized he'd better get moving if he didn't want to be late to dinner with his new neighbor.

He was pretty sure his shirt and slacks from the office were still clean, but he wasn't taking any chances, so he headed into his bedroom to change. Clean pants. His fingers found pants hangers and he chose khakis rather than jeans and pulled out a brown belt, identified by the tiny Braille tag he'd used to label it.

He passed by the suits paired with dress shirts and matching ties on the metal hangers and felt the plastic ones that were his system for locating casual shirts. Better get a clean shirt, too. Showing up with an ink stain or food smeared on his collar wasn't the impression he wanted to make.

He was running his fingertips over the label that clued him in to color when his hand stilled on the knit shirt he'd chosen. Since when did he care about making an impression on a woman?

Quickly he finished dressing and called the dogs. He harnessed Cedar and put a leash on Feather. She tried repeatedly to shove her way between Cedar and him, and when he finally used a stern tone, she skulked behind him as if he'd beaten her with a stick.

"I'm sorry, girl," he told her as he stood in front of Lynne DeVane's door. "I'm doing the best I can to make this work."

"Make what work?" Lynne opened the door in time to hear his last comment.

He forced a laugh. "Sorry. I don't usually stand around talking to my dogs."

"Really?" Her tone held amusement.

He thought about it. "Okay, maybe I do."

"I don't blame you. They pay attention to what you're saying more than people do most of the time." The direction of her voice shifted and he realized she had stepped back so that he could enter. "Please come in and have a seat. But then you have to tell me what you were talking about."

As he entered her apartment, he told Cedar, "Find a chair."

"I didn't realize you taught them things like that," she said as Cedar took him across the room and he found a large wing chair with his outstretched hand.

"Good boy," he said to the dog. To Lynne, he said, "It isn't a formal command taught by the school, but when I first got Feather, another guide dog user suggested that it might be a useful command, along with things like, 'find the door.' Some people use specific commands to find a family member in a large store." He'd chosen finding a chair for the first thing he'd teach Cedar, and already his big black dog was catching on.

"How long have you had Cedar?"

"We just graduated from the training school two weeks ago."

"Oh, my," she said, clearly taken aback. "I assumed you'd worked together much longer than that."

He smiled. "He's a good dog. And having worked with one dog helps. When you get your first dog, both of you have to learn everything together. Speaking of which, where is Feather?" He stretched his hand down to his right side where he'd been trying to teach her to lie, but she wasn't there.

"Oh, I'm sorry," Lynne said. "I was petting her. Isn't that allowed?"

"No, it's fine unless a dog is working," he said. "She's probably enjoying the attention. Since I retired her and got Cedar, she's been getting more and more depressed."

"How can you tell?"

He shrugged. "She's not eating well. Sniffs her food and turns away. And she just seems kind of…lackluster. Dull. She used to be bouncy and her tail was always wagging. I could always tell because her whole body vibrates from the back end forward when that tail's going."

"It sounds funny to think of a dog suffering from depression, but I suppose it makes sense. Did you say you two worked together for eight years?"

"Yes. She just had her tenth birthday." He sighed. "I'm starting to think I should have let her go. A lot of times the original families who raised them as puppies will take them back again, but if not, the school has a waiting list of families who will adopt a retired guide."

"How could you give her up, though, after all that time together?"

She understood. Warmth spread through him. "Exactly. It's not easy for a blind person like me who lives alone to care for two dogs, but I just couldn't send her away. She's a part of my family."

"I can imagine," Lynne murmured. "I don't think I could do it, either." Her voice changed as she bent over and addressed his dog. "You're a beautiful girl, yes, you are. With a beautiful name." She laughed in delight.

"Let me guess. She rolled over on her back and has conned you into rubbing her belly."

"Oh, so you're a belly-rub slut," she said to the dog. "It's disappointing to hear that you'll do this for anybody."

He chuckled. "In a big way." He fondled Cedar's ears as a comfortable silence stretched.

"I apologize for grilling you," Lynne said. "You probably get really sick of people asking you questions about your dog or being blind."

He shrugged. "You get used to it. It drove me crazy the first year or so, but it comes with the territory."

"So you haven't always been blind." It was more a statement than a question. "I thought from some of your mannerisms that you had been able to see once."

"I was sighted until I was twenty-one. While I was in college, I fell over a balcony railing at a frat party and landed mostly on my head."

"Holy cow. You're lucky you survived."

He nodded. "Very."

"A frat party," she said reflectively. "I never went to college. Are those as wild and debauched as I've heard?"

He grinned. "I've been to a few that fit that description. But I hadn't been drinking that night. A guy behind me tripped, and it was just sheer lousy luck that he plowed into me."

"No kidding," she said with feeling. "Did you know right away that you were blind?"

"Not right away." He hesitated as the memories of those early days in the hospital welled up. Kendra had been with him when he'd asked the doctor about his vision.

"Let's change the subject," Lynne said. "I think it's your turn to ask the questions."

He realized he'd been silent too long, and he mentally smacked himself. He really *was* out of touch with socializing. Entertaining clients was a lot different from dating. Even if this wasn't really a date. "Sorry. It brings back a lot of memories. It was…a time of enormous change for me."

"I can imagine," she murmured.

He decided to take her up on her offer. "What kind of work do you do?"

He felt a subtle change in the room, a tension that surprised him. He'd expected that to be a fairly safe question.

"I'm not working right now," she said. "But I have a couple of interviews this week, so I'm hoping to have an answer to that question soon."

"Okay," he said. She'd probably just lost a job, and since that often happened under difficult circumstances even to the best of people, she might feel embarrassed or humiliated. "Let me rephrase that. What kind of work would you like to do?"

"My interviews are at a preschool and at an elementary school as an aide," she responded. "But what I'd really like to do is go to college and learn to teach."

"What age would you prefer?"

"I'm not sure," she admitted. "I enjoy little kids,

but I honestly don't know enough about older children or teens to know whether or not I'd also like those age groups. Hence the job choices."

"So you haven't worked with children in the past?"

"No." He heard her stand. "Can I get you something to drink?"

"Iced tea?" he asked.

"I happen to have some. Sugar or lemon?"

"Just lemon, please." He listened to the pad of her feet across the room and into what sounded like her kitchen, judging from the tile floor onto which she walked. Her place appeared to be laid out just like his, except with the floor plan reversed. The jingle of Feather's tags alerted him that she had followed Lynne.

Was it his imagination or had his hostess become uncomfortable the moment he'd asked about her past? She'd leaped into action right after that, and she certainly hadn't volunteered any information about what she'd been doing before she moved to Gettysburg.

He heard the clink of ice cubes, and a minute later Lynne returned with his tea.

"Is there anyplace in particular you would like me to put this?" she asked.

"Is there a table near me?"

"There's an end table on the right side of your chair."

"You can set it down there."

He heard her moving toward him, and as the glass

settled on the table, a whiff of clean, womanly fragrance enveloped him. She was close.

How tall was she? He thought she was probably pretty tall for a woman because her voice didn't sound as if it was coming from miles below him when she was facing him.

"There," she said. "It's toward the front of the table on the corner closest to you."

He reached out and lightly followed the lip of the table forward until his hand encountered the cool, smooth glass. "Thank you."

"You're welcome. Dinner will be ready in a little bit. I played it safe and baked a chicken."

"I like baked chicken. Any potatoes?" he asked hopefully.

"Also baked. Double-stuffed."

"The kind with sour cream and cheese all mashed up with the potato and then put back in the shell?"

She laughed. "The skin, not the shell."

"Whatever." He dismissed semantics. "Sounds great, especially to someone who eats most of his food out of take-out containers or microwave dishes."

"I guess cooking is difficult," she said tentatively.

He laughed, picking up his tea and taking a sip. "I know another blind guy who's a fabulous cook. He's a partial, which makes it a little easier for him—"

"A partial?"

"A person who still has some vision, although it's usually pretty limited. Some partials have more vision in one eye than the other, some have vision in certain quadrants of their field of vision. I have no vision, so I'm a total."

"I'm sorry I interrupted. You were talking about your friend who cooks."

He smiled. "No problem. I was only going to say that even when I could see, it wasn't at the top of my list of fun stuff to do."

"I always enjoyed cooking, even when I was a little girl. I haven't done much of it in a long time, though."

It seemed like an odd statement, and he wished he could have seen her face. "Life too busy?"

"Something like that," she murmured. "Have you always lived here?"

He recognized an about-face in conversational direction when he heard one. "No. I grew up in rural Pennsylvania, out near Pittsburgh. How about you?"

"A teeny little town called Barboursville in Virginia."

"Is that anywhere near Williamsburg?"

"No. It's above Richmond. Why?"

"One of the partners in my firm went to college at William & Mary. We were high school buddies so I was down there to visit a couple of times."

"I forgot you told me you were with a law practice."

He nodded. "Yes. Brinkmen & Brinkmen. Our offices are right on Baltimore Street downtown."

"I've seen them. It's a very charming little town."

"And convenient, too."

"Convenient?"

"Easy for me to get around independently."

"Oh, right." She paused. "I guess I didn't think about that. You don't drive, so you have to have at least basic services within walking distance." She sounded as if she were talking more to herself than him.

"A lot of vision-impaired people live in large urban areas," he said, "because things are so much more convenient, and there's public transportation close at hand."

"Didn't think about that, either," she admitted.

"Proximity to the things I need was one of the major attractions about Gettysburg. Main Street has a thriving business area thanks to the college and the tourists, so banking and doctors and dry cleaners are all within walking distance. And there's a grocery store and a pharmacy, too, and some great restaurants."

"Do you ever go over to the college?"

He nodded. "A lot of their music and theater performances, as well as the occasional guest lecture are open to the public."

"Oh, good," she said, sounding delighted. "I love music."

"Do you play an instrument?"

"No. I played piano when I was a kid. It's something I've always wanted to take up again." Her voice sounded wistful.

"Maybe this is your chance," he said.

"Maybe it is. So what else does one do in Gettysburg?"

"Well," he said, "I hope you enjoy Civil War history."

She laughed. "Guilty. It was one of the things that drew me to the area. I want to learn more about the battlefield and the whole war."

"I doubt you'll have any trouble."

She chuckled. "What else?"

"The usual things," he said, "with an extra focus on history, perhaps. There's a Community Concert Association, a library, a humane society, performing groups, a bunch of churches, business and civic organizations, stuff like that. If you want to get involved, I guarantee you'll be welcomed with open arms."

"I've never done any volunteer work. I wouldn't know what to do." Her tone was doubtful.

"You don't need prior experience." He felt like a cheerleader, and he wondered why she had so little self-confidence. "If you go to a meeting or two or join a church, it won't be long before you're being asked to help with things."

"That would be nice." He heard her rise. "Dinner should be about ready. Why don't we go to the table now?"

Dinner was delicious and the conversation easy and inconsequential. They lingered for more than an hour, sharing coffee and cookies after the meal. Finally, he remembered that he had an extremely early morning the following day. He was just rising when her telephone rang.

"Excuse me." She stepped away from him and he heard her pick up a handset. "I'd better take this," she said, apparently having looked at the Caller Identification screen. "Hello?" Her voice sounded cautious and cool and although he knew it was rude to eavesdrop, he could hardly help hearing her side of the conversation.

"Hello, Daddy." Her voice lilted with a pleasure he would have given a lot to have aimed at him. "How are you?… Yes. Yes. I know I haven't. Oh." The lilt flattened with what sounded a lot like disappointment. "…I see. When?… Congratulations. No, I don't believe I'm going to have the time…. I'd rather you didn't. No…maybe at Christmas. I'll have to see if I can get away." Her voice had taken on a bleak, distant tone. "Well, thank you for calling. I'm entertaining so I can't chat."

She concluded the conversation with speed and an affectionate word of farewell that sounded more rote than genuine.

As she set the handset back in the receiver, he hastily reached for another cookie so she wouldn't think he'd been listening to her conversation. Even if he had.

She returned to her seat silently.

After a moment that seemed to stretch for a long, awkward time, he finally said, "Is something the matter?"

"My father." She hesitated, then said, "My father's getting married again."

"I'm sorry," he said cautiously. "I take it that's bad news?"

She drew in a shuddering breath and he realized she was near tears. Somewhere down to his left, Feather whined, and he heard her get to her feet.

A moment later Lynne gave a shaky laugh. "Thanks, girl." To him she said, "Your dog just gave me a kiss. I think she's worried about me."

"She's not the only one." Without thinking he reached out and placed his hand over the arm he'd heard her lay on the table, then slipped his palm down until he was covering her hand.

He felt her lay her other hand atop his and gently squeeze, then she slid both hands away. "I appreciate your concern, but I'm all right," she said quietly. "I should be used to it by now."

"Used to…your father not being married to your mother anymore?" Maybe her father had had a case of the forty-something itch and had scratched it with a divorce and a younger woman, not necessarily in that order. Lord knew he saw enough of that in his business.

To his surprise, she heaved an unladylike snort. "My parents were divorced when I was two," she told him. "This lucky lady will be my father's sixth wife."

He knew his eyebrows rose, and he couldn't hide his surprise. "Whoa. That's…a lot of wives."

To his relief she laughed. "And that's the understatement of the decade." She took a sip of her coffee, and the cup clinked as she set it down. "Sorry to let that intrude into our evening. He always manages to shock me when he tells me about his newest relationship, although I don't know why." She cleared her throat. "Feather was very sweet. Has she always reacted to human distress like that?"

He shook his head. "Not in general, although when she senses I'm upset she does the same thing. But as far as I know, you're the only other person to receive the honor of a sloppy canine kiss."

"I liked it," she said. She rose from the table. "Would you like some more cookies to take with you?"

"Maybe just a few," he said. "I have to confess that the first batch you gave me is gone already."

"Better you than me," she said. "I—"

A loud growl interrupted what she'd been about to say.

"Feather!" He looked in the direction of the sound.

"What's wrong?" asked Lynne.

He sighed. "I guess she took exception to something Cedar did or maybe just the way he looked at her. She's not handling being supplanted gracefully at all." He called his guide to him, hearing the jingle of Cedar's tags as he rose from where he'd been lying beneath the table.

"Poor girl," Lynne said. "I can imagine how she must feel." Her voice sounded lower and faraway, and he realized she had bent over and was hugging Feather. "It's no fun being replaced, is it?"

"And watching me walk out the door with him

each morning is hard on her." He shook his head, thinking that having a father getting married for the sixth time, Lynne knew a fair amount about being replaced in someone's affections. "Like I said, I really don't want to part with her, but if she would be happier somewhere else, it isn't fair of me to keep her."

He rose and found Cedar's harness. It still felt new and odd after the softness of the leather on Feather's old one.

Lynne moved ahead of him to the door, and he called Feather to come along. He hadn't bothered with a leash since they were just going across the hallway.

But he didn't hear the familiar jingling of her tags.

"Feather, come."

Nothing.

"What is she doing?" he finally asked Lynne. There had been a time when he'd have hated needing to ask someone to describe what he couldn't see, but he'd passed that point years ago. More or less. He ignored the twinge of annoyance he felt.

"Ah, she's still lying on the rug in the kitchen," Lynne said.

He tried again. "Feather, come." But he still heard nothing. "Dog," he muttered beneath his breath, "if I have to come over there and get you, it isn't going to be pretty."

Lynne sounded as if she were trying not to laugh. "She's welcome to stay."

Stay? "No, thanks," he said. "What an imposition

that would be. Come to dinner, leave a dog behind
for you to take care of."

"I wouldn't mind, honestly." Her voice was soft.

With sudden clarity, he remembered the phone
call she'd just received. She'd been pretty upset by
it, no matter how well she'd pretended to recover.
And Feather had comforted her. Maybe…

"All right," he said before he could think about it
too much more. "If you really want her, she can stay.
You two can have a sleep-over." He turned back in the
direction of her kitchen. "But she still needs to come
when I call her. Feather! Come!" He used the I-am-
not-kidding tone he rarely employed, and this time
he heard her as she heaved herself to her feet, lazily
stretched and shook and finally strolled toward him.

"Smart-aleck," he told her when she reached his
side. He grabbed her collar as she attempted to worm
her way between Cedar and him. "No, girl. Sorry."
He knelt, laying an arm across her soft back. "Would
you like to stay with Lynne tonight?"

"You could get her when you come home from work
tomorrow," Lynne said hopefully. "I have an interview
at one o'clock but I don't expect to be gone more than
an hour, if that. She wouldn't be alone all day."

And neither would Lynne, he thought, reading
between the lines. "Works for me," he said, "if you're
sure that's not a problem."

"Not at all." The lilt in her voice told him she was
being truthful. "I'd love the company."

"Okay." He snuggled his old dog for a moment, then rose and picked up Cedar's harness. "We'll see how she acts when I walk out the door."

He gave the forward command as Lynne opened her front door, and Cedar led him straight across the hall to stop in front of his own door. "What did she do?" he asked.

"She went back to the kitchen and lay down on the rug again."

He chuckled, although he felt vaguely hurt. "Traitor." He extended his right hand, realizing that he was anticipating the touch of hers just a little too much. "Thank you for dinner. And again, for the cookies."

She placed her hand in his, and the physical awareness that had simmered all through dinner hit him squarely in the solar plexus.

Lynne stilled as their hands clasped. Stilled completely, as if she were frozen. His body began to stir to life at the touch of her soft flesh. Her hand was small and delicate, nearly swallowed by his much-larger one, and he simply held it, unable to make himself release her. Slowly he rubbed his thumb over the back of her hand and heard her suck in her breath sharply. Satisfaction rushed through him. She felt it, too.

What the hell do you think you're doing? You're not interested in a relationship.

Chemistry, he assured himself. That's all it was. It didn't mean anything. And yet—he still held her hand clasped in his.

Her telephone rang, shrill in the silence that had fallen between them. He felt her hand jump and let her slide it from his. "That would be my sister," she said, "calling to commiserate. I guess Dad just told her, too."

He followed her lead, not acknowledging the moment that had passed, although he was still acutely aware of her. "I'll let you get that," he said. "How about we meet in the hallway at ten-thirty to take them out for the night? I'll teach you her commands then."

"All right." She touched his arm briefly, hastily. "Thank you for coming over. See you in a bit." She dashed back into her own apartment as the phone rang again, and he heard her door close.

Three

"Feather, do you want to go out?"

Lynne slipped on a light jacket, then picked up the soft leather leash that she'd found hanging on her door. His dog trotted to her, tail happily wagging. Her whole back end was wagging, Lynne realized, and she smiled as she clipped the leash to the D-ring on Feather's collar. "You're a sweet girl, did you know that?"

If a dog could grin, she'd swear this one was.

When she stepped into the hallway, Brendan was already there with Cedar. "Right on time," he said. "She uses regular obedience commands—'heel' to move forward, 'sit,' 'down' and 'stay.' Why don't you follow me out?"

Feather walked calmly at her side until they got outside to a grassy spot near the door.

"Okay, ah, do your thing." She felt pretty silly, walking around in the grass, trying to get the dog to "go."

"Park," he said.

"I beg your pardon?"

"That's the word you use to get her to go. I don't think she'll respond to 'do your thing.'" There was a note of amusement in his voice.

"I can't believe your dogs are trained to go to the bathroom on command. Are you serious?" She was used to pets who were let out into the backyard to sniff around until they found the perfect spot.

"Sure. You don't think I'm going to stand out here when the weather's nasty and wait until my dogs decide they've gotta go, do you?" He walked into the grass with Cedar. "Stand in one place like I am."

She did as he was doing. "I don't have to walk her?"

"Walking is good for her, but right now, no. Just tell her to park."

"Park," she repeated dubiously. "What—" But the reason for the word became instantly clear as Feather finally did her thing. Cedar did, too. Apparently the word was a magic charm. "That's it?" she asked, somewhat incredulous. "Just come out here, stand and tell her to park?"

"Yeah." He laughed. "The only other thing I'd

recommend is that you bring a bag so you can pick up if you need to."

"I didn't think of that." She eyed him. "What else do I need to know?"

"Sometimes she fools around," he said. "Sniffing and goofing off. Then I just tell her we're going in, which usually makes her remember she'd better get with the program or she's going to be crossing her legs all night."

She laughed, finding the imagery apt.

"And she absolutely hates rain and snow. If the weather's lousy, I practically have to drag her behind me. She really hates getting wet."

"Oooo-kay. So how many other things do I need to learn?"

"You have to give her a command to eat. But I can show you that in the morning."

"What about sleeping? Is she allowed on the bed? She hasn't even tried to jump on the furniture."

"She's never really been much for sleeping on the couch or the bed, unlike the big goober here," he said, indicating Cedar. "He was on the couch the first day I brought him home. But it's not off-limits unless you don't want her getting up there. I never encouraged her—that yellow hair is a whole lot more noticeable on my suits than black hair is."

She couldn't help scanning his clothing, then— and she forgot about dog hair almost instantly.

He wore only a pair of sweatpants tied low on his

torso and a disreputable Columbia Law T-shirt that was clearly from his college days. He must work out, she decided, because his chest and abs were heavily muscled as were the bulging biceps straining the arms of the shirt.

Holy cow. She'd thought he was hot before, but now…the sweats weren't tight, but as he turned to go back inside she could see that there wasn't an ounce of fat on him anywhere. His backside looked as hard and muscled as the rest of him beneath the soft fabric.

He grabbed the heavy back door and hauled it open, holding it and standing back. "Ladies first."

"Thank you," she murmured. She started forward, and after a moment Feather moved to her side and trotted obediently up the steps and inside.

As she moved up the stairs ahead of him, she reflected that it was rather pleasant to know he wasn't ogling her. She'd lost track years ago of the number of men who appeared to believe that being a celebrity, especially a model, gave them free rein to slap, pinch, fondle or otherwise handle her body. Granted, most of them were famous men who thought the world had been created solely for their pleasure, but even among the general population there were those who didn't appear to regard a model as an animate being with feelings and emotions.

"Sorry I didn't think about telling you her commands right away," Brendan said from behind her.

She tuned back in to the present. "Well, at least now I know the most important one."

He laughed. "That you do. You can walk her tomorrow if you feel like it, but if you don't have time I'll do it in the evening."

"Oh, no. If you don't mind, I'd love to walk her. But I should tell her 'heel,' not 'forward'?" She was certain that's what he said to Cedar.

"That's only for a dog in harness," he said. "She also knows a bunch more, but those are the only ones you'll need, and some of the others are only things she needed when she was working."

"All right." They were approaching their respective apartments. She fished out her key and turned. "Good night."

He smiled. "See you in the morning."

Well, she reflected as she brushed her teeth a few minutes later, she and her new neighbor had certainly gotten off on a better foot the second time around.

She hadn't mentioned him to CeCe, her sister. During their phone chat, they'd spent most of their time commiserating with each other over their father's lamentable lack of judgment.

"Why does he have to marry them?" CeCe had asked. "Why not just live with them? It's got to be less expensive when he gets tired of them if he doesn't have to pay alimony."

Lynne imagined there was some complex psychological reason for her father's need to marry each new woman, although she couldn't begin to guess at what it was. Nor did she really care. She'd accepted his failings a long time ago.

She winced as she thought of the phone call that would have to be made to her mother tomorrow. Her mother had never remarried, and each time her father found a new woman, Lynne's mother erupted in a spew of spurned anger.

Sighing, she called to Feather. The dog came happily into her room and flopped down on the rug beside her bed. Lynne spent several minutes stroking her and rubbing Feather's satiny belly.

"You're better than a man any old day," she told the dog. "If I had a dog like you, I'd never have to worry about being left alone. You'd be faithful your whole life, wouldn't you?"

She had just finished her yoga workout the following morning when the doorbell rang. Wiping her sweaty face with a towel, she opened the door to see Brendan in a sharp charcoal suit with a white shirt and soft lavender-and-charcoal-striped tie, already dressed for the day.

"Good morning," he said.

"Hi." Instinct had her cinching the arms of her black sweater around her waist before she remembered that he couldn't see her. She still felt fat in her exercise clothes. Sometimes it was hard to recall that she'd gained weight on purpose. "That's a great suit. But how do you know you have on colors that don't clash?" The man certainly was gorgeous. She'd bet that back in his college fraternity days, he'd had girls hanging all over him. Probably still did, for that matter.

"I have Braille labels in some of my clothes," he said. "And I have a fantastic dry cleaner. When I take dirty things to them, I always keep them separated in bags by outfit. So all these things I'm wearing will go in the same bag later. Then the dry cleaner reassembles the whole outfit again in a clean bag before I pick it up."

"Ah. So once you've bought something, you always keep it together."

"Right."

Feather brushed past her then and wove herself joyfully around Brendan's knees. Heedless of the suit, he knelt and petted her. "Hey, old girl. I missed you, too."

Then he rose, and she saw the bag of food he'd set beside the door. "Here's her breakfast and enough for dinner in case I'm late getting home."

"Okay." She seemed to be reduced to words of one syllable as she looked at him again. It should be criminal for a man to look so good.

"Is something wrong?" He cocked his head as if to study her, even though she knew he wasn't seeing her expression.

She expelled a rueful chuckle. "You look so nice that I'm just standing here thanking heaven that you can't see me!"

That made him laugh, too, and she felt less awkward.

"Well, now you've got me curious," he said. And before she realized it, he reached forward and unerringly settled one large hand on her shoulder.

She nearly gasped at the touch of his warm palm. His hand was so big that his thumb rested easily on the hollow at the base of her throat, and she wondered if he could feel her pulse racing.

"Ah," he said, fingering the strap of her sleeveless leotard. "Exercise clothes. What were you doing?"

"Yoga." Back to one-word answers again. Did she sound as breathless and silly as she felt?

"Sorry to interrupt. I'll let you get back to it."

"I'm finished," she said. "I do a brief workout three days a week and then go for a run, and the other three days I have a full-length routine I go through."

"That's only six." He still had his hand on her shoulder, rubbing his thumb lightly back and forth over her collarbone, and she suppressed an outrageous urge to step forward and mold her body to his. What was wrong with her?

"Um…six. Right." *Oh, Lord, help me.* "I take Sundays off, unless I feel like doing something."

"Me, too," he said. "I run every day on the treadmill and I lift three times a week."

"Can I ask another stupid question?" She was going to be rude again, but she was really curious about how he managed so well. She finally moved back just a shade, and to her mingled relief and disappointment, he let his hand drop to his side.

"There are no stupid questions, according to my old Latin teacher, only stupid answers."

"How did you know? Exactly where my shoulder was?"

He looked momentarily puzzled.

"Just now," she clarified, "when you put out your hand, you didn't fumble or grab the wrong body part, or anything. You put your hand right where you intended to."

He laughed. "How do you know? Maybe your shoulder wasn't what I was aiming for."

She shot him a dirty look, then remembered the effect would be lost. "Very funny."

"You'll never know, will you?"

"I will when you answer my question," she said firmly. This flirting was getting out of hand. He was just her neighbor, for heaven's sake. Even if he was drop-dead gorgeous and she drooled every time he threw back his head and laughed like that. She was *not* looking for a relationship. All she wanted was to settle into a nice, small town and a nice, small-town life.

"All right." He finally grew serious. "When I lost my sight, my hearing gradually started to be…I don't know, more than just the hearing that a sighted person takes for granted. Or maybe it's just that I tune in to it a lot more now. I use it—and I imagine many vision-impaired people also do—to gauge height when someone is speaking, or distance." He made a "who-knows" gesture with his hand. "I guess I've gotten pretty adept at it. It isn't something I consciously think about. I just sort of knew where your shoulder would be."

"That makes sense."

He put his hand to his wristwatch, and a moment later a voice announced the time. "I've got to go. I'll check in tonight to get my girl, if that works for you."

"That's fine." How cool was that? A talking watch. She hadn't even imagined all the things that she would have to do differently if she were blind. "Have a good day," she said.

"Thanks. You, too." He put his hand on Feather's head and fondled her soft, floppy ears with his right hand. "See you later, girl. You have a good day with Lynne."

She squatted and picked up the bag of dog food, watching as he turned away and moved purposefully down the hall. He didn't even hesitate at the stairs as he and the dog started down.

What would it be like to depend on an animal that much? She doubted she could ever come to trust a dog enough to just step forward and head down a flight of stairs that easily.

She turned and reentered her apartment as his broad shoulders disappeared. "Come on, Feather," she said. The dog still was standing where Brendan had left her, and if she were a person given to flights of fancy, she'd have said the poor thing looked sad. "Why don't we go for a walk?"

Brendan was anxious to get home that evening. It had been a long day preparing for a trial in which he was the lead prosecutor, and the rest of the week only promised to be even longer. He'd planned to take tomorrow off but he'd be lucky to manage it.

He stopped to pick up his mail, then started up the steps to the second floor. He had barely set foot in the hallway when he heard a door open.

Dog nails clicked rapidly on wood accompanied by a happy canine whine, and his heart lifted at the familiar sound. Feather hadn't sounded that happy since the day he'd brought Cedar home. While he was in class at the training school for nearly a month, she had stayed with his old school buddy with whom he worked. Feather thought John Brinkmen was the greatest guy on the planet and Brendan had no doubt she'd been spoiled rotten in his absence. Brink had brought her back the day Brendan had returned and she'd been thrilled to see him until she caught the scent of a strange dog on his clothing. It had pretty much been downhill ever since.

He caught Feather while Cedar stood patiently waiting for the next command.

"Hey, girl," he said. "Did you have a good day with Lynne?"

He raised his head. Even if he hadn't had Feather

to warn him, he'd have known *she* was there. She hadn't made a sound and she was still too far away for him to catch her scent, but he knew. "Hi," he said.

"Hi!" She sounded jazzed, excited.

"You sound happy," he said, wondering what had put that tone in her voice.

"Guess what I did today?" Her voice was jubilant.

"Won the lottery?"

She laughed. "Not even close. I bought a piano!"

"Whoa. When you decide to do something, you don't waste time, do you?"

She laughed. "It's being delivered Tuesday. And I called the college to see if I could find anyone who would give lessons. I start next week!"

"Good for you."

"I also had an interview with the preschool. They only need someone for about twenty hours a week. And the more I think about it, the more I think I'd prefer that to something full-time. This way, I can look into taking classes and maybe even start in January."

"Will you go to Gettysburg?"

"Can't. The college doesn't offer a teaching degree. But there are several schools within an hour that do. Today I looked at some schools online. Shippensburg University, Wilson College, Penn State's Mont Alto campus and Messiah College are all less than an hour away. And they all offer education degrees except for Mont Alto, but I could do the first two years there if I chose and then transfer. If I wanted to stay at Penn State I'd have to finish at the University Park campus which is more than two hours away, but I don't really want to get settled in here and then move and I don't want to drive two and a half hours one way to school each day for two years, either. So I'm going to visit Shipp, Wilson and Messiah next week."

"You have a lot of energy, don't you?" he observed in a dry tone.

She laughed. "No more than the average person, I don't think. It just seems that way because I'm starting so many new things."

He was dying to know where she'd worked before, what kind of career she'd just apparently walked away from. Maybe it was something as mundane as fast-food work, but he doubted it. Then he thought of something else.

"You do realize," he said, "that working twenty hours a week at what is probably minimum wage is not going to pay for this apartment." Let alone a new piano.

She went still. He might not have been able to see her, but he could tell from the very quality of the air that she'd practically frozen in place. Finally she cleared her throat. "I do realize that," she said quietly.

"I hope I haven't burst your bubble," he said hurriedly, regretting now that he'd said anything at all. She was an adult and her finances were none of his business. "It's none of my business. I apologize."

"It's not a problem," she said. "I should have

realized how it would look to someone who didn't know me." She hesitated. "I'm, ah…" She stopped again and chuckled nervously. "There's no polite way to say it. I'm fairly wealthy."

"That was polite," he observed. "You could have said you were loaded. Or filthy rich."

"I suppose I could have." She chuckled again, and there were far fewer nerves in her tone this time.

"Are you?"

"Am I what?"

"Filthy rich."

"Define 'filthy rich,' please."

He couldn't help smiling. "Smart-aleck. Okay. More than a million."

"Oh." Was that relief in her tone? "Yes."

She was worth over a million bucks? Was she some kind of industrial heiress or something? He couldn't figure out any polite way to ask, so he just let it go. "That's good," he said lamely.

He had fished his key from his pocket and as she spoke he unlocked his door. "Come on in," he said. "So Feather was good for you today?"

"She was delightful." She trailed after him and he heard her shut the door as he bent to remove Cedar's harness. "She just follows me from room to room. I guess she's used to always being close to someone?"

"Yeah. At work my dog lies beside my desk. She's been pretty upset at being left behind every day, even though I was trying to come home at lunch to make sure she was doing all right."

"Well, I don't mind having her hang out with me one little bit. She's more than welcome to come back anyday."

"Thanks." It was nice to know he had someone to call on in an emergency, although he couldn't possibly impose his dog on her regularly.

"Have you been over to the battlefield yet?"

"No. It's near the top of my list, though." Her voice grew warm and amused. "I think it's probably illegal to live in Gettysburg and not know anything about that battle."

"I have an auto tour on CD. You can borrow it or, if you're free tomorrow and you'd like company, I'd be happy to ride along." He was mildly amazed to hear the words come out of his mouth, particularly since he hadn't even been sure he wanted to take the day off. Had he just asked her out? He wasn't sure the casual offer qualified as a date. Still, he hadn't come anywhere near that close to dating since he'd ended his engagement a few months after his accident.

"I would enjoy that," she said. "And I'd love the company. Can we take the dogs?"

"They can come along in the car. Cedar can go anywhere we go, but now that Feather is a pet and not a working guide, I'd have to check. I'm not sure that the Park Service allows dogs on the battlefield."

"I can check," she said. "I'll get online later and

see what I can find out. If I don't get results, we can call the Park Service before we leave in the morning."

"All right. Thanks."

"Thank you. I've been wanting to look around the battlefield. This will be perfect." He could tell she was turning away as she spoke. "I'll go look it up right now."

He followed her to the door. "What time would you like to go?"

"I'm flexible. Is nine too early?"

"Nine's good."

"All right. See you then."

"Lynne." He reached out and circled her wrist before she could pull open the door. "Thank you for caring for Feather today. She means a lot to me, and it was easier to be at work knowing she wasn't alone."

She had stilled at his touch. Then, to his surprise, she turned her hand beneath his until their palms were touching, and she lightly squeezed his fingers. Her skin was warm and so soft he knew whatever job she'd held before, if any, hadn't involved manual labor. He also knew that she hadn't been any more prepared than he for the immediate sexual tension that had leaped between them. He'd felt an intense spike in his pulse when their hands touched, and from her small, stifled gasp, he suspected she'd felt the same.

Still, her tone was calm and her words were prosaic when she cleared her throat and spoke. "It was wonderful to have company," she said. "I didn't realize how solitary I am until I moved here. And I'm determined to change that." She chuckled. "Even if I have to start with a dog." Then her tone changed as she slid her hand free. "Uh-oh."

"What?"

"Feather." She sounded rather chagrined. "She's sitting by the door. I believe she thinks she's going with me again."

"Feather, come."

Silence. Great. It was going to be a repeat of dinner last night. He tried not to feel hurt. After all, from Feather's point of view, *he* was the one who had replaced *her.*

"I'd love to have her stay again," Lynne said hesitantly, "but I know you'd like her here with you."

"Yeah, but I want her to be happy…"

"She'll come around." Lynne's hand touched his shoulder lightly, rubbing a small, comforting circle. At least, he was pretty sure it was meant to be comforting. In reality, every nerve cell in his body leaped to life again at the feel of that small, warm hand.

Relationships had been on the back burner for a number of years now, but his new neighbor with the sexy voice and soft skin was getting to him in a way that was impossible to ignore.

It wasn't that he didn't *like* women, he told himself. He liked them a great deal. He'd loved one once. But after the accident in which he'd lost his eyesight, he'd been unable to believe she would want to stay with him forever. Dumb as it seemed in hind-sight, he'd pushed his fiancée away, had isolated himself behind a wall of self-pity and insecurities.

It had taken him several years of counseling and healing to become comfortable with who he was now, to become convinced that a loss of sight didn't equal a loss of manhood. And by the time he'd figured it out, Kendra had moved on. He'd gone to see her one day—only to learn that she'd married. She'd answered the door of her new home and he'd felt great about the opening of the conversation, until she told him she was married.

There hadn't been much to say after that.

He'd left with the taste of defeat in his mouth, and the knowledge that he'd lost her due to his own stu-pidity. Since then…since then he'd had a few dates with a few very pleasant women and one hilarious disaster of a blind date. Which, in his case, took on a whole new meaning.

But of the more normal dates he'd endured, there had been no one memorable, nobody who had made his mouth water and his pulse race. It had been easy to immerse himself in his law practice, until Lynne DeVane had moved into the apartment across the hall less than a week ago.

And now?

He had no idea what she looked like, but she was memorable, all right. And it wasn't simply sexual, either. Her wry humor tickled his funny bone. She was direct and thoughtful, and she loved his dogs. She didn't even mind dog hair as a fashion accessory, which made her damn near perfect all by itself.

But there was no denying the attraction he felt. *They* felt. Because he was sure it affected her, too. The odd pauses, the pregnant silences, the electric sense of possibility that flowed between them…oh, yeah, she felt it, too.

She made his pulse race and his mouth water with just one whiff of the warm scent that clung to her skin. Her husky laugh made his whole body tingle, and the warmth of her hand made him wonder how it would feel on him.

Yes, it had been a long, long time since he'd felt this drawn to a woman, since he'd felt compelled to seek her out and explore the charged atmosphere between them.

But there was no question that he did now. And he knew exactly what he was going to do about it.

"So," he said, "after the tour of the battlefield, we'll go to the visitor center. Might as well start you out right from the very beginning."

"The beginning of my Gettysburg education?" There was laughter in her voice.

He nodded, smiling back. "The beginning of your life in Gettysburg."

"I like the way that sounds," she said with great satisfaction. "My life in Gettysburg."

Four

She would enjoy herself today.

Lynne pressed a hand to her stomach the next morning, hoping to squeeze the butterflies that were frantically fluttering around in there into submission. She checked her backpack again to be sure she hadn't forgotten anything vital, then glanced at the clock. One minute to go, if Brendan was punctual, and she'd bet her last dime that he was.

There was no need to be so nervous. It wasn't really a date. Just a neighborly excursion. He was grateful to her for her help with Feather and wanted to pay her back for dinner.

It *was* a date. At least, it certainly had sounded like

that when he'd offered his tape and his company. And then he'd planned the entire day. She suspected that as she got to know him better, she'd find a hard-core take-charge kind of guy beneath those dark suits and elegant ties that looked so good on his tall, solid frame.

Right on time, a sharp, definite knock sounded at her door. The butterflies all sprang into action.

She crossed the room and pulled the door open. "Good morning."

Feather pushed past her, and Brendan bent to fondle the dog's ears. "Good morning, and good morning. How's my girl?"

She was pretty sure he wasn't addressing her in the second sentence. "She ate breakfast and seemed content this morning. I really enjoy having her around."

"Good." His smile was broad with relief. "I worry that she's going to think I'm abandoning her."

Lord, but the man was potent. And it wasn't just that smile, although it sure didn't hurt.

She'd thought he looked good in a suit, but today, in a burgundy sweatshirt and faded denim jeans that clung to his strong thighs, he took her breath away. His shoulders looked a mile wide beneath the sweat-shirt, and he'd pushed up the sleeves to reveal muscular forearms covered in silky dark hair.

How had she missed seeing just how big he was over the past few days? She was nearly six feet herself, and she barely reached his jaw, so he had to be close to six-six.

"Are your parents tall?" she blurted.

One dark eyebrow quirked upward in an expression she'd seen a number of times before, as if he wasn't quite sure how the conversation had taken such a turn. "My father is," he said. "My mother's only average height, but she has three brothers who all are over six feet." He stretched out a hand and touched her shoulder. "You're pretty tall yourself. Where did you get the height?"

"My father. My mother is only five-two." She tried to laugh. "It's not easy being the tallest girl in the class until you're in high school. I was taller than my older sister before we were even out of elementary school."

"I like tall women," he said. "My high school girlfriend was the captain of the basketball team."

"I never played basketball." She wasn't touching that first line with a ten-foot pole. "The coach was always after me to come out for the team, but I just wasn't interested. I was a dancer. For a long time I dreamed of auditioning for one of the big ballet companies. But finally I accepted the fact that no one can really use a ballerina who is taller and heavier than all the men who have to do lifts with her."

"You're not heavier than any man I know."

"Um...Brendan? Without being rude, may I ask how the heck you would know how much I weigh? I could be three hundred pounds for all you know."

"Not a chance." The hand that was touching her shoulder clasped the fragile joint, and as before, she was immediately wildly aware of how big his hand was, of how much of her skin that hand could cover if he stretched his fingers wide. "You're skinny," he pronounced, tracing his thumb over her collarbone and sliding it up to caress the line of her jaw. "In fact, I'd say you're almost too skinny."

"I am not!" If he had known her when she was modeling. And then she noticed the grin hovering around the edges of his chiseled lips. She balled her fist and lightly made contact with his shoulder. "You're teasing me."

"I might be." The grin grew broader. "Just about had you, too."

Just about had you. She was almost sure that he registered the double entendre nearly as quickly as she did. His hand stilled, and she wondered what he was thinking. *She* was having a hard time keeping her mind out of the gutter. How would it feel to have those lips on hers? To have those hands sliding over her body, pressing her against his large, hard form?

"I wish I could see your face," he said in a low, intense tone.

"Why?" She was breathless, the butterflies inside sucking all the oxygen away from her lungs.

He turned his palm to cradle the side of her face. "I'd give anything to know what your lips look like."

Her pulse stuttered and sped up even further. Before she could think of all the reasons why it was a bad idea, she reached up and took his index finger in her hand, then placed it on her lips.

Silently he traced her lips as she stood, mesmerized by the strangely intimate sensation of having him touch her face. He slid his finger around her lips, then moved down her chin, lingering for a moment in the slight cleft that she had always despised. Then he continued, tracing along her jaw and back to her ear, where he circled the fragile shell and then tugged lightly at her earlobe, exploring the three small studs he found there. She shivered, a thrill of excited nerve endings, and he left her ear to sweep back over her head. She'd done her hair up in an intricate variation of a French braid that she particularly liked because it held the straight, slippery strands of her hair in place well for long hours, and he lightly ran his hand over it, then found the bundled length of it contained in the knot at her neck. He slipped his hand beneath the coil of hair and cupped her nape. She felt herself sway toward him, but before she could complete the motion his hand was moving forward again, up to her temple, across the wide span of her smooth forehead and down the small, straight slope of her nose. He smoothed over her eyebrows and brushed her eyelashes lightly as her eyes fluttered closed—

And then his hand was gone. She opened her eyes to see him turning away.

"Thanks," he said. "I've been wondering."

"You're welcome." Her voice sounded so normal, compared to the feelings still rioting through her. Chief among them was intense disappointment. She'd wanted him to kiss her, she acknowledged to herself. She was pathetically, ridiculously infatuated with her neighbor of less than a week—and he, while he might be interested in her as a willing female, certainly didn't seem to suffer the same effects that his mere presence gave her.

"I've found that if I ask people to describe themselves, they're usually astonishing unhelpful," he said. "I get a much more accurate picture by touching."

So he did this frequently. Or, if not frequently, at least occasionally when he was getting to know someone.

It's like Braille for him, she told herself. It didn't necessarily mean anything more. It was just his way of learning a little more about me. Only fair, really, since I know what he looks like.

She felt as deflated as a hot-air balloon on the ground. "Well, now you know. Nothing out of the ordinary." She grabbed her backpack. "Are you ready to go?"

His eyebrows had done that quirky thing again at her pronouncement, but he didn't comment. "Sure."

She led the way down to her small SUV. After a moment's hesitation, she asked, "Where should we put the dogs?"

"They can go in the back together, if you put down a blanket to keep the dog hair from getting ground into your upholstery," he said. "Is there any way to keep them from being tossed forward if we were to have an accident?"

"I have a cargo net that stretches from side to side right above the back seat. Will that work?"

"Perfect," he said. "The school teaches us to put them on the floor at our feet, but most of the graduates I've met disregard that because it's too dangerous in the event of a front-end collision."

She popped the back and raised the hatch. Brendan removed Cedar's harness and patted the floor inside. "Hup up." And both dogs leaped in.

"If we were going any distance," he said, "I'd put them in kennels for safety, but since we're only going a mile or so to the battlefield and then driving five miles an hour most of the time, they should be okay."

As she walked to the driver's side, he trailed a hand along the passenger side until he reached the door, and they both slid into their seats at the same time.

"Whoa," he said as his knees practically met his nose. "Somebody a lot smaller than I am was sitting here last time, right?"

She chuckled. "My mother rode along to help me move in. There's a set of automatic buttons along the side of your seat. Press backward on the first one and your seat will move back."

"Here." He handed her a jewel case with a CD inside. "Here's the battlefield tour. Go out 116 toward Fairfield and Reynolds Avenue. Where we begin, is just a little way out of town on your right after you pass the Lutheran Seminary."

She followed his directions and easily found the correct road. Almost immediately after she turned in, the view opened up onto a sweeping vista of fields and stands of trees that sloped gently uphill at its far end. Cannons stood in occasional small formations, and along the roads she could see a number of small plaques and statues. Several miles directly ahead, a large monument with wide stone steps around it looked down over the green expanse, still lovely in early autumn. The Peace Light Memorial, he told her.

"There should be a pull-off along the road around here," he told her. "If you stop there, we can put the CD in and begin the tour. It'll tell us when and where to move."

"How many times have you done this?" she asked him.

He shrugged. "Less than a dozen, but enough to be pretty familiar with it. I've taken my folks and my sister's family, and friends who have come to visit, and my partner's parents and a few others."

"So we probably don't need the tape," she said dryly.

"Well, yeah, we do." He laughed. "I enjoy Civil War history. If you ask me to narrate, the tour might last three days instead of three hours."

They began the tour then, and talked little as they drove. Twice he asked her to describe a certain monument or scene for him. Frequently he added personal anecdotes from the diaries and stories of men who had fought at Gettysburg.

She became utterly engrossed in the saga. He showed her Cemetery Hill, where the Union forces rallied after a humiliating rout on the first day of the battle. There was the Peach Orchard, the Wheatfield, Little Round Top; names she vaguely recognized from her American history class in high school. She'd realized that walking over the grounds where so many had died would affect her. But she had never expected to be so moved by the monuments erected to honor the troops. The larger-than-life, beautifully sculpted memorial at the cemetery depicting the mortally wounded Confederate General Armistead being attended by Union Captain Henry Bingham brought her to tears as Brendan told her of Armistead's friendship with Bingham's commanding officer, Major General Winfield Hancock.

Virginia's state monument, with its clustered soldiers from different walks of life at the base and the stunning sculpture of Robert E. Lee on his horse Traveler atop the column was perhaps her favorite. "It's said to be one of the best likenesses ever done of Lee," Brendan said in a tone of near-reverence.

She smiled. "You really weren't kidding. You know a lot about this place."

"It's fascinated me since I was a kid," he said. "I was here several times before my accident, so I still remember some things."

"How does that work? Your memory, I mean." She hesitated, formulating her thoughts. "Do you still have clear memories or do they begin to fade over time?"

"I do still have memories," he said. "But as time goes by I find they get sort of blurry. Imagine it as an Impressionist painting. I have the general outline and idea, but the details are going. Handwriting was one of the first things to disintegrate."

"But how do you sign credit cards and documents?"

"I don't often use credit cards. They can be double-swiped, switched or the numbers copied and I would never know. I carry cash as much as possible, and I do a lot of ordering from catalogs and shopping at places where I've established relationships and have a monthly account. For documents, which, as you can imagine, I do have to sign quite a bit, I have a little card called a signature guide that helps me write in a given space. If you use one often enough, your muscle memory helps you keep a consistent, legible signature."

There was no anger or even resignation in his tone; he was simply uttering a fact. She marveled once again at how little his life seemed to be hampered by his lack of vision. Despite the considerable changes that had been forced on him, he had overcome most problem issues with ingenuity and grace.

Along the Emmitsburg Road, where Confederate soldiers had been urged to undertake what amounted to a suicidal effort to charge across an open field, up a hill and over Union breastworks, Brendan told her that photographs of the scene after the battle showed men lying in ordered rows where they had been cut down. "It was insane. The Union troops were massed up on the ridge ahead of you. They would wait until the Rebs got close and then they would open fire. Insane," he said again, regretfully. He told her about Pickett's futile charge, after which Pickett returned to Lee bitter and angry. "Lee told him to prepare his division for a counterattack," Brendan said, "and Pickett responded, 'General, I have no division.'"

They got out of the car a number of times to examine monuments erected by states to honor their fallen. She cried again at the sight of the Irish Brigade's tribute, a beautiful Celtic cross with an Irish wolfhound, one casualty of the battle, lying at its base.

At Devil's Den, he insisted they climb among the rocks. They left Feather in the SUV, but Lynne was surprised at how well Cedar maneuvered Brendan through the wild tumble of boulders to the small summit. "What direction am I facing?" he asked her. "It feels like north or northeast."

She had to think for a moment, squinting at the late-autumn sun. "It is. How did you know that?"

"The sun's on my face." He took her by the shoulder and turned her to face slightly to the east as he began to explain troop movements and attacks that determined the outcome of the battle. "The bottom line," he said, "is that if the Union had lost Little Round Top, the Confederates could have taken Gettysburg. In fact, given General Lee's superb leadership and the lack of any really strong, decisive Union general, it's quite likely. The whole outcome of the war might have been different. For that matter, if Lee had accepted Lincoln's request to lead the Union army, I sincerely doubt there'd even have been a war still occurring in 1863."

His face was animated, the sun lighting his blue eyes to an intense hue. She openly examined his face, wanting to touch him as he'd touched her earlier that day. Wanting more than that. She was supremely conscious of his arm, which had slid from her shoulder down her back and now curved loosely around her waist. Even through her clothing, she could feel his big hand on her.

"Lynne?" Brendan's voice was amused. "God, I'm sorry. Was I that boring?"

"No!" she said hastily, jarred from her sensual preoccupation by his assumption. "You're not boring at all. I was just trying to…to visualize it."

"And did you succeed?" He'd turned to face her, far closer than a sighted man would normally come into her personal space, and she watched as his lips formed the words.

"Sort of." She sounded silly and breathless, even to herself. "I guess we'd better get down from here and keep going."

"I guess."

Was that regret in his voice? She wondered, as she picked a careful path down through the rocks for the man and dog, if he had any idea how interested in him she was. It was silly to be so obsessed with a man. The more she was with him, the more she wanted to be with him.

They spent nearly five hours on the battlefield, and she could have spent five more. She'd anticipated missing lunch and had packed apples and ham sandwiches, which they stopped and ate while sitting on the tailgate of the SUV. As the sun began to sink toward the surrounding mountains in earnest, she turned the vehicle toward home.

"Thank you," she said when they had climbed the stairs to their floor. She stopped in the center of the hallway, midway between their doors. "That was absolutely fascinating."

"I'm glad you enjoyed it," he said. "Some people couldn't care less about the history of the area."

"I can't imagine how a person could fail to find it interesting," she said. "Next time, instead of using the tape, I'll just listen to you the whole way."

As soon as the words were out of her mouth, she wanted to sink right through the floor. He hadn't indicated in any way that he wanted to spend more time in her company.

Brendan smiled, though. "It's a deal." His watch announced the time, something she was beginning to get used to. "I'd better get going. I have dinner plans tonight."

"All right." Dinner plans. Was he subtly telling her to back off? "I need to get going, too. I—"

"Lynne." He stopped her with a finger raised to her lips. "Thanks." He captured her other hand and raised it to his lips.

Wow. If he'd been trying, he couldn't have done anything more guaranteed to melt her into a little puddle of need. She was a total sucker for a man who kissed her hand.

She didn't say anything as his warm lips firmly caressed the back of her hand; she couldn't.

Brendan stepped back and released her. "I'll see you." Then he shook his head as he grinned wryly. "Figuratively speaking."

It was only because she couldn't sleep that she heard him come in just before midnight that evening. Pure accident, she told herself, that she'd gotten a cup of tea and decided to sit in her living room and work a Japanese number puzzle until she got sleepy. And she didn't see him at all on Sunday, although she once heard him leave and later return to his apartment in the afternoon when she'd returned from church. She didn't see him Monday, either.

But Tuesday morning her telephone rang almost before she was out of bed. She stopped in the middle of her Pilates and punched the button on the receiver. "Hello?"

"Hi, Lynne, it's Brendan." She already knew that from the Caller ID on her phone. "I was wondering whether you'd be interested in having Feather anytime this week?"

"I'd love to. It's been weird and quiet around here after getting used to having a dog in the apartment."

"I know the feeling. I had to take Feather to the vet once and leave her overnight. It wasn't fun being without my partner, but it was a lot more than that. It was like being away from a member of my family. I hated it." He paused. "Well, I have to run. Bad week. I'll drop her off in a minute."

He was as good as his word. She'd barely had time to wipe her face with a towel when her doorbell rang.

"Hey," she said as she pulled open the door.

"Hey." He smiled. "Thanks a million. I tried leaving her again yesterday and she was in major mope mode last night."

"She's welcome to stay all week if you like."

To her surprise he nodded. "I would really appreciate that, if you're sure. I hate leaving her alone all day except for one brief pit stop at lunch."

"I'm sure."

"Great! Here's more dog food. Gotta run. Call me if you have any questions or problems." He'd given her his card with his contact information on it days earlier.

"We won't. Have a good…day." But she was

talking to his back as he gave Cedar a command and the two moved off toward the stairs.

Hmm. He must not be kidding about being busy.

She attended a meeting of the library's community support group Tuesday evening and promptly got shanghaied into being the treasurer, since the woman who'd been doing the job had just had an accident.

"It's temporary," the president had assured her.

But the vice president had winked. "That's what they told me ten years ago."

Feather was thrilled to see her when she returned, though she'd only been gone a shade more than an hour. She was a little surprised that Brendan didn't call to check on his dog, but she assumed it had just been one of those days.

Wednesday morning, she did her exercise routine in the house, then went for a run out Taneytown Road, which took her past the Park Service's Visitor Center and out through the southern end of the battlefield. Over the three days of combat in July, 1863, Brendan had told her, there had been clashes, conflicts and the final large-scale confrontation nearly all the way around the tiny town. Gettysburg had, at that time, been a significant crossroad, with five distinct highways leading into and through it. All but one were surrounded by or ran very close to some part of the battlefield.

Route 15 lay not far ahead of her, according to a sign. Better turn around. She had also seen a sign for the Boyd's Bear factory and an outlet mall, and she knew both of those were farther than she wanted to go on foot.

As she returned, she slowed and walked the last block to cool down. Once in her apartment, she headed for the shower and the scale. It was still habit to keep a close eye on her weight; although, these days she had the opposite problem from the one she'd struggled with while she was modeling. Now she had to be careful to eat enough to maintain the healthier weight she'd found when she'd decided to end her career.

And Brendan thought she was slender now. If he'd known her then…!

He called as she was getting lunch, but he sounded rushed, and when she assured him Feather was fine, he thanked her and the conversation ended quickly. Thursday and Friday, the same pattern repeated, and by Friday evening she was feeling the smallest sting of disappointment. He hadn't come home by seven, and she decided he must intend for her to keep Feather until Saturday. Then she heard his footsteps in the hall.

She leaped to her feet from the sofa where she'd been curled up reading a book. Feather, lying beside her, looked alert but didn't rise.

And a moment later, while she was hovering in the middle of the room, wondering what she'd say when she opened the door, she heard his door open.

And shut.

Well. It appeared that he wasn't all that anxious to see Feather, much less her.

He never said anything about seeing you.

That was true. But they'd had such a good time together last Saturday. She hadn't imagined the chemistry between them, had she?

Annoyed with herself, she went into the kitchen and spread out the financial records from the Friends of the Library. They had assured her that being the group's treasurer was no big deal, but if she had to authorize payments for a non-profit organization, she intended to thoroughly understand what she was doing.

Five

Brendan called on Saturday morning while she was stretching in preparation for another run. "Good morning," he said. "I bet you thought I had abandoned my dog."

"Not at all. You said you had a busy week." Which he had. She just hadn't expected him to drop off the face of the earth for five days.

"I'm preparing for a trial," he said. "And I've barely had time to eat."

There was a brief pause. She mentally ran through several responses, but before she could figure out what to say next, the silence had stretched uncomfortably.

"Do you have plans for today?" He didn't sound as if he thought her silence was weird.

"No," she said. "Other than going for a run this morning. I thought I might visit the Boyd's Bears factory this afternoon. Teddy bear collecting isn't really my style, but I'm beginning to think about Christmas, and my niece would love one."

"Christmas." He groaned. "Don't tell me you're one of those."

"One of those what?" She could hear the teasing tone in his voice.

"One of those organized people who spends December walking around looking smug while the rest of us try frantically to finish our shopping."

"Guilty," she said. "There's nothing I despise more than shopping in heavy crowds."

"I agree. It's tough enough maneuvering through tight aisles with a dog in harness. Trying to do it during the Christmas rush is impossible. But that's not why I called."

"I didn't think it was." A bubble of happiness at simply hearing his voice rose inside her and she laughed lightly. "Let me guess. You want your dog back?"

"No," he said. "Well, I do, but that's not why I called, either. Would you like to go out for dinner with me tonight?"

A date? Was he asked her out on a date? Completely caught off guard, she didn't answer him immediately.

"Lynne?" She thought there was a note of uncertainty in his normally self-assured tone. "I know it's probably too short notice for you—"

"I'd love to have dinner with you tonight," she said hastily. "Did you have any particular place in mind?"

"The Dobbin House. It's a local restaurant that serves nineteenth-century meals in a period atmosphere."

"I've seen the advertisements for it and thought it would be nice to try. Do you go there frequently?"

"No." His voice altered subtly, a sober note creeping in. "Not often."

What was that about? The mood had very definitely changed. "What time shall I be ready?" She didn't want him to change his mind.

"How about six-thirty?"

"Six-thirty it is. I'll look forward to it."

"So will I. I missed seeing you this week." The warmth was back in his tone, and for a moment she wondered if she'd imagined the brief change. "See you then."

She hung up the phone and stood by it for a moment, then did a quick and silly dance around her kitchen. He'd been busy. And he said he'd missed her!

The rest of the day crawled past. She washed her hair and then had a long, hot soak in the tub with her favorite bath beads late in the afternoon. She'd left herself plenty of time since her hair took a while to dry even using a dryer.

What to wear had her in a quandary. It was interesting, dressing for a date with a blind man. If he touched her, she wanted him to find the feel of the fabric attractive, sort of like she'd take extra care with makeup if he could see her. As it was, she moisturized her skin and put on the barest trace of lip gloss. She'd come here to start a regular life and the less she looked like her former self, the less chance she had of being recognized.

She should tell Brendan. Soon. He knew her well enough by now that her old life shouldn't be an issue or a novelty like it might to someone she was just meeting. But she'd only known him a week and a half, she reminded herself. It wasn't as if she were deliberately keeping a secret. There just hadn't been a good opening yet.

Finally it was six-thirty. Her doorbell rang promptly and she forced herself to walk—not skip or run—from the kitchen where she'd been standing waiting, instead of lurking just inside the door.

"Hi," she said as she pulled open the door.

"Hi." He was holding a large bouquet of roses in extraordinary shades of pink and peach and orange with some accompanying white blossoms mixed in, a sunrise in his free hand, and he extended the flowers to her. "These are for you."

"Brendan!" She was thoroughly flustered. "These are beautiful."

"Good. The woman at the flower shop described some different arrangements for me. This one sounded pretty."

"It's absolutely stunning," she assured him again. "Thank you." They were still standing in the doorway, and she stepped back. "Please come in while I get a vase and put them in water."

She hurried into the kitchen and pulled a large crackle-glass vase from a cupboard. Running the stems of the roses under water, she quickly trimmed them and arranged the lovely flowers in the vase.

Brendan had followed her into the kitchen. As she picked up the vase to carry it into the living room and place it on the narrow sofa table against one wall, he said, "What are you wearing?"

"Clothing or scent?"

"Both." He grinned. "You smell great and I just wondered what you've got on. Describe yourself for me."

"I'm not wearing any perfume. It must be whatever was in my bath beds. I think it was lily of the valley. Describe myself? Well, I'm tall."

"I already know that." His tone was dry. "And thin."

"Slender," she said severely. "My hair is long and really straight…" What else should she say?

"What color is it?"

"Blond. Very light, and my eyes are blue and my skin is quite fair when I don't have any tan. Without makeup on, I'm practically invisible."

"Hard to imagine," he murmured. "Go on."

"What else do you want to know?"

"Hair—exactly how long is it when you wear it down."

"Years ago it was almost to my waist. Right now it's just below my shoulders and I'm trying to continue to let it get longer."

"Sounds pretty."

It's a lot prettier than that curly red was. She had a horrified moment when she wondered if she'd spoken aloud, but Brendan's expression didn't change, and she breathed a sigh of relief. "I have big feet for a woman," she offered.

"Goes along with the height," he said. "I have my shoes custom-made sometimes because it's so hard to find size fourteens. Tell me about your face."

"My face? What about it?" She was mystified, and a little uncomfortable at being the focus of his attention in such a way. She was used to having her physical features analyzed but she'd never been asked to do it herself before. She also was used to her body being noticed, but it had never affected her on a personal level like this.

"What shape is it?"

"Shape? I don't know. Kind of long and thin, I guess. Oval, maybe?"

"And I already know your cheekbones are high and you have a cute little cleft in your chin."

"Which I despise."

"Why? It's sexy."

"At least I don't have to shave it. That would be a real pain."

He laughed. "Now tell me what you're wearing."

"A long skirt. And a silk shirt. I have a corduroy jacket lying on the back of the couch to wear tonight. I know it's warm for November, but it's not warm enough for one thin layer."

"Would you mind if I touched your clothing?"

"No." She took a fold of her skirt and guided it to his big hand.

"Mmm." He made an appreciative sound. "Feels like suede."

"No. I think it's brushed polyester."

Then his hand slid up the fold of skirt she'd handed him. He skimmed lightly over her hip to her back, and rubbed a small circle on her blouse. "Wow," he said. "Silky. Feels wonderful."

She didn't have a quick answer for him. Her body had tightened in anticipation at the brush of his fingers, and she was practically quivering. Good heavens, the man was potent. If he could do that with nothing more than the touch of fingertips, what would it be like if—*stop it, Lynne!* Once again, she reminded herself that she wasn't hunting a relationship. She'd had plenty of opportunities for that when she'd been modeling; not once had any man seriously appealed to her after Jeremy.

Until now.

Well, okay. So Brendan was gorgeous, too sexy to be allowed to walk around free, and more appealing to talk with than any man she could think of. It didn't mean she was going to act on her interest. Of course not.

Since it was a mild evening for November and the weather had been clear and dry all week, they decided to walk the few blocks to the Dobbin House. Brendan left Cedar at home, noting it was hard for the big dog to get out of the way in a restaurant. "His tail has been stepped on every day this week during business lunches," he explained.

He carried a white cane, and she was surprised at how well he was able to negotiate the uneven sidewalks of the old town. "If *I* couldn't see where I was going, my knees would probably be permanently skinned from falling."

His mouth quirked. "It's been known to happen. But I'm pretty careful on these sidewalks because I expect them to be uneven, so I usually do okay. Whether I'm using the dog or a cane, I find I really have to focus."

"How did you learn to use the cane? Did you have to go to some kind of school after your accident?"

"No." He shook his head. "In Pennsylvania, the Bureau of Blindness & Visual Services assigns you a mobility trainer. Unfortunately, it's done strictly by zip code and all the instructors aren't equally good. And I only got three sessions, anyway."

"Three sessions!"

"Yeah." He snorted. "I'm lucky. My family had the resources to hire a private trainer for six weeks. She was enormously helpful."

"I can't even imagine." A moment later her curiosity got the better of her when he didn't elaborate. "In what ways?"

"She taught me how much easier things could be if I learned Braille. A lot of adult-onset blind people never learn it. But now I have a special label maker and I can put special labels on my clothing so I know what matches what, which spices are which, stuff like that. I learned to use a screenreader, which translates typed messages, like e-mail and Web sites, to oral text, and I got a few assisted-living devices like my talking watch. You can't imagine all the things that are available now, although most of them are not really necessary items."

"What was your biggest challenge?"

He didn't even hesitate. "I had to adjust to using my sense of touch a lot more and to memorizing things like distances, placement of furniture. Listening to traffic patterns is another skill that takes concentration to master."

"What about people? Is it frustrating trying to figure out who's talking to you?"

"Not usually." His swinging cane detected the edge of the curb, and he stopped just as she was about to grab his arm. "Let me know when we have the light," he added. "Unless it's someone I haven't seen for years, I've found I'm pretty good at recognizing people's voices."

"I think you're amazing," she said sincerely. "I guess unless each of us is confronted with something like what you've gone through, we never know how we'd react. But I could never do what you do."

"I'm just living," he said mildly.

"Alone," she elaborated. "Independently. You support yourself, you care for two animals."

"You do what you have to do," he said. "If you'd asked me if I could handle being blind when I was a college kid, I never would have been able to imagine it. I'd have said no way."

"I suppose." But she was still doubtful. She'd meant it when she'd said he was amazing. As she got more and more used to being with him, it was hard to remember that he was blind. He was just... Brendan.

They approached the restaurant then, and she quietly directed him through the entry. After they'd hung up their coats and the hostess began to lead them to a table, he turned to her. "May I take your arm? You could guide me to our seats."

"Sure." She didn't hesitate. "Uh, right or left?"

"Left. It's called the 'sighted guide' technique. Just hold your arm close to your side and let me put my hand under your elbow. That way, you're a step ahead of me and I can tell if we're moving up or down steps or ramps, and you can keep me from banging into things."

"Okay." She moved into position and waited for him to take her left arm. He raised his right hand and sought her elbow, and his fingers brushed her rib cage and the side of her breast as he did so.

A bolt of white-hot lightning flashed and she swore she heard a clap of thunder as a surge of heat rushed through her. She closed her eyes. Had she ever been so aware of a man before?

"Lynne?"

His voice was deep and close to her ear. She turned her head to see his mouth only inches from her. What would she give to stretch up the few inches necessary to close the gap between them? She cleared her throat, determined to get her mind off Brendan and back on dinner. "I was just waiting for the hostess to show us to the table," she said lamely, starting forward.

She stopped when he was beside his chair and said, "The chair is directly to your left. The back is next to your left hand."

He put out his hand and grasped the back of the chair, easily settling himself as she moved to her own seat on the far side of the table. But when she glanced at him, he was scowling ferociously. It was the most unpleasant expression she'd seen since he'd fallen over her boxes the week before.

"What's wrong?"

His shoulders moved dismissively. "Nothing."

There was a moment of tense silence, and then he sighed. "It just really bugs me sometimes that I can't do the things I should do for a date, like seating you. Like opening doors."

"That's not important to me," she said. "Although it might be if you could see and you were just too self-absorbed to bother."

That startled a snort out of him, but she noticed his lean features relax as he chuckled. "You sound as if you're familiar with men like that."

"You can't imagine how many dates I've had that have treated me like...like an accessory," she said, thinking of several of her more boring evenings on the arm of whichever spoiled playboy was chasing her at the time.

There was a short silence. "I take it you've dated a lot of men of the 'self-absorbed' persuasion," Brendan said, a distinct query in his tone.

She was shocked to realize she'd nearly forgotten that Brendan had never seen her, that he had no idea who she had been. "Not so many," she said, trying to minimize the damage. "Maybe I just remember them vividly because they were such spectacularly bad dates."

"How about good ones?"

"Good dates? I've had some of those, too."

"Any in particular?" His voice was light but she thought she detected an intensity she couldn't quite define.

"There was one," she said, "that I thought might be a prince, but he turned out to be a toad."

"Frog." Brendan corrected her. "In the fairy tale, she kisses a frog."

"I know, but this one was definitely a toad."

"What did he do that earned him toad status?"

Oh, dear. She chose her words carefully, thinking of how she'd met Jeremy at a post-show party after a large job in Paris. "I met him when I was young and still a bit starry-eyed. He was British, and wealthy. Very wealthy, and I suppose his family had certain expectations for him. I thought he loved me, but it turned out he liked the way I adorned his arm better than he actually liked the person I was."

"How did you find out?"

Her mouth twisted and she willed herself to breathe easily. Jeremy was far in the past. "I was starting to dream about marrying him. When he realized that, he let me know in no uncertain terms that I wasn't suitable for a wife. On the other hand, he'd have been more than happy to keep me on the side after he did get married."

Brendan quietly said a word that had her eyebrows rising. "You deserve better."

"That's what I told myself." Then she gathered her courage and said, "What about you? Any—what do you call female toads? Toadettes?—in your past?"

He smiled. "No. No toadettes. If anything, I was the toad."

"How so?" She cocked her head, curious.

"I was engaged once, too." He paused a moment as if waiting for her reaction. But she carefully didn't respond, finding herself surprisingly resentful that he'd actually nearly married. How silly, when she herself had been engaged.

When she didn't speak, he went on. "It…just wasn't working out, so I ended it. She didn't want to break it off, but I insisted. So I guess I'm the toad."

"You must have had good reasons." Of that she was certain. Brendan was not the type of man to hurt someone needlessly.

"They seemed good to me at the time."

Something in his tone made her wonder…. "But now you regret it?"

"I did, later, and for a long time. But—"

The waitress approached then, and he never finished. Dinner was pleasant; the meal, interesting. Their server wore a long skirt and apron with a period blouse. The food was prepared and presented as it would have been a century ago.

As they ate, the conversation was light and easy. Brendan clearly was done with personal revelations, but she would have given a lot to know what he'd been about to say.

It wasn't as though she could ask, though. If she continued to pry, he might ask questions that would be awkward for her, as well.

And she didn't want to talk about her past. It

would be too easy to slip and say something that would make him realize that she was—or once had been—something more than simply a girl next door.

She would tell him, she promised herself. Eventually. But it was just so nice to be with someone who didn't react to her as A'Lynne, the redheaded supermodel from the cover of *Sports Illustrated*.

Afterward, they walked back to their building. As they climbed the stairs, she said, "Would you like to come in for coffee?"

"Sounds great. I'd love to." Brendan followed her into the apartment and took a seat on the couch as she hurried into the kitchen. Feather immediately appropriated a place to lie down—right across the top of his feet. As Lynne worked in the kitchen, she could hear him talking in deep, gentle tones to the old dog.

Something in the quality of his voice reminded her of the way her father had talked to her when she was small. Her father. She'd avoided thinking of him during the past week. She had gotten very good at that, but Brendan's tone had pushed her mental barriers aside. Whatever else he might be, no one could ever say her father was a man who didn't love his children.

She sighed. Why did he feel compelled to marry again? She wished he'd stop tying himself legally to every woman who came into his life. Not because of any inheritance claims Lynne and her sister might have—heaven knew, Lynne had enough money squirreled away to keep her comfortable for the rest of her life, and CeCe was married to a software development engineer who owned a highly successful company. Josh was a wonderful man she'd met in college who adored her and their two children.

Hmm. That was something to think about. While neither of her parents was a stellar role model for marriage, Josh and CeCe had been married for nine years and had been together for nearly fourteen. And they were as happy as anyone she'd ever seen.

Now, where had that random thought come from? The last thing she needed to be thinking about was marriage. How silly.

She carried a small tray bearing the coffee and its accoutrements into the living room and set it down before perching on the sofa a respectable distance from Brendan.

"Did you get your piano delivered this week?" he asked after she had handed him a steaming mug.

"I did! I can hardly wait for next week!" She felt like a little kid, ready to bounce with enthusiasm. "I've been practicing scales and a few finger exercises I remember from before."

"You'll be a concert pianist in no time."

"I wish. Did you ever play an instrument?"

"Trombone, in high school. But I didn't continue in college."

"I never played anything in a band, although I always thought it would have been fun."

"It was. I went to a big high school with a very competitive band and we actually marched in the Rose Parade one year."

"Wow! I bet that was exciting."

"It was." He chuckled. "Although, I think the anticipation leading up to it was nearly as big a deal. We spent a year and a half before, raising money to get there."

"Sounds like your high school memories are good ones."

"Yours weren't?"

She shrugged. "I was taller than any boy in my class from the beginning of sixth grade on. Even by my senior year there were only a few guys taller than I was. I wasn't much of a basketball player so I didn't have anything that might have given me an identity. I loved ballet but that wasn't a school activity."

"You should have looked into modeling. Isn't height a requirement for that?"

Oh, dear. It was the perfect opening…but she wasn't ready to tell him yet. He seemed to enjoy her company now. Just her—Lynne. Once she told him who she was, she would have no way to ever know again if he was responding to her or to her image.

"I should have thought of that," she said lightly.

Not a lie, since she'd fallen into modeling purely by chance when a photographer had taken her picture at a charity event at which she'd been working for the bank where she'd gotten a job as a teller out of high school. "Add on a pretty older sister who was the captain of the cheerleading squad, and you get a girl who faded into the background most of the time."

"Hard for me to imagine," he said. "I think I would have noticed you. Even in my dopey-teenage-boy stage."

She chuckled. "You think so?"

"I know so." He set down his coffee cup. "I have to get going. I need to work tomorrow morning, clearing up the last details from the trial."

"Oh, I forgot!" She set down her cup and rose with him, following him toward the door as Feather wound around their legs. "Is it over?"

"Ended yesterday." He leaned his cane against the wall and linked his arms above his head, stretching mightily. "Thank God."

"Good outcome, I take it?"

"Of course." He grinned as he lowered his arms. "I wish I was always able to say that. This was a pretty solid case. Insurance fraud."

"Congratulations!" She punched his shoulder lightly, feeling the solid flesh beneath her balled fist. "Why didn't you say something during dinner? We could have celebrated."

"I didn't think of it during dinner," Brendan said. He reached out and settled his big hands on her shoulders, lightly rubbing his thumbs over the silky fabric of her blouse. "I was too engrossed in you."

She was too stunned to speak. Engrossed in her? Before she could summon words, he purposefully slid his arms around her, tugging her closer. "I'm going to kiss you now."

It wasn't a question, but as his face neared and his warm lips found hers, she didn't care. She put her arms around his neck, an action that allowed him to pull her more closely against him, as he took her mouth with a firm, thorough exploration that sent sizzling streams of excitement arrowing through her body.

Had she ever felt this before, this nearly irresistible urge to throw caution to the winds and give herself to this man? Had she ever felt that her flesh was going to leap right off her bones if a certain man didn't touch her?

One hand slid down her back, pressing her into the hard contours of his body, and she couldn't hold back the small sound that escaped from her throat as their bodies slid into snug proximity, fitting together as if they'd been made for that very purpose.

Brendan tore his lips from hers, stringing a feverish trail of kisses along her jaw to her ear, where he found a spot so sensitive that her knees actually buckled when his tongue caressed her there.

"Lynne." He breathed her name against her skin, raising goose bumps along the tender flesh of her arms. "I've been wanting to do this."

She smiled as her head fell back and he slid his mouth along the column of her throat. "I've been wanting you to do this."

He chuckled, then his mouth sought hers again. He kissed her strongly, deeply, repeatedly rubbing his body against hers and setting her afire so that she twisted against him and moaned.

Finally he withdrew in tiny increments, leaving her throbbing and regretful. "I've got to go," he said hoarsely, still holding her loosely against him. "Before I rush you into something you're not ready for."

She was unbelievably touched by his insight. "I'm not," she confirmed. "But you could probably change my mind," she added honestly.

He groaned. Dipping his head, he pressed one last, hard kiss against her mouth. "Do you have to make it harder?"

The moment he said it, silence fell between them. A heartbeat passed, and then he ruefully said, "Poor choice of vocabulary," as he set her away from him.

She laughed, delighted with his frankness. "We'll pursue that another time."

"God, I hope so." His words were fervent and he smiled as he picked up his cane and his hand sought the door handle. "I'll call you tomorrow."

* * *

Brendan paused inside his own apartment. Cedar was kenneled in the kitchen, and the metal rattled as the dog anticipated his release. "I'm coming, buddy."

He negotiated easily through his apartment and released Cedar from the kennel, stroking the broad head as the dog pressed himself joyously against Brendan. "I love you, too, buddy," he said aloud. "But I sure wish there was someone other than you touching me right now."

His breath was still fast and shallow from the moments with Lynne as he clipped on a leash and led Cedar down to the park at the rear of the building. He hadn't been looking for a relationship. In fact, it had been so long since he'd even been interested in learning more about a woman that he had been starting to think that perhaps his lack of interest was related to the fact that he could no longer see them.

Now he knew that couldn't have been more wrong. He just hadn't met the right woman.

He entered his apartment again, still aroused by the mere thought of Lynne's slender curves and sweet mouth. As he removed his pants and his hand brushed against his own hard flesh, he groaned, wishing relief could be that easy. But he wasn't going to be satisfied with anything less than his pretty neighbor stretched out beneath him in his bed, her long, slender legs wrapped around his hips and her body arching against him as he pleasured her.

That would, indeed, be satisfying.

Dropping his hand, he padded naked across the hall to the bathroom. He'd never been a fan of cold showers but tonight might just be the exception to the rule.

Six

There was a message from Brendan on her answering machine when she got home from church the next day. Did she want to go hiking in the Michaux State Forest?

Yes! Her heart leaped at the sound of Brendan's voice, and her fingers trembled as she called him back.

When he answered, he sounded strangely diffident as he repeated the invitation. "There's only one catch," he said.

"What's that?"

"You have to drive."

"Oh, I don't mind driving," she said quickly. If driving meant she got to spend the afternoon alone with him, she'd drive across the country.

The hike was pleasant, as the weather was still mild. The path was a wide, well-traveled one that Brendan and Cedar had no trouble covering. The first half, however, was nearly all straight uphill, and by the time they reached a plateau that looked out over a nearby ridge, she was almost panting.

Brendan, she noticed, didn't even look as if he'd broken a sweat.

"No fair," she said. "How can you make this look so easy?"

His smile flashed. He was wearing jeans today that faithfully hugged the strong contours of his thighs and—though she tried not to stare—closely molded to the bulge in the front of his jeans. His light-green sweatshirt emphasized his tanned skin and dark hair and she knew that her breathlessness wasn't all due to the climb.

"Faithful exercise," he said.

"Hey! I exercise faithfully!"

"Maybe I'm just naturally in better shape than you."

She snorted, showing him her opinion of that, and he laughed. Then he turned and gestured to the view before them. "Tell me what you see."

"How do you *do* that?" she demanded, stepping to his side.

"Do what?"

"How do you know which way is the view?"

"Well, much as I'd like to claim I can sense it," he said, "this one is a no-brainer. We came up the hill, and I turned to talk to you. But Cedar is still standing in the same position he was when we reached the top. And I already knew the open view was straight ahead at the top of the trail since I've been here before."

He reached for her hand and a warm glow spread through her as he laced her fingers between his. "So tell me what you see."

She cleared her throat, trying to think past the surge of her pulse and haze of awareness clouding her brain.

"Ah…the leaves are mostly off the trees now, and the tree bark makes the mountain look sort of silvery. It's a pretty day and the sky is very, very blue. Down in the valley between the two mountains is a river, and since we had a wet summer, the water level is still high and there are splashes of white where a few small waterfalls have formed."

"Very nice images. I had been here with my college roommate before the accident. I can still picture it in my head, but it's nice to hear your description. It really brings it back."

"Did your roommate live in this area?"

"He still does. That's who I work for."

"So that's what drew you to Gettysburg."

"That's what drew me to Gettysburg," he confirmed. He picked up Cedar's harness handle. "We probably should start down again. I have dinner plans this evening—a working dinner, actually—and I have to prepare."

As they hiked back down the hill, she found herself amazingly content. He hadn't invited her to do anything that evening—but he'd told her the circumstances of his outing rather than leave her to wonder whether or not he had another date.

She volunteered for the first time at a local soup kitchen the next day. Her fellow volunteers were mostly retirees who had known each other for years, but they were so warm and welcoming she felt as if she'd been there forever by the time the last dish had been dried and put away. When they learned she was free and interested in volunteering some more, they promptly shanghaied her to help deliver meals to people who were homebound every day for the rest of the week.

She suspected Brendan was having another busy week because she didn't hear from him for two days, and she was glad she was busy. She hadn't heard anything more about the preschool application she'd sent in. On Monday she attended an executive committee meeting of her library group, where she learned more than she'd ever expected to know about the cost of transferring selected historical texts onto CDs. That evening she got out a brush Brendan had sent along with Feather's food and gave her a thorough brushing out in the backyard of the building. She figured if she saved all the hair she collected, in about a year she'd have enough to knit a sweater.

She had her first piano lesson on Tuesday and was working on some new finger exercises that evening when the doorbell rang. She nearly broke her ankle rushing to the door because Feather darted in front of her determined to beat her to it. But it was worth it when she opened it to see Brendan on the other side, looking ridiculously hot and handsome in a black suit with a white shirt and conservative burgundy tie.

"Hi," she said.

"Hey. Did I hear music?"

She nodded, then remembered to speak. "Yes. I had my first piano lesson this afternoon. Would you like to come in?"

He shook his head. "I have to go back to the office this evening. But I wondered if you'd like to go to a community concert with me tomorrow evening. The featured performers are a jazz quartet that's pretty well-known."

"That sounds nice. I'd love to." *He just asked me on another date!*

"I'll knock on your door about seven," he said. "It starts at seven-thirty, so we'll have plenty of time to walk over. It's at the high school."

He was as good as his word the following evening, and they strolled over to the school for an evening of jazz. Cedar lay down at Brendan's feet the entire time, seemingly asleep. At intermission she said, "I can't believe the music doesn't bother him."

"His puppy raisers used to take him to their kids' band concerts. He's a music buff from way back."

She laughed. "A cultured dog."

After the concert they walked home again, and to her utter pleasure, Brendan put Cedar on a stay and then kissed her at her door, leisurely exploring her mouth and urging her closer to his hard body until she had to tear her mouth away and draw a breath.

He leaned his forehead against hers. "You are a potent package, lady."

"Thank you," she said, "I think."

"I'm pretty tied up tomorrow and Friday," he said, "but if you'd like to get together on Saturday, I'm game."

"I need to do some Christmas shopping at the outlets," she said. "Not fun but necessary. You can come along if you like."

"That would be great. You can help me pick out gifts for my mom and my sister."

"But I don't even know them," she protested. "How will I know what they like?"

"I know what I want and their sizes," he said. "You can be my style and color consultant."

"I can give that a shot."

Tuesday evening, Lynne opened her door as he was fitting his key into the lock and invited him for dinner, but he had to pass because he was going back to the office for a seven-o'clock meeting. "Are you going away for Thanksgiving?" he asked.

"Yes. My sister is having Mom and me for the meal." She hesitated. "Would you consider letting me take Feather along? I promise I won't let my niece and nephew harrass her."

"That would be fine." He'd been worrying about how both dogs would do at his parents' house. His dad was driving down to get him tomorrow evening and it had been on his mind.

"That's great!" she said. "I'll only be gone overnight, because I'm not leaving until Thursday morning."

"No problem." He stepped closer, snagging her by the waist and tugging gently. "Come here and kiss me goodbye."

"Goodbye." As his lips met hers, he could feel her smiling.

On Wednesday morning, he had to go down to the Franklin County courthouse in Chambersburg, nearly an hour's drive away. It didn't take as long as it might have, because he caught a ride with a local deputy who was driving down for a trial, and the guy drove as if he was an entry in the Indy 500. Even without sight, Brendan could tell they were moving a lot faster than the speed limit.

The deputy had the radio tuned to a country station and proceeded to sing along at top volume. Off-key. Brendan wouldn't have been surprised if Cedar, kenneled in the back of the big SUV beside the deputy's patrol dog, had started to howl.

As they passed the turnoff for the Michaux State

Forest, his thoughts immediately turned from the case he should be reviewing to the past weekend. To Lynne.

The shopping trip on Saturday had gone well, in his estimation. He'd hated shopping even when he'd been sighted. Now it was torture. But with Lynne, he'd barely noticed the annoyances. She'd matter-of-factly given him directions and if she'd minded the extra time he was sure the trip had taken, it never showed.

In fact, she took his lack of sight in stride better than some people he'd known for years. Like his own mother, who hovered anxiously every time he went home, asking him frequently how she could help him. For a long time it had annoyed him. Now he just let it roll off, knowing his sister was sitting on the other side of the room smirking. His sister, Jeanne, married with two young children, was usually the object of their mother's almost compulsive need to help, so she enjoyed the respite whenever he came home.

Lynne, on the other hand, never assumed he couldn't do something. If he needed help, she responded in a low-key way. She asked good questions when she didn't understand something. He knew Jeanne would like her.

He wanted to take her home to meet his family, maybe at Christmas, although he hadn't told her yet. They'd only known each other for three weeks.

Only three weeks…and in those three weeks, he had quickly recognized that nothing in the life he had led so far had prepared him for the emotions he was beginning to feel in connection with the tall, sweet-tempered woman across the hall.

He was walking through a hallway on the second floor when he heard a woman's voice say, "Brendan?"

He stopped, instantly swept into the past, but unsure if he was imagining things. "Hello?"

"Brendan." The voice drew closer, and he heard a woman's light steps tapping across the floor. "It's Kendra. I thought it was you and then I saw your dog and that clinched it. How are you? What are you doing here?"

A hand touched his forearm, and he automatically raised his own and clasped it. "I'm good. Just down here for a case. How about you?"

"I haven't seen you in so long." She fell silent, and an awkward moment passed as she clearly remembered the last time she'd seen him. "I'm here to get my passport renewed. Joe and I are hoping to travel to Ireland in the summer to visit my grandmother. Remember her?"

He did, indeed. A fiery little Irish lady, Kendra's grandmother had come over for Christmas once while they were in school. "I do. Is she doing well?"

"Oh, yes. We're going because…well, I'm pregnant, due in February, and we want her to see the baby. She's getting too old to want to fly anymore."

"Congratulations." He smiled, meaning it. "You're going to be busy in the new year."

"Yes. I can't wait. I'm sort of hoping for a girl, but

I know once I hold this baby in my arms I'm not going to care one little bit." Her voice bubbled with enthusiasm, but Brendan recognized nerves beneath the bouncy tone.

"I really am happy for you, Kendra," he said quietly. "I wish things could have worked out differently. I was a jerk and I'm sorry for that."

"You weren't a jerk." Her voice was low and gentle. "You were a man dealing with a life-altering event in the best way you knew how." Her voice changed, becoming teasing. "It was the wrong way, obviously, since you weren't smart enough to keep me."

"My loss. Joe's a lucky guy." He smiled. They'd been close once and although their lives had taken paths far different from the one they'd once expected to tread together, he had fond memories of their youthful years together.

"Is this a new dog? Last time I saw you, you had a golden retriever."

"Feather. I retired her not long ago. This is Cedar and he's working out very well." He went on to tell her a little more about Cedar, and after a few more moments of small talk, she stretched up and kissed his cheek and they parted ways.

He got called into court shortly after that and didn't really have time to think about the encounter until the trip home, with Deputy Depree singing "These Boots Were Made for Walkin'" beside him.

When he got home, his father would probably be

waiting, and he and Cedar would be off to his parents' home for a few days. He wished Lynne could go with him.

And he suddenly realized just how much he'd been thinking of her over the past few days. It had been nice to run into Kendra, but there was no pain like the last time, when he'd gone to her house to tell her he wanted her back—and found out she'd gotten married.

No, this time he was genuinely happy for her. He had Lynne now, and the old sting was gone. In fact, there was little comparison between his boyish feelings for Kendra and what he was beginning to feel for Lynne. Holy hell. Was he actually considering the implications of the "M" word?

Marriage. In retrospect, he'd taken Kendra's love as his due. Everyone grew up, fell in love and got married. At least, that had been his distinctly shallow view of the world back then.

He had cared for Kendra. But their relationship had been based largely on sheer sex appeal, like any healthy young animal. With Lynne, there was more. They shared some interests, enjoyed each other's differences. She'd been pleased when he'd won his last case; he'd been delighted that she'd taken up piano again. He tried to make her laugh just for the pleasure of hearing the musical sound, and he appreciated that she didn't seem to view his blindness as something that made him less or different.

He hadn't made love to her—yet—but he was

pretty sure that when he did, the explosion would be able to be seen in Taiwan. So, yeah, the physical attraction was definitely part of it. He could hardly wait to take her to bed, because it would be one more link between them, as well as being the best damn thing that had ever happened to him in his entire life.

Since he'd chosen to walk away from Kendra, marriage had always been a someday-down-the-road occurrence, and he'd been in no hurry to pursue it. But now…now the daydream had a face and a voice. He could picture living with Lynne, sharing the little moments that made up a lifetime together.

And kids. A wild sense of anticipation rushed through him. He hadn't pressured her so far but that was about to change. Both because he wanted to tie her to him so thoroughly she'd never even think of wanting to get away, and because his patience was wearing thin.

He wanted to know everything there was to know about her, but she was amazingly reticent for a woman, and unless he asked directly she rarely volunteered information about herself. He was keenly aware that she still held a deeply private part of herself away from him—away from everyone.

He fully intended to stay with her, to keep her with him until they were parked side by side in rockers on the front porch of a nursing home. So she was just going to have to get past that little tendency to hold part of herself back.

As he'd anticipated, his father was waiting when he returned. And Lynne wasn't home, much to his intense disappointment. He hadn't realized how much he'd counted on introducing her to his father. Feather barked from inside and he called to her through the door before he left, feeling vaguely guilty, though he knew Lynne already loved her and would take care of her as well as he could have done.

But it was with some reluctance that he gave Cedar the "Forward" command and started out of the apartment building behind his father.

Thanksgiving at CeCe's house had been a whirl-wind of parades, pumpkin pies and pesky children who begged her to play games incessantly. "Just one more, Aunt Lynnie? Please?"

How was she supposed to resist that? Her niece was great with Feather, especially once she explained that Feather was an older lady and probably wouldn't want to chase their balls or run around the yard much.

All in all, it had been an extremely pleasant visit. Neither she nor her sister had mentioned anything to her mother about her father's newest marriage, so the holiday had been fairly tranquil. If they could just make it through Christmas, they could tell her—and then she'd have a good while to rant and rave. Hopefully, she would have vented the worst of her outrage before another big family event.

* * *

She knocked on Brendan's door after she brought her luggage up from the car Friday afternoon, but there was no answer. Oh, right. He was probably working.

But she didn't hear his footsteps at all Friday evening or Saturday. He must have gone away for the holiday weekend. Intense disappointment stung her and she caught herself holding back tears several times.

Once again it appeared she had presumed too much.

She remembered vividly the conversation they'd had about Thanksgiving. She'd told him her plans—but she hadn't heard his. In hindsight, it was a pretty clear sign that he wasn't ready for intimacy on a deeper level.

And that was okay with her, because neither was she, she assured herself vigorously. She was just disappointed because they'd been spending so much time together.

She'd talked to her father last night. Well, mostly she'd listened while he babbled on and on about his new bride. He thought he was in love. And, truly, he sounded like it. But she knew it wouldn't last. Which made her wonder how in the world she could ever trust her own feelings.

Right now she felt strongly attracted to Brendan. If she wanted, she could daydream about a house with a white picket fence, two kids and a minivan. The dog was a given. But…

I don't own him, she reminded herself. Nor do I want to.

Right. Fibber.

She sighed. She couldn't deny that she found Brendan enormously attractive—

Bang! Bang! Bang! "I know you're in there."

Brief silence.

Then the overly enthusiastic knocking—which was, she realized, what the banging sound was—began again. "Open up, Brendan." The voice was male, deep and colored with frustration. "I just found out about Kendra's pregnancy, and I know she told you. Are you okay?"

Pregnancy? Kendra who? Why would Brendan be upset about it? A fist clutched her stomach into a painful knot.

Oh, stop it! There could be a dozen explanations.

Feather chose that exact moment to begin to bark.

"Feather!" Lynne hissed the name, trying not to let the visitor know anyone was there. But the dog was beyond hearing. She ran to the door and, in the first such display Lynne had seen her make, began to paw at the kick plate and whine, occasionally stopping switching to high-pitched, happy barks.

The banging on Brendan's door stopped. Then she jumped a foot in the air as the person in the hallway transferred his fist to her door.

"Feather? Is that you, Feather? Hey, Brendan, if you're in there, open the damn door!"

She stood. If the dog liked him, the stranger

couldn't be dangerous. Unlocking the dead bolt, she pulled open her door.

The moment the door opened, Feather shoved her way through it and made straight for the man on the other side. He was about as tall as she was, blond, deeply tanned and rugged looking, with thick eyebrows over piercing, blue eyes. If they weren't in Gettysburg, she'd swear he had just walked off a beach with his surfboard.

"Hey!" he said by way of greeting. He knelt, and Feather rolled over onto her back so that he could vigorously rub her belly. "How's my best girl?" he crooned. "My Heather-Feather. Have you missed me?"

He glanced up at Lynne and grinned, apparently not caring a bit that she'd just heard him speaking baby talk to a dog. "Sorry. Feather and I are special pals."

"I see that." She extended her right hand. "I'm Lynne DeVane."

He rose and clasped her hand in his for a moment, shaking it firmly. "I'm John Brinkmen, Brink to my friends. Brendan and I work together." He openly assessed her from head to toe. "You must be new. Brendan's neighbor, the one I remember who lived here, was small and white-haired, and he, uh—" he grinned "—he sure didn't look like you."

She nodded, unsure what to say, but Brendan's friend barely paused for breath. "Do you know where he is?"

She shook her head. "He was gone when I got back here Friday and I haven't spoken to him."

Brink's easy smile faded a bit. "Then why do you have his dog?"

"Feather's been staying with me most of the time since I moved in." And why was she explaining herself to this man whose eyes were growing increasingly suspicious? "She hasn't been happy about sharing Brendan with Cedar, and she seems to prefer living over here." She knelt and called the dog, and Feather came to sit obediently at her side. "I love having her."

Brink's expression relaxed somewhat as the dog's relaxed manner registered with him. "I see. He told me he'd been having some problems integrating Cedar into the equation. But I wonder why he never mentioned you."

She shrugged. "There's nothing really to mention. He's a good neighbor." *And my nose is probably growing. Nothing to mention, my foot.*

One blond eyebrow rose. "I see."

She sincerely hoped not. There was nothing worse than looking like a lovesick fool, especially in front of the object of your affection's closest friends. "I'd be happy to give Brendan a message when he returns."

"I'd appreciate it if you'd tell him I stopped by." Brink waved a mobile phone in the air. "I've left him voice mails and texts all day but he hasn't answered." Then he paused and looked searchingly at her. "Have we met? You look awfully familiar."

An alarm bell sounded. "No." She spread her hands. "A lot of people say that. I must just have one of those faces."

Brink was still examining her. "I guess." Then he smiled and held out his hand again. "Good to meet you, New Neighbor Lynne. Thanks for passing on my message."

"You're welcome. Nice to meet you, too."

But as she took the dog back into her apartment, her thoughts were consumed by what she'd heard. Who was the pregnant Kendra? And why wouldn't Brendan be okay with it? There was one obvious answer: a man who didn't want to be a father wouldn't be pleased at learning he was about to become one.

Seven

An hour later Lynne was about to head for bed when Feather started to bark and she heard Brendan's footsteps on the stairs. She would let him get settled in, she decided, stifling the urge to run to the door. She would have plenty of time Monday evening to pass on his friend's message.

He was speaking to someone, and she heard a second set of footsteps, both of which stopped outside his door. Deep, masculine voices rumbled for a few moments, and soon one set of footsteps moved off toward the stairs at the end of the hall.

Then, instead of heading into his own apartment, Brendan's footsteps crossed to her door. Feather went wild, prancing and leaping, although she didn't bark as she had earlier.

Sighing, she went to the door. Might as well get it over with. Part of her was anxious to see him. Too anxious. The other part was fighting feelings of hurt and insignificance.

"Hello," she said. "Welcome home."

"Thanks. I missed you." He reached for her, but she stepped back and he only caught her hand. After a moment's awkward silence, he asked, "Did you have a good holiday weekend?" He released her hand and bent to fondle Feather's ears.

"Yes, very nice. You?"

"Pleasant. I went to visit my family. But it's a relief to be coming home to my own place again. And I think Cedar had enough of being stalked by my mother's cat."

She couldn't help chuckling at the image of the big black dog backing away from a cat. Then she remembered she was striving for reserved and calm, and she composed her features.

"How did Feather do on your trip?"

She gave him a quick briefing and then took a breath. "A friend of yours came by today."

"Who?" He didn't sound more than idly interested.

"John Brinkmen."

"Oh, Brink. I don't claim him as a friend." Brendan grinned, and she sensed that he was determined to keep the conversation easy and pleasant. "Although the line loses some of its punch without him around to hear it."

"I let Feather go visit with him. She was having conniption fits in here once she heard his voice."

"I bet. When I got my first dog, some more-experienced guide dog users warned me that almost every dog has some person they react to, some person who makes them lose all common sense and training and act like a total idiot. Brink is Feather's downfall."

"It was rather obvious."

"I finally convinced them both that she had to behave and act like a guide at the office. But at home…" He shook his head in amused dismay.

"He mentioned something about a Kendra, too. He was concerned about you." She tried hard to keep her voice expressionless.

Brendan went still. "Exactly what did he say?"

"Just that he knew you'd found out she was pregnant and he was worried about you. You should probably call him."

Brendan exhaled. "Or maybe I'll just go over there and strangle him."

"What?" She was startled out of the careful calm she'd been cultivating.

He raised a hand and rubbed the back of his neck. "I owe you an explanation."

"You don't have to explain anything to me, Brendan. It's not like we—"

"Lynne." His voice sliced through her babbling. "Do not finish that sentence."

She didn't know what to say in response to that, so she said nothing.

"Give me ten minutes to park the dog and take all my stuff inside. My dad and I set all my suitcases in the hallway."

"All right." She would have offered to help but she sensed he needed the time.

"I'm going to stick my head out the door and yell, and when I do, you're coming over." It wasn't a question.

"All right," she said again. There were times when it just wasn't worth arguing. For some reason Brendan had taken exception to something she'd said and she was fairly sure she was going to find out exactly what it was in about ten minutes.

He yelled across the hall in exactly nine minutes. When she entered his apartment, there was only one light burning, and the room was dim.

"Sit down," he said. "I poured us some wine." He indicated two glasses on the coffee table before the couch.

Silently she took the seat he indicated and shifted to face him as he sat beside her.

Once seated, though, he didn't speak immediately. Instead, he took her hand and sat, rubbing his thumb across the backs of her much-smaller fingers. Finally he said, "I do owe you an explanation. It just never occurred to me that it was important."

He picked up his wine with his free hand and took

a sip. "I mentioned before that I had a steady girl-friend in college. Her name was Kendra."

Lynne's heart sank. So he'd known her for a long, long time.

"We got engaged at Christmas of our senior year. In February I had the accident." He didn't have to elaborate; she knew what he meant. "I also told you I was the one who called off the wedding a few months later."

She managed a noncommittal "Mm-hmm?" to encourage him to continue.

"Kendra got married a couple of years ago. She lives in Chambersburg. I was at the Franklin County Courthouse the other day and I ran into her." He shrugged. "In all honesty, I never would have known she was there if she hadn't said something. It was…nice…to talk to her. She's pregnant and expecting her first child soon."

She was so relieved she couldn't speak if she wanted to. It wasn't his baby! Not that she'd really thought it was…she just hadn't known *what* to think.

"Anyway," he went on, "my obnoxious friend and partner apparently found out, and I guess he thought the news would drive me to suicide. Hence the idiotic trip over here."

She found her voice. "He was just concerned. It was nice of him."

"Huh." In one short syllable, Brendan made it clear what he thought of Brink's concern.

Then he shifted, drawing her closer and sliding his arm around her. "I apologize for not staying in touch over the past few days. I went to visit my family for Thanksgiving. I intended to come back on Friday but my mother talked me into staying through the weekend. I should have called—but I realized I only have your number at my office."

"It's all right," she said. "You don't owe me—"

"Dammit, Lynne!" His voice was explosive, and she jumped. "Why are you constantly trying to downplay what's happening between us?"

"I'm not," she protested. "But I don't have any claim—"

"Maybe I want you to," he said in a low, ferocious tone that caught her totally by surprise. And before she knew what was happening, he jerked her toward him and set his mouth on hers.

He kissed her with a stunning, single-minded intensity that rendered her too shocked to move for a moment. His tongue boldly sought hers, his lips dominated and devastated her pitiful defenses. Finally she put her hands up to his shoulders—to push him away?—but he only reached up with one hand and dragged her arm up behind his head. At the same time he pushed her backward onto the couch, using the broad planes of his chest to lay her down as he slid one hand unerringly up beneath the thin sweater she wore. There was nothing tentative about his touch as he pushed her lacy bra aside and filled his palm with her breast.

And still he didn't speak as he rolled and rubbed her sensitive nipple, fanning a wildfire of desire deep inside her.

She couldn't speak, couldn't move, couldn't think; she could only lie there and *feel.* Brendan slid one muscled knee between her legs, dragging the fabric of her skirt aside so that she felt a rush of cooler air over her lower limbs. He was kissing her again, sapping her will and dragging her under a crashing wave of wanting.

"Brendan." It was the gasp of a drowning woman.

"Lynne. I want you," he said, his voice deep and hoarse. "I've been going crazy wondering if you've thought of me as much as I've thought of you."

The words melted any resistance she might have offered. "I did. I have." But he already had his mouth on hers again, kissing her almost frantically. He slid his lips along the line of her jaw and she felt the hot blast of his breath on her sensitive earlobe a moment before he sucked it into his mouth and swirled his tongue around it. An unexpected bolt of white-hot desire flashed through her, and she sucked in a breath as her body arched against him.

"Wait!" she gasped, not entirely sure what she even meant.

But he only shook his head as his mouth traveled down her throat and sought her breast, beginning to suckle her, right through the fabric of her shirt and bra. "Can't."

A distant part of her felt him reach down, his big hand moving purposefully between them, and then suddenly, shockingly, his hard body was there, the steely length of him pushing at the moist, tender entrance to her body as he pulled aside her thong.

Instinctively she tried to close her legs but he controlled her easily, one big hand pulling her thigh up around his waist. He pushed, pushed, and suddenly her body gave way and he slid into her, pressing steadily forward as her body accepted his hard possession. She felt a slight pinch of discomfort and then her slick readiness eased his path. As he surged heavily into her, she groaned, sure she could take no more.

Just as steadily he withdrew and thrust forward again. She clung to him, her body overwhelmed by his hard aggression, the rough delight of his urgency tightening the need coiling in her belly as he repeated his actions. She lifted her legs higher around his waist, her heels pulling him to her, and the shift in position exposed her to his thrusts in an even more intimate way that caught her off guard as waves of heated pleasure rolled through her in rhythm with his movements.

He pounded into her faster and faster, his slick muscles hot beneath her hands as she pulled his shirt out of the way and ran her hands up his back.

She couldn't think, couldn't breath, couldn't do anything but let the spiraling excitement build. Then she screamed, the sound muffled against his shoulder, as he slid one hand between them and pressed a finger firmly against her. Her back arched and she convulsed beneath him as rhythmic waves of release shuddered through her. Above her, she dimly heard him make a deep sound of pleasure as her body squeezed and clenched his swollen shaft. And then his motions disintegrated into frantic intensity until he froze above her, his arms shaking as he held himself still, pouring himself into her in long, liquid jets of heat until he collapsed onto her in boneless satisfaction, turning his face into her neck and pressing his lips against her.

His back heaved beneath her hands as he gasped for breath. His body was heavy, but when he would have moved she made an incoherent sound of denial and pulled him closer.

He gave a low laugh as he nuzzled her neck and then sought her lips. "Can a person die of pleasure?"

She smiled. "I never thought so before tonight."

He did move then, though she protested, sliding out of her and rolling to one side. Before she had time to feel bereft, he turned and pulled her into his arms. Her body felt heavy and lethargic, and her last thought before her eyes closed was that she would be happy for the rest of her life if she never had to move from this spot again.

A while later—she had no idea how much time had passed—Brendan stirred, his muscled chest moving beneath her head. A finger slipped under her chin and lifted her face to his, and she responded wholeheartedly as he kissed her again and again.

Finally he pulled his head back a fraction. "What have you been thinking for the past couple of hours?" he whispered against her mouth.

"I thought you might be in love with someone else," she blurted. The moment the words hit the air she wanted to crawl into a hole and never come out. She couldn't believe she'd said that aloud.

Brendan had gone perfectly still. She couldn't blame him. Sex, especially to men, didn't necessarily have anything to do with love.

Then he shifted, pinning her beneath him again. "And that bothered you?"

She hesitated, then whispered, "Yes." She'd already blundered; why try to fix it now?

"That's good," he said with great satisfaction, and his hands were tender as they traced the bones of her face. "Because I'm falling in love with you and I'd hate to think I was the only one affected."

"Oh, Brendan…" Her throat closed up and she couldn't speak. She was too happy. It was scary to be this happy, to know that another person could hold your world on the tip of one finger.

He kissed her again, and against her belly she felt his body stirring to life. She reached down between them, and he groaned with pleasure as her seeking fingers circled him, tracing the hard flesh she found from the tip to the crisp thatch of curls at its base.

She forgot any thought of talking then as he lay back and reached for her, drawing her up to straddle his hips. An involuntary shiver of excitement rushed through her at the feel of him solidly nestled against her soft, wet flesh, and he gave a low chuckle of lazy pleasure. "We can talk later. Right now I can think of better things to do."

Brendan was barely through the door of his office the next morning when Brink rushed in behind him. "So just how serious are you about your gorgeous blond neighbor?"

"Who says there's anything serious going on?" He waited a beat, but he couldn't stand the suspense. "Gorgeous, huh? What does she look like?"

"Hot," Brink said promptly. "Very, very hot. Tall, legs long enough—"

"Her face," Brendan said sharply. "Just her face."

"She's pretty," Brink said simply. "She wasn't wearing makeup the day I saw her, and I don't think I'd have picked her out of a crowd right away, but it wouldn't have taken long once I'd gotten a good look at her face. Great cheekbones, full lips, dimples. That damnably sexy dimple in her chin. Nice teeth. Big blue come-hither eyes—"

"Okay. You can stop there."

Brink laughed. "Uh-oh. Jealousy gene kicking in?"

"No need. She's mine."

"Are you kidding me?" Brink sounded astonished.

"Not one little bit. Hands off, buddy boy."

"Damn." Brink sounded aggrieved. "There's no justice in the world. You can't even see her and you still get the hottest woman in this town. You could have found a sweet girl, a girl with a wonderful personality, a girl with wit and charm. It wouldn't have mattered if she was uglier than a mud fence, but no, you have to take one of the pretty ones."

Brendan nodded with satisfaction, laughing hard. From the very day of his accident, Brink had been irreverent and amusing, refusing to dance around the topic of Brendan's blindness. "A mud fence, huh? Thanks so much for thinking of me."

"No problem. What are friends for? So are you going to bring her to the Christmas party?"

"The thought had crossed my mind. Have you managed to snag a date yet?"

"Amanda from the accounting firm across the street."

"The one you've been taking to lunch? The one you said looked like a Meg Ryan who is quiet and mysterious?"

"The very one."

"Way to go."

"Yeah. We're going to have the greatest dates in the room." Brendan heard the sound of his friend's footsteps heading for the door. Then Brink turned around again. "So, you never answered me...how serious are you about her?"

He didn't hesitate. "Very."

"Like rings and vows serious?"

Brendan nodded. "Yeah. But we haven't known each other very long. I don't want to rush her."

"I don't know, bro," said Brink before he headed to his own office. "That is one incredibly gorgeous girl. You'd better not wait too long."

Lynne's cell phone rang that afternoon as she was walking home from a new-member meeting at the church she'd begun attending. She had Feather with her since the pastor had told her it would be fine to bring the dog along. Happiness rose as she glanced at the display: Brendan. He'd insisted they exchange phone numbers and e-mail addresses before they'd parted that morning.

"Hello?"

"Hey, sweetheart. How'd your meeting go?"

"It just ended. I think I am going to join. I really like the church."

"Guess I'll have to check it out."

She almost dropped the phone. What did that mean? *Don't read too much into it, Lynne.* "You're welcome to come with me anytime."

"It's a date this Sunday." He shifted gears. "Do you have plans for dinner?"

"No. I was just going to make a meat loaf." She was still back on the "date this Sunday" line. "Ah, would you like to come over?"

"That would be great. I can't get home before six. I'll be over as soon as I feed Cedar."

"All right. See you then."

"I miss you. I haven't been able to think of anything but you all day."

She stopped dead. "Oh, Brendan. I feel the same way." She lowered her voice. "Hurry home so I can show you how much I missed you." Had she really just said that?

There was a moment of silence on the other end of the connection. Then he spoke again, his voice deep and rough. "I'm holding you to that, sweetheart."

At home she mixed up a pan of brownies and baked them. While they cooled, she put fresh sheets on her bed. Just in case. Then she made the meat loaf and put it in the oven with two baked potatoes. She'd steam some asparagus right before they were ready to eat.

Glancing at the clock, she saw she had time for a quick shower. Good. She pinned up her hair and jumped in the shower. When she finished, she glanced at the clock. Five-thirty. She was in fine time.

She shrugged into her robe and began to take down her hair—and froze as the doorbell rang. Rats. Who could that be? Brendan wasn't due home yet.

But when she went to the door, Feather already stood there, her tail beating a mad rhythm.

She pulled the door open. "You're early!" Then she stopped and looked around. "Where's Cedar?"

"I got away quicker than expected," Brendan said.

"He's already been fed." He shut the door and pulled her to him. "Come here."

As he slid his arms around her, plastering her against his body, she shuddered with raw need. How could he do that? One minute she was fine, the next she felt as if she were going to evaporate in a cloud of steam.

"Kiss me." She wound her arms around his neck, lifting her face to his.

After a moment, though, it was clear that Feather wasn't going to let herself be excluded. With a laugh, Brendan released Lynne and knelt to snuggle his retired guide. Finally he rose and they walked together into the kitchen where he kenneled her.

He turned then and took Lynne's hand. They walked back into the living room and he immediately pulled Lynne into his arms again. But soon he drew back. "What are you wearing?" His hands were already on the belt of her terry cloth robe, pulling it open and sliding inside to caress her bare curves.

"Brendan! We're in the living room!"

"So? Are the curtains closed?"

"Yes, but—"

"But nothing." He began to kiss her again, while his hands roamed over her, stroking and teasing, brushing repeatedly over her nipples with his thumbs until they were tight little peaks and electric sensation shot straight from her breasts to her womb with each touch. She writhed against him, but he only backed her against the wall and continued to stroke her, his hand sliding down the flat plane of her soft belly to brush the tight curls at the vee of her legs.

He shifted one knee against her, pressing until she widened her stance, and she moaned aloud as his warm hand probed deep between her legs, sliding along the tender seam, gently opening her and spreading the slick moisture he found there.

She let her head drop back against the wall and her body sagged in surrender as he bent his head to suckle her. Then she moaned again as she felt the advance of one long finger inside her, slipping in, slipping out, rubbing the throbbing bud that he uncovered at the apex of her thighs.

"Brendan," she gasped. "I can't—I can't—"

"You can," he said with determination, sliding a second finger into her. He rotated the pad of his thumb against her again and she clenched her teeth together to prevent the scream that wanted to escape. And then he touched her again and the world exploded, her body heaving and buckling against him as he ruthlessly drove her over the edge with his hand, prolonging her responses until she quivered with aftershocks. Gently he withdrew his hand, and the simple action made her briefly jerk against him again.

"Wow," she murmured. "If that's how you always come through the door, I'm going to need to take more vitamins."

He laughed, hugging her against him. "Let's make it a habit."

As she rested against him, she realized that while she might be relaxed, he was far from it. And when she slipped her hand down to cradle the bulge at the front of his trousers, he said, "Maybe we should find a bed."

"Or not." Before he could move, she dropped to her knees before him.

"What are you doing?" It was rhetorical, his voice deep with arousal and anticipation.

Slowly she unbuckled his belt, unzipped his pants and spread the fabric wide. He wore blue-and-white-striped boxers beneath, and she slipped one hand into the front opening, wrapping her fingers firmly around him and gently beginning to stroke the taut column of flesh she found.

"Lynne," he said in a guttural voice above her head, "you're going to kill me."

She smiled as she withdrew her hand and tugged the boxers out and down. "I hope not." He was fully aroused, and as he fell free, she leaned forward and caught the very tip of him with her lips. His back arched and his hands curled into fists for a moment, and then he bent and hauled her to her feet. In one smooth move, he lifted her and braced her against the door, then guided himself to her.

There was one breathless moment where she felt that the world was suspended, that everything around her was balanced on a knife-edge of desire—

—and then he took her hips in his big hands and

pulled her firmly down, thrusting forward in one long, smooth stroke until he was lodged deep inside her receptive channel. Bracing his arms against the wall on either side of her head, he began to move steadily, his buttocks flexing as he pushed into her again and again.

She wrapped her legs around his waist, pleasure so intense that she was barely able to form conscious thought. She felt a fist of need drawing tight, deep in her belly. Her arousal was fueled by her awareness of his rising excitement, and as he surged against her in the final moment of his own satisfaction, her body hurled her into climax as well. She bucked and writhed, the wall hard at her back and Brendan hard within her, until both of them were panting.

Brendan began to chuckle. "My knees feel like overcooked spaghetti. Can you walk?"

"I'm not sure." She wasn't kidding.

Slowly he lifted her off him and lowered her until her feet touched the floor. He held her hips until she locked her knees. She started to laugh then. "We need to get horizontal before we fall down."

"Good plan." He stepped out of his pants and shoes, tore off his shirt and socks, and then, gloriously naked, bent and lifted her into his arms.

"What are you doing?" she gasped.

"Give me directions."

"But I'm too heavy. Put me down."

"Directions," he said again, "or we're not going to get to a bed."

"Two steps forward and turn right!"

Eight

The next two weeks were the happiest days Lynne was sure she'd ever known in her life. She and Brendan ate dinner, cared for the dogs and spent every night together, usually in her apartment. The weekend following the first night they'd made love, Brendan came running with her.

Neither of them was exactly sure how well it was going to work. Brendan still ran on a treadmill but he hadn't jogged outside since his sighted days. But he told her there was another guide dog user in one of his online groups who had run the New York Marathon with her husband. They used a sighted-guide technique, although it was different from the typical right-hand-to-left-elbow position for walking.

So after consultation with the woman, they set out one morning for the long, straight roads that ran through the battlefield. Because of the huge volume of tourist traffic in the summer, the roads were kept in good repair. But in mid-December, there was next to no traffic.

They walked out to the battlefield to warm up, and stretched. It felt odd not to have Cedar, but the guide dog school that had trained him had given him strict warnings about not running with his dog. It was too easy to overheat a dog who was already wearing a harness, and too dangerous. He had no wish to circumvent the school's dictates on such an important issue. It was, he told her, a little different than letting the dog claim a spot on one piece of furniture.

Brendan produced a wide cotton band he'd gotten for their purpose, and they tethered themselves loosely together, her left wrist to his right.

Since each of them needed to be able to establish a steady breathing pattern, they worked out a system of non-verbal cues. He ran slightly ahead of her so that he could respond to tugs on his wrist. Her job was to cue him as well as to be sure there were no potholes or uneven spots in the road surface, and to be sure he was out of the path of oncoming vehicles.

"That was amazing!" He sounded utterly jubilant as they slowed to a walk and regained enough wind to speak again. He grabbed her with his free right arm and hauled her against him, seeking her lips. "Thank you so much. I never expected to be able to do that again."

"We can make it a regular habit," she told him when he released her. "Although from the sound of things, it might get tricky to find a safe time to run during tourist season."

"Probably. These roads get unbelievably congested." He nodded as they walked briskly back in the direction of their building. "You haven't really lived in Gettysburg until you've been here when the tourists are. It's like a plague of locusts."

"It will be interesting. I've never lived anywhere that was such a distinct tourist attraction." She couldn't wait to experience the summer season. It would mean that she'd been here long enough to really put down roots, and she'd feel more as if she really belonged in the community and less as if she were still on a long-term visit.

She awoke in the middle of the night that night, realizing he was awake, also, though he hadn't spoken. It was still a thrill to fall asleep in his arms and awake the same way. She supposed one day that would change, although she couldn't imagine it, she decided, basking in the bone-deep contentment that had infused her.

He lay on his back with her snuggled into the crook of his arm, one of her legs twined with his.

With his free hand, he idly wound a lock of her hair around and around.

"Brendan?"

"Hey."

"What are you doing?"

He abandoned her hair and reached over to tilt her face up to his for a leisurely kiss. "I was just lying here thinking about how lucky I am to have met you."

Her heart expanded a little more at the tender words. "It's a mutual feeling."

There was a comfortable silence. Then he said, "We never finished a conversation we started a couple of weeks ago."

"What conversation?" She was sleepy, sated and supremely comfortable.

Beneath her cheek his chest moved up and down as he laughed. "At the risk of being tacky by bringing up another woman's name while we're in bed together, we were talking about Kendra."

"Oh." She considered it. "Tacky, but I'm listening."

"I'd really like to tell you about her." His voice had grown serious.

She lifted her hand and caressed his cheek. "Of course."

"She was great after the accident. Very supportive, very determined not to let me sink into a pit of self-pity. She's actually the one who suggested I get a dog."

"Okay. Maybe I like her after all."

He smiled and tugged on her hair. "I still cared for

her but at the time I was totally immersed in myself. All I could think about was how my life had changed."

"Understandable."

"Maybe. Anyway, after about six months, I told her I couldn't marry her. I had this dumb idea that now that I had such big physical challenges to live with, I couldn't be the kind of husband she deserved."

"That was remarkably stupid."

He winced. "I know. I really hurt her. The one thing she asked me to promise her was that I'd go to counseling after we broke up. So I did. The psychologist I saw had also lost his vision in his twenties, and he was a big help in getting me to move past the 'why me?' stage and start living my life again. I got on the list for a dog and about six months later, I was matched with Feather."

"So why didn't you get together with Kendra again?" She lay back down in the circle of his arm. "Not that I'm complaining."

He smiled. "I felt guilty for ending it so badly, for a long time. And then I got to thinking that maybe I could fix it." He rubbed her hair absently between his fingers as he spoke. "Looking back, I think it was more the familiarity of the known relationship than anything, but I decided I wanted her back."

She tensed. She knew it, but she couldn't help it. Brendan hesitated, but then he simply went on with his story. "She was still living in the same condo she'd been in, and I just showed up there one day. I

rang the bell—and some guy I didn't recognize
answered the door. As soon as he saw me, he yelled
for Kendra. Turns out she'd just gotten married."

"Oh. Bad timing."

"Yeah. I felt like an idiot. For a long time, I
thought I still loved her. I was mad at myself for
losing her, and mad at her for giving up on me, even
though I know that's not rational since I was the one
who pushed her away."

"Feelings aren't always rational."

"When I saw her the other day, it actually felt
good to realize I didn't care for her anymore. I didn't
resent her and I didn't want her." He tightened her
arm, bringing her closer and kissing her temple. "I
had moved on. I had met you."

A bubble of happiness expanded within her,
threatening to float her right up to the ceiling.

"I never felt this way about anyone," he said. "I
thought I loved Kendra, but I never felt about her the
way I feel about you. I love you, Lynne."

The happiness turned to apprehension, though, as
she remembered that she had yet to share her own
secret. She had to tell him who she'd been. She
couldn't imagine that it would matter, but…it wasn't
the kind of secret she should be keeping from the
man she wanted to spend the rest of her life with.
And she *did*.

"Sweetheart?" He shifted her to her back, looming
over her in the darkness, a large silhouette with

shoulders that blocked what little light there was. "What are you thinking?"

"Make love to me," she said. She had to think about how to explain why she'd kept such a secret, before she just blurted it out. Deliberately she raised her knee where it was snuggled between his legs and rubbed it lightly back and forth, feeling him shudder as his sensitive flesh was stimulated, and when he moved to cradle himself between her legs, she immediately began to rock against him. His shaft was growing steadily, filling, throbbing and hot against her, and when he arched back and she felt the smooth head probing her tender opening, a spear of arousal went through her. She placed her feet flat on the bed and pushed up and he sucked in a startled breath as her action pushed him deeply within her.

He cupped her bottom in his big hands, tilting her up to receive his steady strokes, and as she felt the sweet surge of desire preparing to break over her head, she clutched at him, crossing her ankles behind his back to hold him deep and tight. *I love you, too,* she thought, but she couldn't say it aloud until she'd been honest with him. *I love you, too.*

They put up a Christmas tree in her apartment one Friday evening. Brendan couldn't be bothered with decorating his own apartment.

"It's not that I don't like Christmas," he told her. "But I can't see any of it, and it's a hassle to get out a bunch of stuff and then have to put it all away again. I'll be happy to help you, though."

"All right," she said, "but you at least have to let me put a wreath on your door. And help me decorate my place."

"I'll play Christmas CDs and eat cookies."

"Such a selfless volunteer."

He laughed, pleased that she wanted him to share preparations for the season. "It's a deal."

They took her SUV out to a local fast food place that had set up a Christmas tree lot. Wandering through the rows of trees, Brendan squeezed her hand through the mittens she wore. It had gotten steadily colder since they'd run the previous week, and snow was predicted for the weekend. "This is great," he said, inhaling deeply of the frosty air redolent with the scent of pine. "Brings back good memories from my childhood. My family always used to go out and cut down our tree together."

"That sounds nice." She was a little wistful. "We always had an artificial tree. My mother said it was too difficult for a single woman and two little girls to put up a real tree."

"So now you put up a real tree of your own," he said.

"So does my sister. I do it just because it's fun. She also does it because she's determined to give her children a real Christmas holiday."

"You didn't feel like you had a real one as a child?"

She shook her head. "Mother never spent much

time doing anything beyond what was necessary for CeCe and me. Don't get me wrong—she's not a bad person. But she was too absorbed in her hurt and anger at my father to focus on us."

"Do you remember them ever being together?"

"Not really. I have a few vague memories of him playing with us, but no specific ones of my whole family together. He came back for about a year after he divorced the second wife, but by the time I was nine he had left again. Then he had three more wives during my teens and early twenties, and now there's number six, the one he's just about to marry."

He was a little stunned to think of what her childhood must have been like. "He must really like alimony."

That startled a laugh out of her, and she leaned her head against him for a sweet moment before they told the sales attendant which tree they'd selected.

Back at the apartment, he helped her carry the tree upstairs and set it up in her living room. Since she had him to help, she told him, she could get a bigger tree than she normally did. He liked the way she assumed he could do most things unless he told her differently. He hadn't helped with this particular part of the Christmas ritual since he'd lost his sight, and he found it deeply satisfying to be more than just a bystander. And he was even happier to get the damned tree up the steps without breaking either of their necks.

She had delicate wooden snowflakes from Germany that felt fragile beneath his hands, a variety of balls and other ornaments that she told him were mostly red, silver and green, fluffy-feeling garland and a collection of Waterford crystal ornaments from Ireland. "My father has given CeCe and me one each year since we were born," she said, putting a smooth, cool piece of glass into his hand.

Exploring it, he realized that it was an angel, and it felt as if there was writing etched into one side. "What does this say?"

"Baby's first Christmas, with my name and birth-date. They all have my initials and the year on them."

"A nice tradition," he pronounced. "We all have Christmas stockings made by my mother. And a lot of the tree ornaments were made by her at one time or another. If there's a kind of needlework she can't do, I don't know what it is."

"I think it would be lovely to have things like that."

"Sorry, but I don't do needlework," he said, making her laugh.

When they were done, he reached for her and drew her close, feeling the rush of pleasure he always got when her long, slim curves settled against him. "Thank you for making me do this. It feels like we're creating some traditions."

She kissed his jaw. "I like the sound of that. Traditions."

"Things we'll do every year," he clarified, wanting

to be sure she understood how important she was to his life. Funny, but in just under two months, she'd become as necessary to him as…as breathing.

He felt her take a deep breath. "My sister has invited me to spend Christmas with her," she said, "but I haven't answered her yet."

Hearing the question she hadn't voiced, he said, "I guess we'd better talk about how to handle the holiday. I want to meet your family—"

"And I want you to meet them. Actually, CeCe has threatened to withhold my presents unless I bring you along for Christmas dinner."

He chuckled. "I want to introduce you to my family, too, but why don't we make our plans first and then I can explain to my mother when we'll be there."

"It would be nice to spend Christmas Eve here," she said. "And attend my own church for the first time."

"That would be nice," he said. "Church should be over by nine or so. Would you want to drive to your sister's after that?"

She shook her head. "I'd rather spend Christmas Eve right here with just the dogs and us. We can get up early in the morning and drive to CeCe's."

"And then head for my family's house sometime in the afternoon?"

"Sounds like a plan." He could hear amusement in her voice. "Although we might not fit into our clothing if we eat Christmas dinner at both places."

"I'll risk it if you will." He dropped his head,

kissing a line down the sensitive column of her neck until he could nuzzle the hollow above her collarbone. "Are we done with the tree? Because I have a present I want to give you."

She laughed, sliding her hand down the front of his body to explore the growing shape of his arousal. "I can't wait. Can I have it right now?"

Brendan's office Christmas party was held on the third Saturday of December at a local country club. Lynne was thrilled that Brendan wanted her to attend with him and meet his friends and co-workers. He'd already been to church with her twice and they'd met a number of people there. It was an intimate feeling to know that others regarded them as a couple.

Still, this party made her horribly nervous. She wanted to look good for Brendan, even though he couldn't visually appreciate it. The fact that those who knew him would be examining her was reason enough for her to want to do her best for Brendan.

But dressing up, wearing makeup and doing her hair, brought nerves and fear back to the surface. She felt like she had in the first weeks after she'd quit modeling. She'd come home to live for a while until she could find a place of her own. Every time she left the house, she had felt like a field mouse venturing out of hiding, exposing itself to predators. She'd been certain someone would figure out that she'd been a sort of celebrity, terrified someone would recognize her face.

But as time wore on, she was struck by one utterly astonishing fact. Most people were far too wrapped up in their own lives and concerns to think much about the new face they'd just met. Every once in a while, someone would look puzzled, as Brendan's friend Brink had, and ask if they'd met before. Not a single person had ever made the connection.

She would tell Brendan soon, she promised herself. Before Christmas. Then they could start the new year with nothing hidden, nothing standing unspoken between them. Although, really, she was beginning to wonder if she was being paranoid, assuming someone was going to recognize her.

It was the coloring, she had concluded months ago. Without makeup, her eyes were unremarkable and the facial emphasis was on her bone structure and porcelain skin. But with makeup...with the right makeup her eyes became dark, sultry pools. When she painted her lips in the bold colors that the red hair she'd had demanded, her mouth became pouty and eye catching. And then there had been that hair, a bright, curly explosion of attention-grabbing proportions. Without the hair, she was a whole new person.

It had just taken her a while to relax and realize it.

But now she had a quandary. She needed to dress up for the party. Dressing up meant wearing some makeup, making some effort. And taking the chance that her face might trigger someone's memory.

Still, she didn't feel she had a choice. She couldn't dress down. Brendan had told her that after Brink's father retired in another year, Brink had offered him partnership in the firm. It was a wonderful opportunity for him, and she needed to support that.

So she did what she could to camouflage herself. As A'Lynne, no last name needed, she'd nearly always worn the red hair loose and flowing to show off the curl. For the party, she pulled it up into a smooth, severe French twist.

She'd usually worn black, as well, since the hair precluded a number of other colors. Brendan was wearing a tux so she needed to wear something long. She still had some striking gowns, but instead she drove an hour to her sister's house one day and borrowed a deceptively simple pine-green velvet gown. It was sleeveless and fitted, with a draped cowl neckline, but it plunged to the waist in the back. She knew the texture and the cut would appeal to Brendan's sense of touch, and it certainly drew attention away from her face.

Her face. There was little she could do except go light with the application of color. She chose subdued earth tones rather than the brassy pinks and plums they'd used on her for photo shoots, did the best she could to make herself look attractive and classy without making her face unforgettable and promised herself she was not going to agonize about it all night. Not much, anyway.

When he crossed the hall and knocked on her door, Brendan looked handsome and imposing in a severe black tux with a black shirt and tie. He didn't have Cedar with him. He'd debated about bringing him, he told her, but had finally decided to let his guide relax at home, since they would largely be sitting at a dining table.

Brink and his date picked them up. The party would be attended by several law firms in the area. Each firm's dinners were small affairs, held either in private rooms at the country club or elsewhere around town. But after dinner, there was a dance in the club's elegant ballroom, to which all the guests had tickets regardless of where their dinner party had been held.

As Brink pulled into their parking lot, Brendan said to her, "You do realize it will be your job to let me know if I drop food on my lapels."

"Oooh," she said as he helped her into the back seat of Brink's Mercedes, "I guess that gives you some incentive to be nice to me."

He walked around the car, folded his cane, took his place beside her and slammed the door. While Brink was seating Amanda, Brendan leaned over and growled, "I intend to be very, very nice to you later, sweetheart."

"I can't wait," she purred, sliding one finger upward from his knee along his muscled thigh.

"Ah-ah-ah." He grabbed her hand and linked their fingers. "Unless you want to embarrass us both, that's a really bad idea. It's only a short ride to the country club."

Dinner itself was pleasant. They were seated at a table with Brink and Amanda, and the two men's office assistants and their husbands.

The other two women gave them a run-down of who was who in the room, with commentary from Brink, who seemed to be a one-man talk show. She was glad, actually, since it meant she didn't have to talk much and people's attention was focused elsewhere.

After dessert, the tables were cleared and the live band began to play. It was an excellent group and as the notes of the first slow song began, he rose and took her hand. "Dance with me."

It was heaven. She hadn't known him long enough to take being in his arms for granted. And she loved to dance. Brendan was a strong partner and with a minimum of direction from her to keep them from plowing into other couples, they moved extremely well together.

During one break from the music, he asked Brink a low question, and when his friend answered, Brendan's head swiveled to the left. After a brief nod, Brendan turned to her and said, "I want to introduce you to Mr. Brinkmen, Sr. His own father opened this firm and he took it over when Brink's grandfather retired. Now he's looking at Brink to do the same thing."

"And then you will become a partner?"

Brendan nodded. "Brinkmen & Reilly, Attorneys-at-Law. Has a pleasant ring, don't you think?"

She laughed. "I do."

His voice deepened. "Sort of like Mr. & Mrs. Brendan Reilly also has a nice ring to it. Even better, Lynne Reilly. I like that particularly well."

Was he asking her to marry him? Completely thrown, she said the first thing that came into her head. "I love it, but since no one named Reilly has asked me to marry him, this is all hypothetical."

Brendan laughed so hard people around them turned to look. "Trust you to cut straight to the heart of the matter." He slid his hands up her arms to cup her elbows. "Lynne, I didn't intend to do this tonight. I haven't bought a ring yet. But since we seem to be standing here tiptoeing around the most important topic we might ever discuss together... will you marry me?"

Her head was reeling. She had to remind herself to breathe. "Brendan—are you sure? Wait! I didn't mean that."

He laughed again. "I'd take a one-word answer right about now."

"Yes," she said hastily. "Oh, yes!"

Unaware, and probably uncaring of the curious stares of those around them who sensed something was up, Brendan slid his arms around her and kissed her, bending her backward so that she was clinging to his strong neck, depending on him to support her.

When he raised his head, he said, "Hey, every-body, this beautiful lady has just agreed to marry me."

Around them, clapping, whistles and cheers erupted.

"Way to go, buddy!" Brink was there slapping Brendan on the back, while one of the office assistants threw her arms around Lynne.

"Congratulations, dear. Brendan is one of the finest young men I know."

She opened her mouth to respond, but her mobile phone, in her small evening bag on the table, began to play its distinctive tune. Startled, she said, "Oh! That's my phone. Excuse me."

Concern filled her even before she flipped open the top and spoke. She really kept the phone with her only for family emergencies, or so that her mother could reach her if needed. She honestly couldn't even remember the last time it had rung since she'd moved to Gettysburg.

"Hello?"

"Lynnie?" It was CeCe, and Lynne immediately realized she was crying.

"Cees, what's wrong?" She felt her stomach drop as if she were in a plane that had just hit an air pocket. "Are you okay?"

"I'm okay," CeCe said, "but Lynnie, Daddy's in the hospital. Can you come?"

"Of course." Immediately she reached for a napkin and began to scribble down directions. "What happened?"

CeCe cried harder. "He went jogging with the new wife-to-be. Apparently she's a serious marathoner and they ran ten miles—and Daddy collapsed. They think he might have had a heart attack."

"Ten miles!" Their father was in excellent shape, but— "Didn't he tell her he's never run more than three or four in his life?"

"You know Daddy," CeCe said, her voice slightly calmer. "He'd die before he'd admit he wasn't as strong and fit as a younger man."

There was a sudden silence as she realized what she'd just said, and then she began to cry again. "Can you come right away, Lynne?"

"Of course."

Without hesitation, Lynne agreed and went to tell Brendan what had happened, disappointed and distressed at the dramatic turn of events. How could the best moment of her life suddenly become the worst?

Nine

On Monday morning Lynne called Brendan at the office. She'd kept in close touch since she'd rushed out of town Saturday evening to be with her father. As it turned out, he had, indeed, had a mild heart attack.

Lynne had been overwhelmed with concern after speaking with her sister, frantic to get on the road, and Brink had driven them home immediately. There was no question of Brendan going; he needed to care for the dogs.

She'd been a whirlwind back at the building. He was pretty sure she'd changed, packed and rushed out the door in under five minutes.

"Good morning," he said in response to her greeting. "How's your dad today?"

"Doing much better." There was a wry note in her voice. "He's getting boatloads of loving attention from Alison, the newest attraction. He might have faked getting sick before if he'd realized how much attention he'd get. Kidding," she added with a laugh, "I think."

They talked for a few more minutes about her family, and Brendan reassured her that the dogs were well.

"I miss you," he said. "Sleeping alone has no appeal anymore."

"I miss you, too," she said. "Daddy's being discharged this afternoon, so once he's back in his apartment with Alison to take care of him, I'll head home."

"I'll look forward to it," he said. And he would. He'd spent two hours at the jeweler's down the street from the office today, selecting a ring. He'd taken his office assistant with him and he hoped he'd chosen a ring that Lynne would treasure. He'd get some flowers on the way home, and tonight they could make their engagement official.

After a few more minutes they hung up and he turned his attention back to the brief on which he was working. He'd been immersed in it for thirty minutes when he noted Brink returning from the court appearance he'd had in the morning.

He'd already tuned the distraction out and gotten back to work when his office door burst open.

"I finally figured it out," Brink crowed. "You sly dog."

"Good morning to you, too. Figured what out?"

"You know. Lynne."

"What the hell are you talking about?" He finally stopped the screen reader and gave Brink his attention. "Figured what out?"

"You know…Lynne. Who she really is."

"Oh, you did, huh?" His tone was dry. "Wanna share this revelation? I'm sure it'll be good for a laugh."

There was an odd pause, making him wish he could still read his buddy's expression. "You're joking. Right? She's A'Lynne. From *Sports Illustrated*."

"Allan who?"

"No, not Allan. Ah-LIN, and not a guy. A supermodel—only one name. She was on the cover of *Sports Illustrated*'s swimsuit edition a couple of years ago. You knew," Brink asserted. "You're just jerking my chain."

"No," he said carefully, "I am not kidding. You really believe this model Lynne resembles is her?"

Brendan heard the thud of a magazine on his desk. "I keep all the old *SI* swimsuit editions. It's the same woman. I even asked Dad and he agreed."

He was silent for a moment. Finally he said, "You're crazy. What makes you think it's her?"

"I almost missed it. She looks different now. She used to have this wild, curly red hair. It was kind of her trademark. And she was tanned and of course, wearing a boatload of makeup. But I am telling you, Brendan, it's definitely the same face. Bone structure, the shape of her eyes and lips… And the body matches. Tall and slender, although she looks a lot skinnier in the magazine. Think about it," Brink urged. "The name's similar, just Lynne with an extra *A*-apostrophe. Are you telling me you don't know this?"

"She's never mentioned it, *if* it's even true." He feigned unconcern, though his heart was racing. "I'll run it by her tonight. I imagine it'll give her a good chuckle. But, thanks. It's pretty flattering, I guess, that you mistook my girlfriend—my fiancée now—for a supermodel."

There was silence in the wake of his words. Finally Brink said, "Okay. Must be my mistake. She'll think it's an amazing coincidence." He sounded relieved when his assistant called from behind him that he had a phone call. "I'll talk to you later, man."

She had missed Brendan more than she'd ever thought possible. As she unlocked her door and let herself in that evening, she could hardly wait to drop her bags and rush across the hall into his arms.

But she didn't get the chance. As she came out of her bedroom, the front door opened and Brendan strode in.

"Hello!" she said. "I was just coming to you." She crossed the room and wound her arms around his neck to kiss him—

And he stepped away.

Too shocked to react, she just stood there.

Brendan tossed a magazine on the table beside the door. "Explain this."

Automatically she glanced down at the magazine. And froze.

There she was, clad in sand, a deep tan and an extremely skimpy azure bikini, on the cover of *Sports Illustrated*. It was one of the most coveted assignments in the world—and she could still remember how unhappy she'd been at that time. Separated from her family, distressed by the shallow pleasures so many of her friends chose to pursue, deeply depressed by the ending of her relationship with Jeremy, with whom she'd really thought she'd found love… She didn't even know what to say. "Where did you get this?"

"It must have been amusing for you," Brendan said furiously, "hanging with someone who would never be able to figure out who you were."

"It wasn't amusing! It was…wonderful." She was bewildered by the depths of his anger. "I know I should have told you before, but—"

"Gee, you think?" His heavy sarcasm cut across her explanation. "Brink thinks I'm an idiot. And I guess I am. I expected honesty from the woman I cared for—"

"I never lied to you!"

"Omission is a form of lying," he retorted. "You deceived me. Deliberately."

"It wasn't deliberate." But she had known it was wrong to keep the information from him. Guilt bit deep, and defiance colored her response. "When we met, I owed you nothing other than my name. And Lynne Devane *is* my real name." She was fighting tears of distress and of rising anger at his accusations. "And then as we started getting to know each other, I just…I enjoyed knowing you liked me for me, not because it was cool to be with someone *famous*."

"That sounds nice," he said, "but it still doesn't explain why you didn't tell me. *I asked you to marry me!* Didn't it occur to you that perhaps I ought to know what I was really getting?"

He was shouting by the time he finished, and she shrank back, folding her arms and hugging herself, holding herself together as the dreams she'd built since she'd met him began to drift away like wisps of smoke. "You think you know it all, Mr. Perfect," she said, a sob catching her voice. "But let me tell you what the life of a top model is like. You can't leave your room without people chasing you around asking questions and taking pictures. You never know if the people you meet are genuine or if they only want to get close to you because they think some glamour might rub off on them. Your manager fusses about every bite you put in your mouth and you have to fight to keep from doing what three-quarters of your co-workers do, which is eat like fools and then purge, or else starve themselves because they're convinced they're fat. You're offered drugs and asked on dates by creeps who assume that because you're an international celebrity you'll have sex with them. And sometimes one of them is nice to you, and sweet, and gentle and you really think maybe this one is different—" she had to swallow another sob "—and then you find out he's not different at all, that he just wants you because you increase his own status." She poked him in the chest with a finger. "Don't you *ever* dare to judge my reasons for trying to keep a low profile."

She slid past him, careful not to touch him, and reached for the doorknob. Then she turned back to him and said, "I thought you were different. I thought you loved me for *who* I was, not *what* I was."

"I did!"

"You go right ahead and tell yourself that. You're as bad as Jeremy in a different way. He wanted me for what I was. You *don't* want me for the same reason. Now get out."

"Lynne—"

"Get out!"

She couldn't stop crying. All night, she sobbed, on and off, until at daybreak she finally quit trying to sleep and got up. She paced around her apartment, Feather following anxiously behind.

At seven-thirty, reality struck her with the force of a blow. It was over. There was no going back from the angry words she and Brendan had exchanged last night. What was she going to do? How could she stand to live across the hall from him, see him casually again and again? How could she bear knowing what he thought of her?

The answer to the final question was clear: she couldn't bear it. At least, not if she had to be confronted with his scorn. That, she could do something about.

She rushed back to her room and hauled out a bigger suitcase than the bag she'd taken when her father was ill, haphazardly tossing in a variety of clothing items that would get her through a week or so. She would contact the Realtor from whom she'd rented the place and see about a sublet. She could stay with CeCe for a few more days while she figured out what on earth she was going to do next. Clearly she couldn't stay in Gettysburg.

She should have been warned when she learned that his engagement hadn't been broken off for the reasons she'd assumed. Instead of being dumped, Brendan was actually the dumper—and for a stupid presumption that he wasn't good enough for a sighted wife. He said he'd gotten over it and she'd believed him.

But he'd made another stupid presumption about her "motives" for getting involved with him, a presumption that showed her his uncertainties still existed. Like the fact that he couldn't see had actually had a single thing to do with her reasons for not telling him about her past career. If he'd been sighted and hadn't figured it out, she would have done exactly the same thing. Maybe it *was* deception but it hadn't been malicious.

She loved him, dammit! Rage and despair lent impetus to her actions, and the suitcase was filled in mere moments. Slamming the lid shut, she grabbed the toiletries case that she hadn't even unpacked yet. She was halfway to the door before she realized she couldn't just leave Feather behind.

And she couldn't take her along, she realized with a heavy heart. Feather wasn't hers.

Sad and angry, she sank down onto the edge of the couch and bent to wrap her arms around the old dog. Fondling her ears, she said, "I'm sorry, girl. You know I'll always love you. But I have to go."

She rubbed the silky edge of Feather's ears, tears streaming down her face. The only thing she could do was leave the door unlocked and call Brendan to come over and get her after she was gone.

He heard her apartment door close and her foot-steps recede down the hall, but he was too angry to talk to her again for a while.

And hurt. He could admit that. She hadn't trusted him. He'd been willing, even eager, to give her his heart, and she hadn't felt the same way. If she had, she would have confided in him weeks ago.

How many weeks ago? You haven't even known her eight weeks yet.

And in that short period of time, he'd fallen deeply in love. For someone who'd lived the life he now realized she had been immersed in, she was remarkably unassuming. Her tastes were simple, her desires few. She was even tempered rather than arrogant, loving and tenderhearted rather than expecting adulation.

Good God. He'd had a supermodel taking care of his dog. It was hard to even comprehend. Although he'd made his peace with his loss of sight years ago, every once in a while he bitterly regretted not being able to see. This was one of those times. Perhaps if he could see Lynne, compare her to that magazine—

Why? So you'd have proof that she was someone different?

Different on the surface, perhaps, but the very fact that she'd walked away from that lifestyle and chosen this—*chosen him*—spoke volumes about her character.

The telephone rang. He leaped for it, willing it to be her. "Hello?"

"Brendan. You need to go across the hall and get Feather. I left my door unlocked. Her toys and lead and bowl are in a bag on the counter."

"Lynne, you don't have to give her back—"

"I'm not going to be living there anymore. I'm sorry, but I won't be able to take care of her for you." She rushed on before he could react. "I've enjoyed her. Thank you for that. Goodbye."

And in another instant there was a dial tone in his

ear. She'd left! She'd left for good. Moved out. Well, obviously she hadn't moved out yet, but she intended to.

He sank onto the couch with his head in his hands, anger suddenly forgotten as the finality in her stricken tone sank in.

Dear God, what had he done?

He left nine messages on her mobile phone in the first two days, but she never called him back. He was frantic, wondering if her father's health had taken a turn for the worse or if the only reason she was staying away was because she was so hurt.

Tuesday dragged by, then Wednesday and Thursday. By Friday he was wondering if she ever planned to return. The weekend passed in a dull haze of sadness. And anger—anger at himself. He knew better than to let a knee-jerk reaction dictate his behavior. He'd been trained to stop and think things through.

How could he have been so stupid?

I thought you loved me for who I was, not what I was.

Funny how much sense that made now that he was past the initial hurt and anger he'd felt. There had to be a way to talk to her. To make her understand that he was sorry for the things he'd said. But…for an attorney who'd passed the bar exam with one of the highest scores in the state, he felt pretty clueless, because he hadn't come up with one viable idea for getting Lynne to speak to him again.

Monday evening he trudged up the stairs. He'd been home at lunch to let Feather out, but Lynne still hadn't come home. He would know the minute she arrived. All he had to do was keep an eye on his dog.

He'd never seen Feather so subdued. She'd been depressed and annoyed when he'd retired her and she'd had to deal with a new dog in the house, but now she was so different he was starting to worry in earnest. She didn't even get to her feet when he arrived home anymore. Yesterday he'd made an appointment with the vet because she'd eaten so little in the past few days he was worried about her weight.

He unlocked his door and entered his apartment. "Feather," he called. "Hey, girl. Where are you?" No sound betrayed her presence. "Feather?" He called her name four times before he heard a deep doggy sigh and the sound of her feet shuffling across the floor toward him. His heart broke a little more as her unhappiness hit him almost as a physical blow. She was a golden retriever, a breed that practically was listed in the dictionary beside the word *bounce*. But she hadn't shown any sign of vibrancy in days.

"I'm sorry, old girl." He knelt as she approached, and when her head came to rest against his chest, he massaged her silky ears. He hadn't cried since he was a child but he caught himself swallowing a lump lodged in his throat at the palpable misery his beloved old friend exuded. "I want her back, too," he whispered.

Suddenly, with energy Feather hadn't shown in

days, the dog reared back and tore away from him. He heard her nails frantically clacking across the floor to the door, and then she began to bark. Cedar followed her, less excited but interested in whatever had gotten her so worked up.

Hope rose faster than he could get to the door. Feather acted this way when Brink was around, but just maybe… He rushed after her, misjudged the distance to the door and nearly slammed into it face-first. He caught himself with a hand against the wood mere moments before his nose would have met it. There was a tremendous bang as the door trembled in its frame.

Hell! For a moment he wasn't sure whether to pray it was Brink so that Lynne didn't figure out what an ass he'd just made of himself, or whether Lynne would be kinder than Brink, who would tease him unmercifully for days.

"Brendan? Are you all right?"

It was Lynne's voice! His knees suddenly trembled as if they were about to give way, and a sweeping relief carried him along as he yanked open the door and rushed into the hallway right behind Feather. Cedar, agitated at the near accident, hovered close beside him.

"Hey." He tried for casual, but was afraid he failed miserably. "I'm fine. I'm glad you're back."

There was a taut silence. "I'm not staying," she said, and her voice was subdued. "I just came to get a few important things that I don't want to risk getting lost or damaged when the movers come." He heard her kneel, and as Feather quieted he knew she must be cuddling the dog.

"The movers?"

"They'll be here Friday."

"Friday." He felt as if the words were bouncing off the surface of his brain, incomprehensible. "This Friday?"

"Yes." He could barely hear her.

"But…you can't move," he said.

Another silence. He waited, hoping for a response, any response. But she made none.

"Please come in and see Feather." He didn't care that he probably sounded desperate. "She isn't eating well. She misses you."

Lynne knelt on the floor, rubbing Feather's silky ears, resting her forehead against the old dog's. "You be a good girl," she told her in a low voice. "No more of this picky-eater stuff. And be nice to Cedar." Her voice broke and she cleared her throat as she rose. "No, thank you," she said. "I need to get started." This would probably be the last time she would ever see Brendan, and she drank in his familiar features, wishing there was a way to go back two months and start over.

"Lynne," he said, "I'm sorry."

His head lowered and she couldn't quite read his

ANNE MARIE WINSTON   175

expression. She blinked, unsure she'd really heard
him right. Sorry for what?

"I know it probably doesn't change anything now,
but I want you to know that I really am sorry. I had
no right to judge you without asking you why you
felt it necessary to be anonymous."

She swallowed, her throat so choked that she
could barely speak. "Maybe not. But I was wrong to
deceive you in the first place so I apologize, too." She
couldn't take another minute of polite, earnest regret,
so she turned toward her door. "Goodbye, Brendan."

"Where are you going?" He was standing between
her and her apartment door and he didn't budge.

"I already told you I was moving. The landlord is
subletting my apartment here for the remainder of my
lease." She tried to smile. "I asked him to be sure it
was someone who loved dogs."

He stepped forward, and she moved to the side so
that he could pass her. Instead, with the uncanny in-
tuition she'd observed before, he reached right for
her, his hands sliding down her arms to link her
fingers with his. "Don't go."

"I have to." She couldn't hold back the tears.

"No," he said. "You don't." He gathered her
against him and she wanted to be there too badly to
struggle away.

"I do," she said. Throwing pride to the wind, she
cried, "I can't stay here. I'm not strong enough to
help you with Feather, to see you every day, to live

across the hall from you and never be able to be with you again." She pushed out of his arms. "I appreciate your apology, I really do, and I will always wish I had done things differently, but—"

He put his arms around her again. Lowering his head, he covered her lips with his, cutting off her protests. He kissed her as he always had, exploring and devouring her, eliciting a helpless response until she raised her arms and cradled his head, kissing him back with no regard for her heart's protection.

When he finally tore his lips away from hers, it was only to transfer his mouth to her neck. "Make love with me," he said against her skin.

"No." She struggled again, desperate to get away before she completely dissolved into tears. Was he enjoying making this so difficult?

"Why not?" He was relentless. "That's exactly what it would be—making love. I love you, Lynne." His voice grew passionate. "And I know you love me. I was wrong. The woman I fell in love with is no different from the woman you've been all your life. If I've learned anything, I learned that."

She bit her lip. She wanted to believe him, wanted to let go of all the sadness and heartache of the past few days, but… "I do love you." She cleared her throat. "But, Brendan, I can't change my past. I'm always going to have been a supermodel."

"Do you still want to be one? Because if you do,

or if you decide you might like to go back, I'll support your decision."

"No!" That was one thing of which she was certain. "I just want to be a regular person with a regular life."

"Okay. We can do that." He lifted a hand and cradled her cheek, and she felt her doubts begin to slip away. "I want to make you happy, sweetheart. And I don't think you're going to be happy if you leave me."

"I don't think I am, either," she confessed. "But can you really be happy with me now that you know I'm not just the girl next door?"

"No problem." He drew her against him again, his big body warm and solid against her. "I don't want you to be the girl next door, anyway. I want you to be my wife."

Tears stung her eyes. "I want that, too. Are you sure?"

He smiled as he took her hand and drew her into his apartment. "I have something for you. I was going to wait until Christmas morning, but now I think I'd better not."

She allowed him to seat her on the couch and watched as he went to his bedroom and returned with a small package wrapped in silver and gaily tied with soft red ribbon. Her heart skipped a beat as hope rose within her.

Taking a seat beside her, he found her hand and turned it palm up, setting the small box there. "Open it."

"Now? I don't have your presents wrapped yet." She wanted to open it badly, but her hands were shaking, and she pressed the small box tightly between them.

"After the way I behaved, the only present I want is you," he said. He slid from the couch to one knee and loosely cradled her hands in his. "I already asked you to marry me once, but I'm asking again. Will you marry me?"

For the first time, she felt a glimmer of happiness return. "Oh, Brendan, are you sure?" Her throat closed on the words.

"Absolutely," he said. "There is nothing you could tell me that could make me change my mind. I already learned the hard way that having you in my life is more important than anything that could come between us."

"Does it bother you that I'm independently wealthy?" Might as well drag every skeleton out and make sure it wasn't going to fall apart at her feet later.

He snorted, and she knew her fears were needless. "You mean, is my masculinity threatened? Nah. Just as long as you can't run faster, jump higher or leap buildings in a single bound. That might put me off."

"You're in no danger." Happiness allowed her to respond in the same jesting manner. "Physical fitness was not my best subject in school. I run now to keep in shape, but there's no speed involved in the activity. And I certainly do not bound."

"That's settled, then." He squeezed her hands lightly. "So open this."

She took a deep breath. "All right." Slowly she pulled off the ribbon and carefully pried open the wrapping paper without tearing it.

"What are you doing?" Impatience rang in his tone. "Don't tell me you're a paper saver!"

"I most certainly am."

He sighed. "Wake me when you're ready to open the box."

But she'd already slipped the small jeweler's box from the square white one, and as she flipped the lid, Brendan's head snapped up.

He didn't move—and neither did she.

Finally he said, "Well?" and there was uncertainty in his voice once again.

"It's...incredible," she said in a small voice. And it was.

"You like it? I told the jeweler what I wanted and he helped me with the details."

"I love it," she said fervently. "There's a large diamond in the center with two smaller ones on each side and the whole band in studded with tiny chips. It's radiating light like I can't even describe."

He reached for the box and removed the ring, then picked up her left hand and found her ring finger. Sliding the ring into place, he asked, "How does it fit?"

"It's perfect!" She held out her hand, unable to believe she was wearing such a lovely ring.

"Good," he said. "It will match my wife. Perfect."

"I love you, too." She laughed. "Yikes. Nothing like high expectations to live up to!"

"You're not going to have any trouble." He paused, and drew her into his arms. "I love you, sweetheart. The day I fell over your boxes was the best day of my life."

She laughed, her lips skimming over his face. "Just think of the story we'll have to tell our children of how we met."

"Our children. I like the sound of that." He rose, drawing her up with him and linking her fingers with his. "We should get started."

"Telling the story?"

"No." He pulled her against him, fitting his hard frame to the softness of her yielding body. "Making the children."

"Brendan! We're not even married yet!"

"So? At the very least, we should practice. We want to be sure we get it right."

And as his hands slipped beneath her sweater, seeking the soft, warm skin beneath, she tugged his tie loose and started opening the buttons of his dress shirt. "By all means, let's make sure we get it right."

* * * * *

0108/10/MB120

Red-Hot & Ruthless

Steamy...
Dangerous...
Forbidden...

Three passionate tales of sexy, fiery men who will stop at nothing to get what they want...

**Available
21st December 2007**

Dana Marton, Anna DePalo, Wendy Etherington

Tall, Dark & Sexy

Rich...
Gorgeous...
Irresistible...

Three strong, powerful men – and the beautiful women who can't resist them...

**Available
4th January 2008**

Helen Bianchin, Margaret Way, Caroline Anderson

100 Reasons to Celebrate

2008 is a very special year as we celebrate Mills and Boon's Centenary.

Each month throughout the year there will be something new and exciting to mark the centenary, so watch for your favourite authors, captivating new stories, special limited edition collections...and more!

www.millsandboon.co.uk

2 Books
and a surprise gift!

We would like to take this opportunity to thank you for reading this Mills & Boon® book by offering you the chance to take TWO more specially selected titles from the Desire™ series absolutely FREE! We're also making this offer to introduce you to the benefits of the Mills & Boon® Reader Service™—

- ★ **FREE home delivery**
- ★ **FREE gifts and competitions**
- ★ **FREE monthly Newsletter**
- ★ **Exclusive Reader Service offers**
- ★ **Books available before they're in the shops**

Accepting these FREE books and gift places you under no obligation to buy, you may cancel at any time, even after receiving your free shipment. Simply complete your details below and return the entire page to the address below. You don't even need a stamp!

YES! Please send me 2 free Desire books and a surprise gift. I understand that unless you hear from me, I will receive 3 superb new titles every month for just £4.99 each, postage and packing free. I am under no obligation to purchase any books and may cancel my subscription at any time. The free books and gift will be mine to keep in any case.

D7ZEF

Ms/Mrs/Miss/Mr .... Initials ....

BLOCK CAPITALS PLEASE

Surname ....

Address ....

....

.... Postcode ....

Send this whole page to:
UK: FREEPOST CN81, Croydon, CR9 3WZ